CULTURED

ALSO BY D.P. LYLE

The Jake Longly Series
Deep Six
A-List
Sunshine State
Rigged
The O C

The Cain/Harper Series
Skin in the Game
Prior Bad Acts
Tallyman

The Dub Walker Series
Stress Fracture
Hot Lights, Cold Steel
Run to Ground

The Samantha Cody Series
Original Sin
Devil's Playground
Double Blind

The Royal Pains Media Tie-In Series
Royal Pains: First, Do No Harm
Royal Pains: Sick Rich

Nonfiction
Murder and Mayhem
Forensics for Dummies
Forensics and Fiction
Howdunit Forensics: A Guide For Writers
More Forensics and Fiction
ABA Fundamentals: Forensic Science

Anthologies
Thrillers: 100 Must-Reads (contributor); *Jules Verne, Mysterious
Island Thriller 3: Love Is Murder* (contributor); *Even Steven;
For the Sake of the Game* (contributor); *Bottom Line*

CULTURED

A JAKE LONGLY THRILLER

D. P. LYLE

OCEANVIEW PUBLISHING
SARASOTA, FLORIDA

ISBN 978-1-60809-618-3

Published in the United States of America by Oceanview Publishing

Sarasota, Florida

www.oceanviewpub.com

10 9 8 7 6 5 4 3 2

ACKNOWLEDGEMENTS

To my wonderful agent, Kimberley Cameron, of Kimberley Cameron & Associates for her unwavering guidance, advice, dedication, and friendship. KC, you're the best agent ever.

To Bob and Pat Gussin and the great folks at Oceanview whose dedication, professionalism, hard work, and creativity made this book better in so many ways.

To my always first reader and editor, Nancy Whitley.

To Nan for everything.

CULTURED

CHAPTER 1

MY LIFE IS GOOD. No, let's go with great. At least that's the view from where I sit. Which was in a lounge chair nestled into bright white sugary sand. The warm day, not a cloud in the sky, meant that the beach was crowded with sun worshipers and swimmers and boogie boarders and Frisbee spinners. I had a glass of sweet tea in my hand and not a single care. Yes, life is good.

One would think that nothing could disrupt such an idyllic day, but I said my life was good, even great, not perfect. Since perfection isn't attainable, the natural next step after achieving greatness is for things to go downhill.

I'm Jake Longly, ex-pro baseball player and owner of Captain Rocky's, a bar and restaurant in Gulf Shores, Alabama. It's popular with locals and tourists who come for the Gulf views, the food, and the drink—particularly the drink. The best things about Captain Rocky's? It gives me something to do and rakes in enough cash to keep me financially afloat while not working. This slacker's dream job is possible thanks to my manager, Carla Martinez, who actually runs the place. My definition of a win-win. A good thing since keeping books and balancing ledgers and stocking inventory and all that other stuff required to run a business are not part of my skill set.

Everyone has a gift. Mine is that I'm good with people. It's true. People like me. Most people anyway. Not my father, Ray, but that's a long story. My incredible, yes incredible—ask Nicole, or Carla, or Pancake, but not Ray—charm makes me the face-man and chief schmoozer at Captain Rocky's. The best job description I know.

Which means that basically I do nothing.

Well, except for hang out with Nicole. That's her sitting in the lounge chair next to me, shaded by a bright yellow Captain Rocky's umbrella. Nice, huh? The red bikini helps, but Nicole needs little assistance in attracting attention. She often pulls gazes her way and stops conversations, even traffic. Just last week, as we walked along a sidewalk in Fort Walton Beach, Nicole, in white shorts and a tangerine halter top, caused a fender bender. Her outfit, and those incredible legs, distracted some dude in a Corvette, and he rear-ended an SUV. The Corvette lost the battle, its hood buckled like a wadded sheet of aluminum foil.

The paperback thriller I had been reading lay in my lap, and I downed the last of my tea. It was midafternoon, the hottest part of the day, but this was tempered by a slight onshore breeze. Nicole's chair faced the water, and mine faced the opposite direction so I could monitor happenings at my restaurant. It was busy and noisy as the late lunch and early happy hour crowd packed the interior and the beachfront cantilevered deck. I flopped one leg over the chair's edge and dug my toes in the soft, warm sand. Nicole had her nose in the pages of her next screenplay, a work that had been in progress for the last two months. She scratched notes between muttering to herself. Things like "That doesn't work" and "What was I thinking?" Seemed like a lot of aggravation to me, but she loved it.

Her last screenplay, *Murderwood*, had been produced by her uncle—Charles Balfour—a Hollywood giant to giants, and starred Kirk Ford—another giant with a worldwide, almost cultlike, following. No surprise that it became a box office smash. *Murderwood* had been based on an unsolved L.A. murder, but I didn't know that until shooting started because Nicole wouldn't tell me. True to form, she wouldn't tell me what this one was about either. She can be difficult.

Another thing good about my life is Pancake, my best friend since childhood. He appeared at Captain Rocky's at random times to hang with Nicole and me and devour the free food. His consumption prowess was the stuff of legends, so when I saw him, I knew it was feeding time. Which for Pancake was less like three squares a day and more like six or seven feasts with snacks scattered here and there.

He lumbered his six-five, 280-pound frame down the deck stairs and rumbled across the beach toward us. It's amazing the stairs and the sand could support him. He wore tan cargo shorts, a red Hawaiian shirt with a green and yellow floral design, and aviator sunglasses. The light breeze lifted his unruly red hair.

"Pancake's here," I said.

"Does it look like good news or bad?"

Pancake had called a half hour earlier, saying he'd be by to talk with Nicole and me. He wouldn't tell me more, only saying, "You'll see." History suggests that when Pancake is secretive, nothing good follows.

"He's smiling that smile," I said.

"Definitely not good." She raised an eyebrow. "For you anyway."

Pancake's a happy guy and people love him. But he has one smile that reflects a certain mischievousness, which is part of his makeup. Been that way since we were kids.

Pancake created a trail of deep footprints in the sand until he reached us, his bulk casting shade.

"What's up?" I asked.

"I have greetings from Ray."

That settled the good news, bad news issue. Greetings from Ray never ended well. Hell, it never even started well.

Ray, my father, is a no-nonsense P.I. who doesn't agree with my career choices. I mean, my baseball career he got behind but a bar owner he couldn't quite grasp. He felt I should do something "worthwhile." For me, Captain Rocky's was worth all the while you ever wanted.

"Oh good," Nicole said. "A case?"

"I'm hungry," Pancake said.

No earthshaking news there.

"Me too," Nicole added.

Also, not earthshaking.

One of the many things that amazes me is that Pancake and Nicole could pack away the groceries and never change an ounce. I think Pancake reached his biological limit years ago and physics didn't allow his weight to move upward. But he seemed to try with every meal. Nicole? Annoyingly able to eat anything, and a lot of it, and never waver from perfection. I mean, I'm also lucky that way, but these two defy nature.

"What time is it anyway?" I asked.

"Time to eat." Pancake jerked his head toward the deck. "Carla's setting up a table for us."

Nicole gathered her materials, stuffed them in her dark green canvas bag, stood, and tugged on her gauzy beach cover. Not like it hid anything, but then Nicole, being more or less an exhibitionist, never tried to hide her assets. We followed Pancake up the stairs to the corner table near the railing. My table. Carla had long ago attached a permanent "reserved" sign on the umbrella pole. Three margaritas waited for us. No doubt ordered by Pancake, which meant he needed us partially sedated and compliant before rolling out the bad news.

Here's what I knew for sure. Whatever news, or greetings, or message Pancake had would involve a case. A Ray case. Nicole would jump in headfirst and I'd get dragged into it. For some reason that's how these things always went. Well, the reason I got involved wore a red bikini right now. Another thing I knew was that whatever Pancake dropped on us would lead to some scary, convoluted, and potentially lethal situation. It always did. See? That's why I prefer Captain Rocky's to Ray's world.

Nicole took a sip. "So, what is it?"

So it begins.

"Ray wants you to join a cult."

CHAPTER 2

LUNCH TOOK ONLY a half hour. Just enough time for Pancake to demolish half the menu. On my dime. I never charged Pancake for food or drink. He was family, and besides, I liked hanging out with the big guy. He spent as much time here as he did at Ray's, the head-quarters of Longly Investigations, where he worked. I think Ray approved of that since the more time Pancake deposited himself elsewhere the slower Ray's fridge emptied. At Captain Rocky's we had several refrigerators and freezers. A couple as massive as Pancake.

After lunch I went over some inventory purchases with Carla, acting like I knew what she was talking about. Something about ribs and hot links and beer and margarita mix. That ploy didn't fool her for a microsecond. She went through the motions though because she wanted to make me feel like I played a part of the management of my restaurant. A total facade. She knew it, I knew it, hell, everybody knew it.

On the way out, I chatted with a couple of the customers, and waved at a few more, face-man being my main role at Captain Rocky's.

We climbed in Nicole's white SL550 Mercedes, top down, and fol-lowed Pancake's black dual-cab Chevy pickup the four miles to Ray's beachfront stilted home. We found Ray at Longly Investigations' de facto office—the umbrella-shaded teak table on his deck. Ray's laptop and several stacks of papers sat before him, a Mountain Dew nearby. To Ray, a frosty Dew was mother's milk. Though he'd deny it, it was for sure an addiction, witnessed by the half a dozen crushed cans in the trash can to his left. Maybe he should go to DA—Dew Anonymous.

"What took so long?" Ray asked. "Trouble getting Jake away from his bar?"

Ray literally hates Captain Rocky's. He considers it the main symbol of my "slacker attitude." That's a direct quote from Ray.

"Actually, we had to feed Pancake," I said.

"Figures." Ray took a sip of Dew.

Nicole pulled out a chair and sat. I took the one next to her.

"So what do you have for us, boss?" she asked.

Runners to your mark, set, go, and we were off and hurtling into Ray's world. Sure, Nicole wrote successful screenplays, but she also sort of, kind of worked for Ray. Courtesy of Pancake, she even had a laminated card to prove it. I'm not sure whether she did it because she liked solving riddles or to aggravate me. Maybe she saw it as a way to gather info for her next movie. Whatever the reason, she always eagerly jumped onboard.

"The client is the mother of a missing young lady," Ray said. "She, the daughter, apparently joined a cult near here. Around a year ago. Then three weeks ago, she stopped communicating. The mother went to the place, talked with the dude who runs it, and was told her daughter met someone and left. According to the mother, he said that wasn't unusual. That one of the perks of working there was that the girls could meet successful guys and who knows after that. Anyway, according to the mother, they told her other girls had done the same and each was doing okay and that she shouldn't worry."

"Did they tell her where her daughter went?" Nicole asked.

"She asked but was told that they didn't know. The *they* being the leader and his sidekick. A woman he works with."

"Seems odd they wouldn't know," I said.

Ray sipped his Dew. "Or aren't telling."

"No sign of her since then," Pancake said. "No activity on her credit cards, ATM, or passport."

"You're thinking something happened to her?" Nicole asked.

"Smells that way," Ray said. "Of course, we need to prove that that's the case and if so find out the who, what, when, where, and how." He shrugged. "The usual."

"What do you need from us?" Nicole asked.

"There is no *us*," I said. "I don't work for Ray."

"Yet, here you are," Pancake said. That smile again. "Someday you're going to have to accept your lot in life and roll with it."

"That's what I tell him all the time," Nicole said. "I mean, what's more fun than being a P.I.?"

"Sitting on the beach and watching a sunset," I said. "That's a lot safer."

Was it ever. Each time I became entangled in Ray's business, dangerous and chaotic situations popped up with an uncomfortable regularity. It always became a game of whack-a-mole, except the moles were armed to the teeth and in nasty moods. I'd end up throwing baseballs and rocks, even a snow globe once, at them to prevent Nicole and me from getting shot, or worse.

Does that sound like fun?

For some reason the joy escaped me; to Nicole, it was all ahead flank speed.

"Now that we've completed Jake's little psychotherapy session, let's get back to business," Nicole said. "What do you want us to do?"

I hate to lose battles before they even start. Which also recurred with an uncomfortable regularity. Nicole explained it to me, more than once, because she wanted to make sure I understood the concept. In the world of boy-girl, the dude's a sprinter, the girl a marathoner. The guy might win, or at least think he did, the battle, but would lose the war as she would always outlast him and grind him into submission. Frantic sprinters had no chance against relentless marathoners. More often the dude lost the battle before he even knew there was one. Nicole's solution was to simply go with it and not whine.

I never whine. Almost never.

"This cult," Ray began, "it's not one of those religious deals. It's more a self-help group." He glanced at Pancake.

Pancake picked it up. "There're just north of a hundred and twenty members that have come to the group for life coaching and confidence building and for creating a path to success. It says so right on their website."

"Who's the leader of the group?" Nicole asked.

"Jonathon Lindemann. He has a law degree and did some estate and property development and things like that until he found a better way to fleece clients. Joining the group isn't cheap."

"Meaning?" I asked.

Why did I open my mouth? I didn't care about any of this.

Nicole smiled at me.

Pancake gave me his "gotcha" look.

He slid a page in my direction. "A hundred-and-twenty K buy-in and then twenty percent of profits after that. If there are any. From what I've found so far, Lindemann charges his clients nothing if there are losses or no profit is realized but takes the twenty percent from what he makes for them."

That actually sounded fair to me. More so than most brokers who win regardless of whether their clients do or not.

"This missing girl?" Nicole asked. "What's her name?"

"April Wilkerson."

"Did she have that kind of cash?"

"Her mother, Clarice, is wealthy," Ray said. "Very much so. On paper. April is too, or will be in a few years when her trust pays out. Her mother apparently blocked any transfers from her trust for the time being."

"The daughter filed a lawsuit but it was tossed," Pancake said. "Apparently the trust was ironclad and she wouldn't take over its administration until her twenty-fifth birthday. She's twenty-two."

"A lawsuit?" Nicole asked. "Against her mother? I guess you can say they have issues."

"That was a year ago," Pancake said. "After the judge slapped it down, they made peace. According to the mother anyway. *Harmonious* was the word she used."

"So how did April get in the door?" Nicole asked. "If she couldn't buy her way in?"

"She's an employee. Apparently part of their marketing team."

"How'd she manage that?" I asked.

"Her mother says because she's young and beautiful."

I didn't like the sound of that. "You're thinking there's a sexual angle to this group?"

Pancake shrugged. "Isn't there always? From Jim Jones to NXIVM."

"I knew a girl that got involved in NXIVM," Nicole said. "An actress wannabe. Fortunately, she figured it out and bailed on the program before she got branded or pimped out."

"The concern here is that this might be a similar situation," Ray said.

"There's no evidence of that," Pancake added. "But the mother fears that's the situation."

"My thinking is that you two go check it out." Ray nodded toward Nicole and me. "Get an inside view."

"Why would I do that?" I asked.

"The usual," Pancake said. "Nicole will and you'll follow."

"Cool," Nicole said. "I've never been inside a cult before. Do they wear special outfits? Or dance naked around a bonfire? Any fun stuff?"

I looked at her.

"What? You've seen me dance naked before." She ruffled my hair.

Have I ever. But not around a bonfire and not with a group of brainwashed idiots. I thought that but said nothing. I'm smart that way.

But, against my better judgment, I did ask, "Why would they welcome us into their secret society?"

"Because you're both famous," Pancake said. "You the ex-baseball player and restaurant owner. Nicole the big-time screenwriter. Exactly what these types are looking for."

"People with wealth and celebrity," Ray added.

I didn't feel like I was wealthy, but I honestly didn't know, not being overly watchful of those kinds of things, and damn sure didn't want to be a celebrity. I felt more like a sacrificial lamb in another of Ray's schemes. Not so Nicole.

"We're all over it," she said.

Of course we were.

"Where is this place?" she asked.

"Up near Magnolia Springs," Pancake said. "It's called Lindemann Farms. It's a couple of hundred acres and Jonathon Lindemann's the sole owner. He calls his program The Lindemann Method or TLM for short."

"Sounds like a fitness or weight loss program," I said.

"The fear here, with April Wilkerson missing from there, is that it's some sort of psychological manipulation," Ray said. "That they get the followers all wound up about self-improvement and moneymaking, and before they know it, they're part of the cult." Another slug of Dew. "If history tells us anything, it's that in the end many cult members don't fare well."

I gave that some thought. "What if it really is as advertised? A group that teaches self-improvement and financial security?"

Ray opened his hands. "Possible. But if so, why are they stonewalling the mother?"

"Are they?" I asked.

"The mother thinks so, and we'll run with that until proven otherwise."

"So, what do we do?" Nicole asked. "Go knock on the gate?"

Ray and Pancake exchanged a glance. Uh-oh. I knew that look. Something not good was coming. Not good at all.

"We can arrange an introduction," Ray said.

"How? Who?"

Ray gave Pancake a nod.

"By someone who looked into membership and knows the players and the lay of the land."

"Who?"

"Tammy Horton."

CHAPTER 3

Tammy Horton.

Just freaking perfect. The only person in my life more aggravating than Ray.

Remember I said my life was good, but not perfect? This wasn't even close to perfect. This adventure was not yet off the ground and it'd already veered into chaos. The chaos being Tammy.

It reminded me of the old Vanguard rocket. Back when the U.S. locked horns with Mother Russia to lead the parade into space by placing a satellite in orbit. That was before my time, but I had seen all the videos. Russia took the lead with Sputnik, the Vanguard having blown up. Twice. One reaching the amazing height of four feet, the second flying for nearly a minute. Not stellar efforts and definitely not orbital. Took the Alabama-developed Jupiter C to finally place our own "grapefruit" in orbit and the race was on.

I felt like I was strapped to a Vanguard and launch control had lit the fuse. At any moment I'd be a ball of fire bouncing across the launch pad. That might sound a little dramatic to the uninitiated, but anyone who had ever entered Tammy World would know the ride is nothing like Disneyworld.

You see, Tammy's my ex. I affectionately call her Tammy the Insane because, well, it fits. She damaged my bank account during the divorce, married her attorney, and yet still thinks I'm her go-to for any and all of the problems that threaten her domain. A realm where rational thought is a foreign concept. None of Tammy's problems are ever earthshaking—but rather simply Tammy being Tammy. Things like she can't get her favorite nail polish because the boutique no longer carries it, or she gained two ounces despite doing her yoga and Pilates every day, or Walter's prostate requires nocturnal visits to the bathroom, which interferes with her sleep. She truly believes I can solve these problems, so she calls. Often. To say her worldview is skewed toward the delusional and self-absorbed doesn't do it justice.

The irony is that now Nicole and I would have to ask Tammy for help. Thankfully, that wouldn't happen until tomorrow. I felt like the governor had called to delay my execution.

After leaving Ray's, we returned to Captain Rocky's for drinks, to watch the sunset, and go through the stack of materials Pancake had gathered. Only a dozen pages but as it turned out, they were dense. It gave me a headache so I let Nicole go through them and give me the thumbnail. That seemed fair since she sort of worked for Ray and I was merely collateral damage.

Clarice Wilkerson, the concerned mother, was forty-three and a former beauty queen, winning a bunch of titles in and around central Florida. She finished college at Florida State with a degree in business, and then married Robert Wilkerson, an uber-wealthy real estate mover and shaker. He was also thirty years her senior. After that, Pancake found no evidence she'd used her business degree, preferring to hang out at the country club and travel with her husband and their only child, April. A good life until Robert slumped into his office chair dead from a heart attack. That was ten years ago, when April was twelve. Mother and daughter then abandoned Orlando and rolled over to Jupiter on the Atlantic coast. Not a neighborhood for those with thin wallets.

April, also a beauty who won several contests, followed her mother's path and enrolled at FSU. A year ago, she graduated with a degree in liberal arts, which meant she partied more than she studied. To be fair, my college experience was similar.

Nicole slid her photo toward me. April was a fresh-faced blonde with blue eyes and cheekbones that matched her mother's. She looked young. The date near the bottom revealed it had been snapped three years earlier when April was nineteen. Her life took a turn shortly after graduation when she hooked up with TLM. Three weeks ago, her trail evaporated. No calls or texts. No Facebook or Snapchat or Twitter or Instagram. No credit card or ATM use. Poof. Gone.

"What's to like?" I asked.

Nicole examined April's photo again. "I don't like any of this. Something bad's happened. I can feel it in my bones." She glanced toward the water. "She ran away to a cult." She looked back at me. "Did she then run away from the cult?"

"It's happened before."

"Why not back home to her mother? To a security that's measured in the millions?"

"Not to mention the trust fund that's headed her way," I said.

"That too."

"Maybe after the lawsuit the mother-daughter relationship was too fractured to repair," I said. "Toss in the rift created by her joining TLM and the fissure might've been too deep to bridge."

Nicole thought about that. "But her mother hired Ray to find her."

"Fear trumps pissed. Or disappointment, or whatever. The mother's concerned, sure, but April might not be ready to put a bandage on things."

"Or she can't," Nicole said.

Which was exactly what I was thinking.

We then dug into the information on the most interesting character in the play—Jonathon Lindemann. The founder of The Lindemann Method, TLM.

"Good-looking guy," Nicole said "Sure doesn't look forty-two."

She handed me his photo. He did appear younger. Tanned, fit, blue-and white-striped dress shirt, open collar, and a casual, friendly smile. His teeth were perfect and blindingly white. Light brown hair fell over his forehead and faint crow's feet guarded the corners of his brown eyes.

"He doesn't look like a fiend," I said, passing the photo back to Nicole.

"They never do."

I leaned back in my chair, propping one foot on an empty one, and stared out at the beach, sipping my bourbon. Nicole continued giving me the highlights.

Lindemann was a Florida boy, born and raised in Tampa. He only used his law degree for a few years until, like the late Mr. Wilkerson, he entered the world of real estate brokerage and development. His property portfolio staggered the mind, or had before he sold it off. His Dun & Bradstreet showed a net worth of ten figures.

"Two years ago," Nicole continued, "he sold out to his partners. Guys named Charles Parker and Martin Gaines. Their company was LPG Investments and it looks like Lindemann walked with about forty mil plus two properties. Both are Tampa-area condo projects that are very high-dollar and boutique." She flipped to the next page. "He formed Lindemann Property Management. LPM for short."

"He likes initials," I said.

"Apparently."

"So he took a bag of money and still has an income stream?"

"More like a river," Nicole said. "One property has thirty units, the other sixty-five. Both are sold out, the lowest for just over a million and the penthouses near six."

"His income stream is from the HOAs?"

"Twelve hundred a month per unit."

I tried to do the math but lost track quickly. Math and I were never close friends.

Nicole had no such problem. "Pencils out to around 1.4 million a year."

"That'll water the grass and trim the hedges."

"And then some." She flipped through a couple of other pages. "Since he didn't have much to do, except cash the checks, he started his self-help and investment deal. It sprouted in Tampa around the time he left LPG. He tagged it The Lindemann Method. Then a couple of years ago he bought property up in Magnolia Springs and built his retreat."

"Why there?" I asked.

Nicole shrugged. "Privacy?"

"Magnolia Springs offers that."

Magnolia Springs, a few miles north of Gulf Shores and not far from Fairhope, was mostly farm country. Definitely cheaper and with more breathing room than Tampa.

"He calls his two hundred acres Lindemann Farms."

I mulled that over. Good-looking guy, obviously smart, with a ton of cash, creates a program and ropes folks with more money than brains into following him into the wild. Not really that wild but definitely off the radar. Where he can work his magic and drain their wallets. Clever. Unless he was legit. From what I had seen so far, except for a young girl who just might simply have run away from mommy, he seemed like any other successful businessman. Well, except for that self-help deal that does feel cultish.

"Looks like the farm has a membership of around a hundred and twenty."

"They live there?" I asked. "On the farm?"

"From the online images it doesn't look that way. Seems more like a resort than a community."

"How does Pancake come up with all this?"

"He's Pancake."

That was true. He could uncover anything. I figured that if he put his mind to it he could find the Treasure of Sierra Madre, maybe the Holy Grail.

"So, what's your plan?" I asked.

"You mean our plan?"

"I don't have a plan. This is your deal. I'm just along for the ride."

"You always say that."

I shrugged. "I like riding."

"Which is a problem. I do too." She smiled. "Tomorrow we'll talk to the mother and then pay Tammy a visit."

Tammy. I had almost forgotten.

"But, right now, speaking of rides, let's grab a bottle of tequila and head to my place."

Oh yeah.

CHAPTER 4

I'M A TECHIE, and a computer guru. Not to Pancake's level, but then no one I know, or had ever known, can rummage around in the cyber world like he does on a regular basis. Still, I felt ahead of the average. I sat next to Nicole on her deck, staring at her laptop screen, my third cup of coffee in hand. A meager attempt to shred the cobwebs in my brain, the remnants of last night. Too much tequila, too much Nicole, if the latter was possible.

She connected to one of those video chat deals. Zoom, Doom, Boom—something like that. Okay, so Nicole did all the keyboard work and I more or less sat there, but I had showered, shaved, and dressed, playing my role as face-man. That's it—FaceTime.

April Wilkerson's mother, Clarice, lived in Jupiter, Florida. Down in south Florida on the Atlantic coast, Jupiter was home to a lot of celebrities, pro athletes, and mega rich folks. It was way too far from Gulf Shores to drop in for a chat, so here we sat doing this video thing. I'd never done one but it seemed simple enough. For a techie like me.

It was eight a.m., nine in Jupiter.

As soon as Nicole opened the program and clicked a couple of things, the two of us appeared on the screen. She, of course, looked great. Me, not bad considering last night's gymnastics. I swiped my hair off my forehead.

"Quit primping," she said.

"I'm not."

"You are. This isn't a photo shoot, it's an investigation."

"Just trying to keep up with you," I said.

"I don't primp."

That was true. Of course, she didn't need to. She rolled out of bed looking perfect. I might be annoyed if I didn't really, really like it. Come to think of it, she was perfect rolling into bed too. But that's another topic.

Nicole completed the connection and Clarice Wilkerson appeared on the right half of the screen. The photos Pancake had found didn't do her justice. Long dark hair, high cheekbones, full lips, and a long, elegant neck circled by what appeared to be a string of pearls. A floppy, unstructured hat shaded her face, which was mostly hidden by trendy, expensive, and oversized round sunglasses. She, too, seemed to be outside, witnessed by the palm trees, the pool, and the Atlantic Ocean behind her.

Nicole made the introductions and Clarice thanked us for calling.

"I hope I'm not overreacting here," Clarice said. "But I have an uneasy feeling about all this. I'm somewhere between panicked and pissed. Either she's in some kind of trouble or she's trying to get back at me." She adjusted her sunglasses. "That'd be just like her."

Not the reaction I expected. Was Clarice primarily worried about or angry with her daughter? I couldn't tell.

"Tell us what you know," Nicole said. "Or think you know."

"April is twenty-two. She's a very independent soul. Always was. Something I guess she got from me and probably why we butted heads so often."

"True of most teenagers," I said.

"Isn't that the truth. Particularly one as headstrong as April. About a year and a half ago she hooked up with Jonathon Lindemann's group. It's a self-enlightenment and financial security group. He calls it The Lindemann Method or TLM. They were based in the Tampa area, which is where April met him, but he moved his operation up to Magnolia Springs, Alabama, where he started this commune-like place he calls Lindemann Farms."

So far, nothing new. I wanted to tell her that we already knew that, but Nicole sensed I was ready to interrupt and touched my arm. Her way of saying, *Keep your mouth shut and let her talk, and get comfortable and relaxed.*

Clarice continued. "April followed him there. That was a year ago. Then, three weeks ago, she disappeared. Since then I've gotten no calls, texts, or contact of any kind."

"Would that be unusual for her?" Nicole asked. "Not to contact you for that long?"

"Definitely. Look, after she hooked up with Jonathon's group, she became even more difficult. More angry and combative. She felt she knew everything about life and that I was backward and not forward-thinking enough." She sighed. "She became secretive about what she was doing and in particular about everything at TLM. The big rift came a year ago when I refused to let her take money from her trust to join that cult. They wanted a hundred and twenty thousand. Can you imagine? I blocked it. She blew up, ranted and raved, and then packed up and left for the farm. After she sued me for her trust money. Can you imagine? A freaking lawsuit. Regardless, we still talked several times a week, even though half of those chats descended into arguments about one thing or another. Usually how I was a witch for keeping her money locked down."

"We understand she won't get control of her trust until she's twenty-five," Nicole said.

"That's right. Her father and I decided that twenty-one was too young for that kind of money. I wanted thirty, but we finally settled on twenty-five."

"What are we talking about here?" I asked. "If you're comfortable with discussing that."

"Her trust is fourteen million."

Fourteen million? Dollars? What would I have done with that kind of money at twenty-one? Would I have bothered to play baseball, or buy a bar, or really do anything? That's the kind of money that could alter your life's trajectory. Maybe not for the good.

"That's an adult number," I said.

"It is. And based on her recent actions, she's far from that. Thank God we didn't give it to her earlier. She probably would've already given it to Jonathon by now."

"So she's really into this?" Nicole asked.

"To a point that I don't think is healthy."

"How did she hook up with him and his group?" Nicole asked.

A young man moved into the frame behind Clarice. I couldn't see his face, but he appeared to be tanned and bare chested. He placed a cup of coffee next to her, muttered, "Here, my love," and moved off-screen. She nodded a thanks.

Clarice sipped the coffee. "It was my fault. After my husband, April's father, died, we were both lost. It was ten years ago now but the pain remains."

In the background, I saw the man circle behind the pool. He was indeed young, early twenties would be my guess. Surfer-like blond hair, lean and fit body, he wore a bright red Speedo, a towel flung over one shoulder. The morning sun reflected off a gold chain around his neck. He again disappeared from view. Obviously catching some morning sun. I guessed he was there to soothe Clarice's pain, though to me she seemed more angry than anguished. Was I being too cynical? Probably, but it appeared that way to me. I mean, he didn't look like a pool guy, or a gardener, or her attorney, or the postman. For sure he wasn't a neighbor over to borrow a cup of sugar.

"Robert left us well off, but without him we both felt adrift. April was twelve and she took it very hard. She and her father were close.

She remained in a black funk for two years. At first she became quiet and withdrawn but this evolved into more defiant and angry behavior. I actually liked it better when she was locked in her room listening to music and whatever else she did up there. Then it was like one day she snapped out of that and began acting out. That led to trouble at school, and here at home. I wrote it off as teenage angst made worse by the loss of her father."

"Two things that can have profound effects on anyone," Nicole said. "Particularly a teenage girl."

"I know. I regret not taking it more seriously and getting her some help."

"Would she have accepted that?" I asked.

Another sip of coffee. "Probably not." She sighed. "You asked how she got involved with Jonathon. That's on me."

"How so?" I asked.

"It was two years ago. I was feeling lost and had no focus, no ambition, no anything. Then I read some stuff online about Jonathon Lindemann and his program. He was in Tampa then. I attended one of his weekend retreats. I loved his energy and even his process for improving self-worth and financial stability." She removed her sunglasses, gave a headshake. "God, I was so stupid and naive and didn't see it for what it was."

"Which was?" Nicole asked.

"Look, Jonathon made money for people. And for himself. He did for me before I cut ties."

"You belonged to TLM?" I asked.

"No. I never joined, but I did hire Jonathon as an advisor. Back then he had a few private clients and I was one of them. But as TLM grew, he pressured each of us to join. Many did, but to me that seemed wrong so I walked."

"Those types prey on the vulnerable," Nicole said.

"At that time, I was definitely vulnerable."

The young man reappeared in the background. He had a pool net and seemed to be removing some debris from the water. At least he earned his keep. Again, the cynical me felt his only duties weren't leaf removal.

"So it was the initiation fee that put you off?" I asked.

"That plus there was something smarmy about the farm, and the girls that worked there. It felt cultish and to me the girls were the window dressing. And Lord knows what else."

"You think he was using the girls to entertain clients?" Nicole asked.

"I do. And to recruit new ones."

"Are you sure?" I asked.

"If you mean do I have any proof, then no, but it felt that way. Why else would Jonathon mix a bunch of wealthy men with beautiful young girls? That's one of the many reasons I became so upset with April becoming part of it."

"How did she get involved?" Nicole asked.

"A few months after April finished her degree at FSU, early I might add, I took her to another of his Tampa-area retreat. She was twenty at the time. That's when I began to see cracks in his program. Its manipulative nature." She settled her sunglasses back in place. "But April completely bought into it, which became another source of conflict between us. Her point was that I had thought it was cool, and that I had brought her there, and that just because I no longer wanted to be part of it didn't mean she couldn't. She of course played the adult card." She shrugged. "As I said, the big blowup came when the judge quashed her lawsuit and I wouldn't release the money from her trust so she could officially join."

"My impression is that most of his clients are wealthy," I said. "Why did he offer April membership? She didn't have a job or anything."

"The trust," Clarice said. "Both mine and April's. He knew about them so he saw me as a current target and April as a future one. He wanted both of us in the fold."

"But you didn't join and refused to give April the money," Nicole said.

"Exactly. I don't think he was happy and I for sure know April wasn't."

"So she moved to the farm," I said.

"Ultimately. We banged heads off and on for a few months. She wanted to join TLM, I refused to release any money, and on and on it went. After one big fight, she packed up and moved up to Orange Beach."

"Did she have the money to do that?"

Clarice nodded. "The trust provided her with a monthly stipend, which kicked in when she was eighteen, but she doesn't get the entire amount until she's twenty-five. Her father set it up that way and I saw no reason to change it. Particularly now that she was acting like a spoiled child and buying into a group I didn't trust." Someone, presumably the young pool dude, said something to her. She turned that way, waved a hand, and said, "Not now, darling. Thanks." Then back to us, "April got a job at some restaurant down there so overall she was doing OK. After a few months she headed up to TLM's farm in Magnolia Springs."

"Since she didn't have the money to join, they hired her on as staff, right?" Nicole asked.

"Yes. She said she was doing marketing, which I suspect covers a lot of activities. Most of which I don't want to think about. Jonathon has quite an entourage at the farm. Mostly pretty young women like April."

I couldn't disagree with Clarice. Nothing about the entire arrangement sounded good. Why would a man who was looking for wealthy investors need young attractive women around? The answer was as old as time.

Clarice continued. "I was sure that some sort of exploitation was going on. What, I wasn't sure, but I do have a vivid imagination."

"As a so-called staff member," Nicole asked, "what were her duties?"

"Officially, to help run the farm, tend to guests, make them feel at home, that sort of thing." She looked down for a full minute. "My fear is exactly what that entailed. I know she traveled a lot. All over the country. What she called 'recruiting trips.'" Clarice shook her head. "Why would a twenty-two-year-old girl be needed for the recruitment of an investor?" A sadness crept over her face. "I can only think of one reason."

Me too, I thought. "Was she on one of these trips when she disappeared?" I asked.

"Not that I know. April always told me when she was traveling and where she was going. New York, L.A., Las Vegas, once to Vancouver. After a week of no contact, I tried to reach her. I called TLM but got nowhere. I traveled to the farm and met with Jonathon and his assistant, Rhea Wilson. Where Jonathon is charming, she's all business. Maybe that's not fair. She was nice and all, but with an undercurrent that business trumped all."

"Where did they say April was?"

"They didn't know. They said she wasn't happy there and left."

"Unhappy about what?"

"About not being a full member, about being an employee, about life. They actually told me it was my fault for not giving her the money so she could join. I told them that was none of their business. It wasn't a good meeting."

"Have you talked with them since then?" Nicole asked.

"I tried but they never returned my calls or acknowledged my emails." She rubbed her neck. "I went to the Sheriff's Department up in Bay Minette. They said what you'd expect. That April was an adult and can come and go as she pleases."

"What do you want from us?" I asked.

"To find her and bring her home. Alive and well."

CHAPTER 5

NICOLE SHUT DOWN her laptop and we sat in silence for a minute. I sifted through my feelings on everything Clarice Wilkerson had said. A lot of layers there.

"I don't like any of it," I finally said.

"What's to like?" Nicole responded.

"I don't think she just ran away."

"She didn't."

"So, what happened?" I asked.

She glanced at me. "You want the good, the bad, or the ugly?"

I looked toward the Gulf. The water lay calm, no wind or surf this morning. I didn't answer Nicole's question. I didn't need to since it was rhetorical. We each knew the answer. The good would be her falling into some high-paying job offered by a big-buck TLM member. Or her TLM travels led her to some solid-citizen, handsome, and of means gentleman and she was blissfully happy somewhere. Or maybe she simply met some random nice guy and moved on, escaping her mother's shadow. None of that really worked for me. Despite their ongoing mother-daughter conflict, she would have told her mother if any of these were the truth. Sure, April might be pissed about her mother keeping her inheritance under lock and key, and who knows, maybe she wasn't happy with her mother's apparent boy toy, but to run off somewhere and not tell Clarice, or at least fire a parting shot? It didn't make sense. According to Clarice, even when their war of wills blazed the hottest, April always kept in touch.

The bad? She was working and maybe traveling as a high-dollar TLM prostitute. We hadn't seen any real evidence that that was happening at TLM, but from what Clarice had said the possibility existed. April is a beautiful young lady, and maybe she decided using her God-given assets to make her own way could give her the independence she apparently craved and also extract her from her mother's grip. Maybe she figured it would just be until her trust fund fell into her lap. Not a great career choice, but at least she would maintain some degree of control of her life and make her own choices. Was her maternal rift deep enough to push her that far? Would that imply that TLM had nudged her down that path? Having lost access to Clarice's wealth, perhaps the Jonathon Lindemann/Rhea Wilson duo felt that keeping April embedded in all things TLM was a sound business decision. Building for the future.

Again, we had no evidence of that. I mean, TLM might have hired young attractive girls as part of their marketing strategy—didn't every TV ad, car show, and sporting event do the same? Sort of like cheerleaders. That didn't mean that TLM expected more than a pretty face and a friendly attitude from the young ladies they hired. Or did they?

The ugly? She was dead, or captive, or being trafficked somewhere. It's a big bad world with many dark corners.

The main question was—Did any of these scenarios mesh with April's disappearance? Was she in a happy relationship, a working girl, or in dire straits, or had she simply dropped off the grid because she was pissed at her mother?

The other question was—Did any of these roads lead to Jonathon Lindemann? Did he have a hand in her disappearance? Even a benign one. Did he introduce her to the love of her life, or pimp her around the world, or sell her to some foreign national? Had he killed her? A case could be made for each.

Or was all of this my imagination kicking into high gear? One thing for sure, I felt that Clarice had every reason to be concerned.

I hated that I was now hooked on finding the answer. Which of course was Ray's plan. Pancake's and Nicole's too. It was a conspiracy that seemed to repeat itself too often for comfort.

Maybe my life wasn't so good after all.

Nicole picked up her laptop and stood. "You ready to go chat with Tammy?"

No, I wanted to scream that I'm never ready to talk to Tammy. Can't I have a root canal instead? I stood. "Might as well get it over with."

She ruffled my hair. "Poor baby. I'll be there to protect you."

She's funny. Really, she is.

Nicole lived in Uncle Charles' mansion on The Point. One of the many multimillion-dollar homes that lined the beach of the exclusive enclave. Tammy and Walter Horton lived a few hundred yards down the same road. In Nicole's white SL550 Mercedes and Nicole behind the wheel, it took all of three minutes to blast down the slope, around the curve, and skid into Tammy's drive.

Tammy Horton's house was the last place I wanted to be. Anywhere else would be better. Not an exaggeration—I mean anywhere. A burning building, a sinking boat, a spiraling airplane, you get the picture.

The house was massive, glass, steel, modern. I felt like I owned part of it. Tammy, and her then attorney Walter, had gouged me for seven figures. Adult money to anyone. Good thing the Texas Rangers had paid me well. The silver lining was that it was worth it. A cool million to drop Tammy in someone else's lap? A deal I'd take again.

Tammy opened the door to Nicole's knock. She wore black yoga pants and a tight gray tee shirt. Her blonde hair wadded behind her head, pinned by a decorative chopstick.

"Hey, Nicole," she said. "Did you really have to bring Jake?"

So it begins.

"The kennel was full so I had no place to leave him."

I should've gone to Captain Rocky's where people like me.

"Too bad," Tammy said. "Come on in."

Tammy led us into her living room. Floor-to-ceiling accordion windows stood open to the massive deck and pool, and beyond the beach and the Gulf. We continued to the deck and sat at a round teak table. A warm breeze stirred from the water. A pitcher of lemonade and three glasses sat before us. "I made some lemonade in case you're thirsty."

"That'd be nice," Nicole said.

Tammy filled each glass, sliding one toward me. I took a sip. "Good. Thanks."

"Thanks for agreeing to talk with us," Nicole said.

"I love the irony here," Tammy said. She stabbed me with her gaze. "You coming to me for help after all the times I've asked you for help and you were a dick."

This is Tammy's World. No basis in reality but revolving tightly around Tammy. The help she referred to would be the constant stream of inane calls asking me to resolve her problem of the day. Tammy attracted complications like a black sweater does cat hair. The truth is that I almost—almost—always gave her answers but rarely the ones she wanted, so here I am, the dick. To me, the issues that wound her up were stupid, childish, and none of my business. I have a hang nail—buy some clippers or see your manicurist; I've gained a half a pound—skip dinner and work out an extra hour; Walter won't let me buy that thousand-dollar purse—use a paper bag; why is "fill in a name here" being such a bitch to me—go look in the mirror. You get the idea. Okay, so some of my responses leaned toward sarcastic, but when you get half a dozen calls a week, you run out of clever answers . . . and patience.

"But he's cute," Nicole said.

"He thinks so."

I knew this was a bad idea.

Tammy wasn't finished. "His major problem. His cuteness allows him to be an ass and still have friends. Pancake, anyway."

"We aren't here to talk about my charming personality," I said. It just came out. I hate it when I do that. I should be hunkering in the foxhole and avoiding incoming ordnance but, no, I had to jump right in it.

Tammy smirked. "You're not that charming. Or cute. Or whatever else you delude yourself with."

My brain finally got the message. This wasn't a battle worth fighting since in the end I'd lose. Guaranteed. It was the same with Nicole, and Pancake, and apparently Ray. Otherwise, I wouldn't be sitting here talking with Tammy The Insane about some cult.

I kept my mouth shut.

Nicole to the rescue. "Let's get to business. We want to learn about TLM and Jonathon Lindemann and your experience with them."

"I'm afraid I don't know a whole lot," Tammy said.

"But you know Jonathon?"

"A little. I heard about his TLM program around six months ago from someone in my yoga class. She raved about it so I checked it out. It looked pretty cool so I went to one of his three-day retreats over in Pensacola. It cost twelve hundred bucks, and Walter wasn't happy, but I went anyway. I also visited the farm Jonathon has up in Magnolia Springs a couple of times."

"But you never joined, right?" I asked.

"No." She frowned. "Walter wouldn't let me. He said it was too much money. He checked them out and said it looked like a scam. I don't know where he got that. Everyone I met said they had made good money with Jonathon's help. Sometimes Walter can be so narrow-minded."

Score one for good old Walter. He might have skewered me, but he also saved my bacon last year when I got sued. A long story. But, one thing about Walter is that he's smart and no one's fool.

"What did you think of it?" Nicole asked. "The program?"

"It's great. He teaches both self-improvement and how to make money. A winning combination to me."

Tammy needed the former, not the latter. Just look around the house I helped build and you'll see. I was sure the massive pool and deck were paid for with the money Walter had gouged from my bank account.

"That's fairly vague," Nicole said. "What's the gist of the program?"

"They teach people to look at what's not right about their life. To identify the things that are blocking happiness and success. Jonathon calls them 'toxic elements.' He shows you how to isolate and remove that stuff. Sort of like cutting out a cancer." She took a sip of lemonade. "Mentally, anyway. Then you reexamine everything and see if removing this problem makes things better or not. Or as Jonathon says, 'Is it merely your excuse for not being successful.' If fixing that problem doesn't help, look for others until you find the one that's blocking your path. Jonathon says everyone has roadblocks and that once those are removed, you're free to focus on what works for you and use that to create success and wealth."

Sounded like every self-help guru I'd ever read about. Every preacher, too, for that matter. Quit being an asshole or come to Jesus and your life will be fantastic and problem free. Oh, and send money. Cynical? You bet.

"Can you give me an example of how that works?" Nicole asked.

This should be fun. Tammy discussing her roadblocks. Maybe I could help here. Insanity, self-absorption, petty rivalries, pretense, gossip. Let's start with those and then move on down the list. Maybe Tammy sensed my anticipation because she talked about someone else.

"Sure," she began. "A woman I met there—her name was—you know, I can't remember—and we got along so well." Her brow furrowed. "We were going to get together but apparently I forgot to call her." She shrugged. "Life gets in the way, I guess."

Life such as yoga classes, manicures, hair styling, watching HGTV, and shopping. Plus, making harassing phone calls to your ex and your calendar fills quickly.

"Margarita Kellerman," Tammy said. She snapped a finger. "That's her name. She lives over in Orange Beach. She's a single mom and lives off a trust fund and property of some kind her husband left. She was having trouble with her kids. A boy and a girl, I think. Rebellious and angry and all that."

Sounded like Clarice Wilkerson. Inherited money, kid problems.

"Jonathon, actually his assistant Rhea Wilson—that's who this woman mostly worked with—showed her that she couldn't resolve her kid conflicts until the kids themselves matured enough to behave like adults. Then these conflicts would correct themselves. The son was already away at college and the girl would be leaving the next year. So, that would fix things. You know, out of sight, out of mind."

So, the great Jonathon Lindemann's advice is to ignore the problem until it went away? Where was the self-help part? Not to mention this didn't feel like sound parenting to me. Ignore your kids until you could shove them out the door and then life would be good. What could possibly blow up there?

"Rhea told Margarita that her main problems were boredom and a lack of direction. She told her that she needed to focus on herself, on something worthwhile, like growing her wealth. Margarita did and was ecstatic with the results." Tammy shrugged. "That's all I wanted to do. Make some money myself and not rely on Walter so much. He works too hard."

I started to say it only appeared that way but that in reality he hid in his office to avoid her. I mean, I would. Hell, I did. Not the office but the ballpark and the Rangers' training facility. My teammates thought I was a fitness fanatic and the hardest-working man in baseball. I actually hated working out, but I'd have eaten glass to avoid too much time with Tammy. That's what I wanted to say, but once again, I kept my thoughts locked up.

"Is that typical?" Nicole asked. "That he helps solve problems by offering financial advice?"

Tammy considered that. "I only met a few people, but yeah, that would fit."

Still sounded vague to me. But isn't that always the case with these self-help types? And again, preachers. They talk in parables and superlatives and make it sound like they're actually saying something. All the while passing the donation plate. Maybe I'm too cynical but whenever someone says they're going to make me a better person, make me richer, or save my soul, I immediately go to what's in it for them. I suspected that Jonathon Lindemann, like a sleight-of-hand magician, waved the shiny thing, the self-help, feel-good-about-yourself stuff, with one hand while convincing followers to fork over funds with the other.

"Does he pay for all this with his seminars?" I asked.

"Yeah. That and donations. Plus he takes a percentage of the profits people make."

Bingo.

"How does that work?" Nicole asked.

"Once you join, Jonathon works up a personal investment strategy. He's sort of a stock guru. Once you deposit funds into your account, he invests it. He then takes twenty percent of the profits. If there're no profits, then there're no fees. That's better than what Walter does. He pays his guy regardless of the outcome."

That exactly matched my thoughts on this subject. Which meant I agreed with Tammy. I didn't like it and felt I must be missing something big. No way my brain and hers could ever be in sync.

The take-home lesson here is that that's how they hook you. Paint a rosy picture of all the money you'll rake in, the big house and the yacht you'll own, and the fabulous trips you'll take to the far corners of the world. All your dreams will come true if you simply fork over your cash and let them play with it.

Of course, I'm no expert in the financial world. I don't invest. I don't buy stocks or funds or anything. Cash and CDs only. Mainly because I don't understand any of that other stuff. Does anyone? My take is that, like Vegas, Wall Street is run by criminals with computers.

"How can we get inside?" Nicole asked.

"You want to? Will you talk some sense into Walter? We'll all join." She glanced at me. "Even Jake. Though he'll probably screw it up."

"I'll keep a firm hold on his leash," Nicole said.

"Won't do much good," Tammy said. "I can call Rhea and set something up if you want."

"That would be great."

Tammy might be crazy—no might about it—but she wasn't stupid. She looked at me, then Nicole. "Why are you interested? I mean, I know Jake's way too cynical for this but what about you?"

"This goes no further," Nicole said. "Okay?"

Now she had Tammy's attention. Nothing got her going like secrets and gossip. She leaned forward. "What?"

"There's a missing girl. Her mother hired Ray to find her."

"She was there? On the farm?"

"Last her mother heard. That was three weeks ago."

"Was she a member or part of the staff?" Tammy asked.

"Staff," Nicole said. "Her mother wouldn't let her join."

"She sounds like Walter."

"What does the staff do?" I asked.

"Help run the farm, the seminars, help with recruiting, entertain clients, that sort of stuff."

"How many staff members are there?" Nicole asked.

Tammy's brow furrowed. "I don't know for sure but I'd guess around a couple of dozen. They're all young and attractive, which fits with the whole vibe of TLM."

"Do they travel?" I asked. "Go on recruiting trips?"

"I think so. Other trips too."

"Oh? For what?"

"I'm not sure. I told you I don't really know all that much. Maybe if Walter had let me join I could help more, plus I'd have made some money."

Well, Jonathon Lindemann would have.

"Did you happen to meet a girl named April Wilkerson while you were there?" Nicole asked.

Tammy shook her head. "I don't think so."

Nicole handed her the photo of April that Pancake had given her. "What about her?"

Tammy examined the picture. Her brow furrowed before she gave a slight nod. "Maybe. I'm not sure. She looks like a lot of the staff there. But I think she and a couple of other girls were with Rhea once when

I visited. For sure I never met her but I might've seen her." She handed the photo back. "Is she the missing girl?"

"Yes."

"Do you think she ran away or something?"

"We don't know," I said. "But her mother's worried."

"Maybe she's off on a recruiting trip or something like that."

It's the "something like that" that's troublesome. Young women traveling to either recruit or entertain for a con artist left me with an uncomfortable knot in my stomach. What had Ray dragged us into this time?

"The woman you met," Nicole said. "Margarita. Do you have her phone number? We'd like to talk with her also."

"Sure. I have it in my contacts."

Tammy gave us the info and we left, Tammy promising to call Rhea and arrange our visit.

CHAPTER 6

"You THINKING WHAT I'm thinking?" I asked Nicole.

"I am."

"Back to your place for some wild sex?"

She backed down Tammy's drive. "That's not what you're thinking."

"It's what I'm always thinking."

"Silver-tongued devil."

"I am. Maybe go see Walter first."

"But hold that other thought for later."

She accelerated up the road. The tires of her SL550 protested as she took the curve and roared past her place. I held on. You'd think I'd be used to it by now, but Nicole behind the wheel was always a thrill ride.

"He might be busy," I said.

"He'll see us."

"You sound sure of yourself."

She glanced at me while taking a turn at seventy plus. "Walter likes you."

"No, he doesn't."

"You and he have a common bond. Tammy."

Bond? Maybe in a perverse way. Walter was married to her, while for me Tammy was more like gum stuck to your shoe. Something annoying that you could never completely remove and that could trip you at any minute.

"Don't you think that alone would create animosity?" I asked.

"He seems happy with her."

"Which makes me question his judgment, common sense, and sanity."

"You married her," Nicole said.

"I was young and stupid. Walter is neither."

Nicole whipped the car off Peppermill Road and onto Beach Boulevard, Highway 182, toward Gulf Shores and Walter's office. She slowed, checked for cross traffic, then blew through a stop sign before veering off on a two-lane shortcut. The SL ate up the road while I tried to keep all my organs in place. My stomach proved difficult. Luckily, we made it to Walter's without tangling with a plane, train, or automobile, completing another successful flight on Air Nicole.

Constance Streelman, Walter's receptionist, greeted us from behind her desk.

"Mister Longly. Nicole. What brings you by?"

"We need to chat with Walter for a minute."

She glanced at her watch. "He's with a client but should be wrapping that up about now. Then he has about fifteen minutes. Would that suffice?"

"It would," I said. "Thanks."

"Coffee or a soft drink?" Constance asked.

"We're good," Nicole said.

"Loved your movie."

"Thanks," Nicole said.

Nicole's movie *Murderwood* had been a huge success worldwide, which included Gulf Shores.

"I mean, Kirk Ford," Constance said. "How could it not be good. He's so handsome."

"Kirk is definitely that. Plus, he has box office clout. I got lucky having him as the star."

"It was a very good thriller. I think it would've worked even without him. But, for sure, his face doesn't hurt."

Walter appeared, along with a neatly dressed woman. He nodded to us as he spoke to the woman. "I'll have the documents ready in a couple of days. We'll call and set up a time to get them signed."

She thanked him and left.

"Jake and Nicole need a minute of your time," Constance said.

"Don't tell me you're being sued again?" Walter asked.

Several months back I was sued by a drunk who got horsey with my staff, threatened me, and when my manager, Carla Martinez, took his car keys so he couldn't drive, he became angry and threatening. Pancake settled him in short order with a bear hug and we stuck him in a cab, which I paid for, and held his keys until he could return sober the next day. He sued for a bunch of stuff including car theft, assault, kidnapping, and a couple of other bogus charges. Walter got the judge to toss the case.

"No," I said. "I've been a good boy."

"Not that good," Nicole said.

Walter laughed. "Come on back."

Walter Horton was an expensive dude. Not just his office decor and his fees, but his clothing. He wore a designer gray suit with a pale blue shirt and blue- and gray-striped tie, none of which could be found on the rack. Good thing his practice was large and his fees excessive since he needed to pay for all this, plus Tammy, who could go through money like a barracuda through a school of fish.

He glanced at his solid gold Rolex as he sat. "What can I do for you?"

"Jonathon Lindemann," I said.

He gave me a quizzical look. Apparently not the topic he expected. "What about him?"

"We understand Tammy wanted to join his little cult but you halted that," Nicole said.

"I did."

"You looked into him?" I asked.

"I take it you talked to Tammy," Walter said.

"Yes," Nicole said. "She said you called him a scam artist or something like that."

"I did." He leaned back in his chair and adjusted his shirt cuffs exposing gold cuff links. "Why are you asking?"

"This stays here in this room," I said.

"Okay. Now I am intrigued."

"A girl who worked on his farm, retreat, whatever it is, as part of the staff has disappeared. Her mother hired Ray to find her."

"Do you think something has happened to her?" Walter asked.

"We don't know," I said. "We're just beginning to look into it."

"Have you been to his farm? Or met him?"

"Not yet," Nicole said. "We're still doing background so we'll be prepared."

Walter nodded his approval of that approach. "I've never met him either. Tammy has and she's been to that farm of his and a couple of his seminars. You might say she was enthralled. When she wanted to pony up a hundred and twenty thousand to join the group, I looked into it."

"And?"

"I suspect you know he teaches all that touchy-feely, self-improvement crap."

I don't know why, given our past history, but I liked Walter. He was a no-BS kind of guy. He didn't waste time and didn't suffer fools. Well, except for Tammy. I guess everyone has a personal blind spot.

"Yes," I said. "He also promotes some get-rich program."

"From what I found, the former feeds the latter."

"In what way?" Nicole asked.

"Are you familiar with the old poker expression that says if you can't spot the pigeon at the table, it's you." He shrugged. "I think Jonathon Lindemann is adept at identifying pigeons. If you think about it, once he gets someone to post up the entry fee, he has them. Then when he dumps his investment scheme on them, they're already hooked. I suspect he makes them feel like insiders on the gravy train."

Well put.

"Does he make money for them?" I asked.

"From what I found, which isn't a lot, he does okay and seems to regularly pay dividends to his investors."

"Not all of them?"

"Not that I could find, but digging out that stuff, without a subpoena, isn't my forte."

That would be Pancake's domain.

Walter continued. "Obviously these dividends are a tiny fraction of the total investment. Just enough to keep everyone happy. What happens to the principal I never found."

"Sounds like a Ponzi scheme," Nicole said.

"It does," Walter said. "Like Madoff and others."

"How'd you find all this out?" I asked.

"I have a guy at a bank in Mobile. He helps me when I need to track down financial assets. Wills, contracts, divorces, and the like. Of course, without the blessing of a judge he could only go so far. But he was able to track some of the funds and that's what he found. How much money Lindemann actually controls and where it is, I don't know." Another glance at his watch. "Regardless, there were enough questions for me to say no when Tammy wanted to hook up with this guy."

"Seems like a smart move to me," I said.

"I don't see how this could be related to your missing young lady," Walter said. "Or am I missing something?"

"We don't either," Nicole said. "But you never know. Gurus, money, and young women can be a dangerous stew. For the women."

CHAPTER 7

ORANGE BEACH, ALABAMA, just east of Gulf Shores and near the Florida border, was a combination of upscale and tourist-grade properties, including a row of high-rise condos along the sand. Margarita Kellerman lived on a spit of land sandwiched between Arnica Bay and Bayou St. John. Her home hung off South Bayshore Drive and faced south.

Her house, maybe the largest in the neighborhood, wasn't modest, which was saying something. The driveway lapped a four-tiered fountain nestled among bright red and yellow flowers. Up a half a dozen steps, a massive dark oak front door stood ajar. Nicole rang the bell.

I heard footsteps, the door swung open, and a forty-ish woman with long dark hair that fell down her back in a braid greeted us.

"That didn't take long," she said.

As we were leaving Walter's, Tammy texted Nicole, saying she had called Margarita and she would be happy to talk with us. Nicole called Margarita who said her morning was free, and gave us her address. It should have taken a half hour to get there, but Nicole's driving cut that in half.

"Not much traffic," Nicole said.

Not exactly how I remembered the trip. Maybe not stop-and-go but still thick enough. Of course, Nicole sliced and diced them so here we were. Early.

"I'm Margarita. Please come in."

She led us into a massive living room that was modern and beach chic. I got that from some show on HGTV about folks buying beach properties. A wall of windows looked over a massive pool and beyond a long pier that ended at a sizable boathouse. Farther still were Bayou St. John and Ono Island, another well-heeled neighborhood.

"Can I get you anything to drink?" Margarita asked.

We declined and sat on a sofa, facing her across a tastefully distressed wooden coffee table.

"Thanks for speaking with us," Nicole said.

"Tammy told me about you both. Impressive. An ex–Major League Baseball player and a big-time movie executive."

"She might have oversold us," I said.

"Looking at you two, I doubt it. She also said you were interested in joining TLM."

"We're exploring it," Nicole said.

"It's wonderful," Margarita said. "Jonathon's such a kind man. He's smart and he makes money."

"That's what we hear," I said.

"He's helped me in many ways."

"Such as?" Nicole asked.

"I have a son and a daughter, both in their early twenties now. But they're still as difficult as they were when they were teenagers." She shook her head. "Maxwell, my late husband, completely spoiled them. The more he let them get away with, the more stuff he bought them, the more difficult they became. He and I had more than a few disagreements over that." She gave us a tight smile. "But I guess that's a common dynamic. One parent spoils, the other disciplines."

My mother didn't spoil or pamper me, but compared to Ray she was a piece of cake. Ray had rules. Hell, even his rules had rules.

"I think that's universal," Nicole said.

"Maxwell never said no so I was left keeping them in check, which made me the bad guy. Or as my daughter often said, 'the wicked witch of the Gulf.'"

"Jonathon Lindemann helped you with that?" I asked.

"Not directly, of course, but he showed me how to be more independent. How to be a free thinker and not feel guilt over my kids' antagonism toward me. He encouraged me to step back and see the bigger picture. To let them be adults and run their own lives and for me to do the same."

"Not easy to do," Nicole said.

"Very true. But it's not like they were tossed on the street. When Maxwell died, I of course retained the bulk of the estate and the property, but the kids each received a sizable trust so they aren't suffering. Far from it. It isn't a money problem."

"A control issue?" I asked.

"Exactly. It was hard for me to let go, stop being a parent, and stop worrying day and night if they were okay." She glanced toward the wall of windows. "Your imagination can be a tough taskmaster. Particularly in the dead of night when you don't know where your children are and what they're doing."

I liked Margarita. She was evidently still damaged by losing her husband and by all that had happened with her children. How could she not be? But she also seemed strong. Did the damage make her vulnerable and an easy target for the likes of Jonathon Lindemann? Or did he add to her strength? Help with her perspective?

"How did you find out about TLM?" I asked

"A couple of years ago, while I was struggling with all this—" she waved a hand at nothing in particular— "the kids, Maxwell's death, trying to figure out how to run the property business, I attended a seminar he put on over in Pensacola. I was impressed. I met a few people who belonged and when he set up his retreat in Magnolia Springs, I visited and ended up joining. That was nearly a year ago."

"What's that place like?" Nicole asked.

"Magnificent. I don't know how many acres he has but the property is beautiful and restful with rolling hills and lots of trees. He has a fabulous lodge and maybe two dozen cabins where members and potential members can stay. There's a dining hall–like restaurant and the food they turn out rivals five-star resorts. My favorite part is the huge patio, shaded by magnificent trees. I could spend all day there. In fact, I have."

"Sounds wonderful," Nicole said.

"It's very relaxing. Your blood pressure drops ten points as soon as you drive up. I've been there several times. Once I stayed for two weeks and in the end didn't want to leave."

"We understand TLM requires a fairly large financial commitment," I said.

"It is. But well worth it."

"In what ways?" Nicole asked.

"Aside from all the personal stuff he helped me with, Jonathon's a master at investing. He knows where to put money to make money."

"We were told the buy-in is over a hundred K," I said. "Is that part of the investment, or is it simply a membership fee?"

"Both actually. Jonathon says he only deals with people who are committed to the program. No small-time investors or those unwilling to buy into TLM. He says that a steep initiation fee keeps the membership exclusive."

No doubt about that. The average Joe driving his pickup to work wouldn't qualify. Probably wouldn't fall for it either. I suspect most guys who drove a pickup to work were as cynical as me.

Margarita continued. "Only half of the one hundred and twenty thousand is a true initiation fee. The other half he invests. It's yours and you can remove it at any time."

"So sixty K isn't refundable, so to speak?"

"No. But again, it keeps the noncommitted away."

"You don't have to answer if you're uncomfortable with it," Nicole asked. "But how has your investing experience been with the other sixty thousand?"

"Oh, that's the minimum. Most members invest much more." She shrugged. "I've invested a total of five hundred thousand so far."

"And?" I asked.

"It's worked out very well. I get a regular quarterly dividend check. It pencils out to around two percent per quarter so that would be eight percent each year. I think that's good."

"So, you'd do it again?" I asked.

"Absolutely." She laughed. "In fact, I'm thinking of adding more cash to my portfolio."

"That's a lot of money," I said.

"Not really. There're some big players who are way up the money tree."

"What are we talking here?" I asked.

"I've heard several members are up to six or seven million and a few much more than that. A little rich for my blood."

What this meant to me was that Walter had balked at more than a mere hundred and twenty thousand. Knowing Tammy, there's no way she'd enter at the minimum. That wasn't in her nature. The best clothes, hotels, champagne, cars, you name it. Tammy saw herself at the top of the food chain. I suspect Walter knew that all too well and knew that once she got in the door she would hammer him to climb the ladder. Better to cut the legs out from under it early on. Smart move.

"We understand that besides members, TLM has a permanent staff," Nicole said.

"They do. A group of very bright young people. They don't have the financial clout to join—not yet anyway—but Jonathon employs them to help run the day-to-day stuff, while educating them in his personal development programs and investment strategies. He says he's building the next generation of TLM members. One of the many admirable things about him."

"What do they do exactly?"

"Help run the seminars, make the members and guests comfortable, help Jonathon and Rhea with recruiting. Lots of stuff from what I can tell."

"We talked with the mother of one of the staff. A girl named April Wilkerson. Did you ever meet her?"

"I did. She's a beautiful and bright young lady. Her mother should be proud."

"She is. But she said she hadn't heard from her for a few weeks."

"She's probably busy as most of the staff is. Maybe she's off on a recruiting trip." She sighed. "My kids don't call me often either."

"When did you see her last?" Nicole asked.

A wave of concern swept over Margarita's face. "When I was last there. Maybe six weeks ago."

"We'll try to look her up when we're there," I said, hoping to offset any curiosity she might have about our line of questioning. It seemed to work as her face lit up.

"So, you're going to visit?" Margarita asked.

"We are," Nicole said. "Tammy Horton's trying to set up a meeting with Rhea Wilson for us," Nicole said.

"Rhea's delightful. Tammy, too, for that matter."

My mind was screaming, "No, she isn't. She's a psycho." I managed to rein it in. But her thinking Tammy was delightful knocked some of the shine off my image of her.

"You'll like Rhea. Smart, together, pleasant," Margarita continued. "I'll also give her a call and tell her I heartily approve of you both."

"That's very kind of you," Nicole said.

"We have to keep TLM growing."

I guessed the "we" meant all the current TLM cult members and the "growing" reflected the fact that Ponzi schemes always need a fresh and continuous influx of money. Otherwise they collapse under their own weight.

We thanked Margarita and left.

CHAPTER 8

NICOLE BLASTED BACK down Highway 182 toward Gulf Shores. The SL's top was down and the warm air swirled around us. When traffic finally slowed her to somewhere around the posted limit, I could speak and be heard.

"A half a million is adult money," I said.

"Seven mil even more so."

"If Jonathon Lindemann's a scam artist, he's a good one."

"I'd bet Pancake knows the answer to that," she said.

"We'll know soon enough."

"Sooner if these people will get off the road."

These people were the ones obeying the law, which made her crazy and me nervous. She wasn't above a daredevil shoulder pass.

"We have time. Pancake won't be there for another fifteen minutes."

"Really?" She glanced at me. "Have you ever known him not to be early for lunch?"

She had a point. The plan was to meet him at Captain Rocky's at noon. Nicole did indeed pass a smoking and rickety pickup on the right and we pulled into the lot five minutes early. Pancake's truck sat near the entrance.

"Told you," she said.

We found the big guy at my private corner table on the deck. Being the owner did have certain privileges. In truth, Pancake used it more than I did. It was his office when he wasn't at Ray's.

"About time," Pancake said as we sat. "I'm hungry."

"We aren't late," I said. "Besides, when did that ever stop you from eating?"

"I'm turning over a new leaf and trying to be more polite."

A mission doomed to failure.

"When did this program begin?" I asked.

"On the way over. This morning Ray said something about gathering more info with sugar rather than intimidation."

"Ray said that?" I asked.

"He did."

"Ray doesn't use sugar. Ever."

Pancake's brow furrowed. "You're right. Hell, I could've already ordered."

So much for the new and improved Pancake.

Our waitress appeared. Not my manager, Carla, who usually took care of us, but the new girl I had hired just two days ago. The truth? I met her after Carla had interviewed and hired her. She was young, eager, blonde, cute, and perfect for Captain Rocky's. She placed a menu on the table, not yet knowing we knew it by heart.

"Well, look at you," Pancake said to her. "Where'd you come from?"

"This is Libby Sagstrom," I said. "It's her second day."

"I can tell you right now you're better than anything on the menu," Pancake said.

"Ignore him," I said.

Libby laughed. "Carla's already warned me."

Pancake twisted toward her. "Why don't you take a seat on my knee and tell me what the specials are."

She laughed again. "I don't think the boss man would like that."
She winked at me. "Besides, everything here's special."

"Good answer," Nicole said. "I think you'll do just fine here."

"I worked at the Flora-Bama for a year," Libby said. "This place is
an oasis by comparison."

A Gulf Coast institution, the Flora-Bama is a massive, piecemeal,
slapped-together plank structure on the sand just steps over the
Alabama-Florida state line. Famous for alcohol, multiple live bands,
unruly crowds, and insanity.

"In that case," Pancake said, "bring me two from page one and two
from page two. Surprise me."

Libby raised an eyebrow. "Love an adventurous man."

Yes, she will do well here.

Nicole and I ordered and Libby drifted toward the kitchen.

"What'd you find out today?" Pancake asked.

I went over our conversations with Tammy, Walter, and Margarita
Kellerman. Nicole added her own thoughts. Tammy would love to
join and Margarita seemed satisfied not only with Jonathon's help
on the domestic front but also with her investments. Walter revealed
less enthusiasm.

"I think Walter had serious concerns about TLM," I added. "He
felt it was a scam."

"That was my take, too," Nicole said. "Margarita did say that she'd
received regular dividend checks so that's something."

"She dropped a half a million in Jonathon's lap," I said. "She said
others had given him much more. In the multiple millions."

Pancake listened, considered everything, nodded. "That's what
I'm seeing."

He went through what he and Ray had uncovered so far. Jonathon's
personal net worth was just over forty million. A combination of
selling his previous real estate business to his partners and the rental

properties he still held. Plus the land in Magnolia Springs, which he owned personally and rented to TLM.

"He rents the farm to himself?"

"More or less," Pancake said. "TLM is a separate entity. Obviously, he owns it. He also gets paid as the director and CEO. Rhea Wilson is the CFO and she's also salaried."

"What are we talking about here?" Nicole asked.

"He's paid a million a year and Rhea a half. That's the base, but they each seem to have unlimited funds for travel, teaching, recruiting, whatever."

"TLM is very good to Jonathon and Rhea," Nicole said.

"Not unusual," Pancake said. "Most of these cultlike organizations rake in cash for the principals. Remember that Rajneesh dude? Up in Oregon?"

"The one that tried to poison the town?" Nicole asked.

"Yep. Folks came to his cult to find enlightenment and self-worth. Of course, that required signing all their worldly goods over to the Baghwan. That was his name—Baghwan Rajneesh. Which they happily did."

I remembered him now. "Didn't he buy a bunch of Rolls-Royces?"

Pancake nodded. "Nearly a hundred."

"Do you think Jonathon Lindemann is like that?" Nicole asked.

"Not really." Pancake glanced toward the water. "His followers aren't all bound up in a compound. They're free to come and go, and I don't see a religious component to TLM."

Our food arrived. Libby placed Nicole's taco salad and my BLT on the table. Behind her, two of the kitchen guys carried four plates for Pancake. A rack of ribs, half a smoked chicken, a pile of onion rings, and, for good measure, a cheeseburger.

"Perfect," Pancake said. "It's like you read my mind."

"Carla helped," Libby said.

"She's truly a good person."

Pancake felt that way about anyone who gave him food.

"I have a basket of French fries coming," Libby said.

"Dump some chili on them," Pancake said. "And a couple of hand-fuls of cheese."

"Will do. Back in a sec."

Like a starving lion on the Serengeti, Pancake tore apart the rack of ribs and went at it. Pancake's scorched-earth approach to food was always a sight to behold.

He pointed a gnawed rib bone at me. "What I'm finding though is that his investing strategies are a bit suspect."

"Oh?"

He shoved an onion ring in his mouth. "Around eighty percent of the money is offshore. Singapore, the Czech Republic, and St. Lucia."

"Really?" Nicole asked. "That sounds sketchy."

Pancake's chili fries, mounded with cheese, arrived. Libby found an open spot on the table to set them down, saying, "Those look good."

"They are," Pancake said. "Take a seat. Have some."

She laughed. "Tempting, but I might get fired."

"Don't worry," Pancake said. "I know the owner, and I have decades of dirt on him."

"Not to mention he's a wimp," Nicole said.

Welcome to my life.

Nicole ruffled my hair. "But he's an okay boyfriend."

"Okay?" I said, looking at Nicole. "Just okay?"

She laughed. "Outstanding. Stupendous. Nonpareil."

Nonpareil? I made a mental note to look that up.

"I'll check back in a few and make sure everything's okay," Libby said. One corner of her mouth lifted. "Or nonpareil."

Did everyone know the definition of that word except me?

Pancake attacked the chicken. "So most of the investment money Lindemann's taken in is stashed in countries known for hiding cash. Places where it's hard to trace and quantify. The other twenty percent is invested in very conservative stuff. CDs, cash, and a few mutuals. Nothing earthshaking."

"You think he's using those funds to pay the so-called dividends?" I asked.

"Bingo. Can you say Bernie Madoff? As long as he keeps his investors on the reservation, the money continues to pile up."

"And the endgame?" Nicole asked. "When the house of cards comes down?"

"He's off to wherever. Some place with no extradition." He shrugged. "It's an old and repetitive story."

"That's what's happening?" I asked.

Pancake swiped his face with a napkin. "I don't know for sure yet but it sure smells that way."

Nicole's phone buzzed an incoming text message. She picked it up and glanced at the screen. "Tammy. She set up a meeting for us with Rhea Wilson and Jonathon Lindemann tomorrow morning."

Pancake laughed. "She going to be there?"

"That's all we'd need," I said. "Trying to impress the power brokers while juggling Tammy's insanity."

"Based on her text, I don't think she'll show up." Nicole handed me her phone so I could read Tammy's lengthy message. "She asked us to lean on Jonathon to let her join without the down payment."

"She apparently thinks we owe her that," I said. I handed the phone back to Nicole.

"I thought she owed you," Pancake said.

"You mean for her house?"

Pancake gnawed another rib. "That and your shaky mental health."

CHAPTER 9

THE NEXT MORNING just after nine a.m., we rolled into Magnolia Springs, Nicole actually keeping below the speed limit. This after a harrowing trip north on Highway 59 and west on Highway 98. Our appointment with Rhea Wilson and Jonathon Lindemann was at ten, which gave us enough time to stop by and see Bobby Taylor.

Taylor owned and worked a farm near Magnolia Springs. We had met him while investigating the murder of Emily Patterson over in Fairhope. Pancake's sixth-grade sweetheart, Emily was headed toward divorce when she ended up dead. One of the suspects, Charlie Martin, who had been dating Emily at the time of her death, was Taylor's cousin. Taylor had been forthcoming and helpful. Now I hoped he could offer us some inside scoop on Lindemann Farms since he was deeply rooted in the community and knew everyone and everything about the goings-on in the area. I had called earlier and asked if we could swing by to talk about TLM and Lindemann Farms. His response: "Oh yeah, those folks."

Nicole pulled up in front of his home, a wooden structure with a slanted green metal roof and a gallery porch that extended the width of the house, a large red barn beyond. Bobby Taylor squatted in a patch garden next to the house. He stood, turned our way, dusted dirt from his hands, and walked toward us.

"How're you doing?" I asked.

"Busy as usual." He nodded toward the thirty-foot-square garden. "I've got some tomatoes, beans, and squash working."

The plants appeared healthy and lush, a few green tomatoes visible.

He tugged a red cloth from his back pocket and mopped his brow. "How about some tea?"

"That'd be good," I said.

Bobby settled us on a porch swing, disappeared inside, and returned with three glasses of sweet tea. He handed one to Nicole, then me, and flopped into a rocker.

I took a sip. "Good."

"Hard to screw up tea."

"How's your cousin Charlie doing?" Nicole asked.

Bobby shrugged. "Getting by. He's still tore up over what happened to Emily. But I'd say all things considered he's handling it pretty well. He's been seeing another girl, but it's not the same. He really loved Emily. This one, seems to me, less so."

"Time will help," I said.

Bobby nodded. "That's what I been telling him. Not sure he listens all that well."

I thought of Pancake. Emily's murder tore a hole in Pancake's heart too. We hadn't seen her since sixth grade, since she and her family left Gulf Shores and dropped anchor in Fairhope, but for Pancake, she was that first love. The one that stays with you forever. He too was still dealing with Emily's death. Though he'd never show it, I knew it was there, chewing on his insides. I imagined it was even more so for Charlie Martin. His wounds were much fresher.

"So you want to chat about that Lindemann Farm group?" Bobby asked.

"We do."

"Why?" Another sip of tea. "If you don't mind me asking."

I hesitated. Did I want to tell him the truth? That a young woman was missing? Risk our cover being blown? Would he talk about it with his friends in the bars and restaurants? What if it got back to the TLM folks? They'd know we weren't simply interested parties, looking to join their little cult, but rather had another agenda. That could close a lot of doors. I wrestled with what to say. Nicole didn't.

"A girl who works there," Nicole said. "She and her mother had a falling-out. Typical mother-daughter stuff. The girl won't return her calls or texts and the mother's frantic. Guilt and all that. She asked us to sit down and have a chat with her daughter. See if we could at least get her to call."

Bobby stared at the floor for a beat, then gave a slow nod. "I see."

I wasn't sure he bought that story. Even though it was partially true, I'm not sure I would have either. Sure, the mother had lost contact with her daughter and was worried, but hiring a P.I. firm to get your daughter to call home probably seemed excessive.

"The mother's a little goofy," I added, an attempt to explain, or soften, the half-truth. "She's wrapped too tight, probably overreacting, and that might be why the daughter doesn't want to talk to her. But we said we'd at least go say hello and deliver her plea."

Bobby looked up. "Family shit. It's always the worst."

Isn't that so.

"We're headed over to the farm to see her," Nicole said. "We thought you might have an opinion about them so we'll know what we're walking into."

"What they are is a bunch of rich folks. I've never seen so many Mercedes, BMWs, even a couple of those Bentleys. Those things cost more than my entire farm. They drive too fast and aren't overly patient when it comes to working folks." He shrugged. "Tractors can only go so fast."

"Any issues?" Nicole asked. "Other than that?"

"For the most part they stay to themselves in that private compound, but when they have some event going on, they sure clog up the
roads." He scratched one ear. "But they do spend money at the few
restaurants we have around here and those over in Fairhope so there is
that. But, for us out here on the farm, they sometimes get in the way."

"Any real confrontations?" I asked.

"Not that I know. I haven't heard anyone complaining anyway. I
just wish they'd stay down on the coast where they belong. Or Florida,
or Atlanta, or New York, or wherever they're from. From what I hear,
they come from all over." A sip of tea. "Sure seems odd they'd end up
here in Magnolia Springs."

"They're probably attracted by Jonathon Lindemann's seminars
and retreats," Nicole said.

"Yeah, I heard he was some self-help dude." Another gulp of tea.
"Seems like someone's always trying to save folks from themselves.
I've never seen any of that work out all that well."

Isn't that the truth. Self-help books and seminars are big business.

"If I'm hearing you right," I said, "other than them driving too fast,
they've been OK neighbors?"

He nodded. "I'd say that's true. For me anyway, and I ain't heard
anything that contradicts that."

"What do you think?" Nicole asked once we said our goodbyes,
thanked Bobby for seeing us, and were back on the road.

"Other than being irritated at the occasional traffic they drag in,
he didn't seem to have any issues with the group. If anyone else did, I
think he'd know. News and gossip out here in these small farm communities spreads like a bad virus."

Nicole turned onto Magnolia Springs Highway. "We'll see for
ourselves soon."

We crossed the Magnolia River, and she hung a left on Richards
Lane. Soon, Lindemann Farms materialized.

CHAPTER 10

THE IMPRESSIVE ENTRANCE sported two eight-foot stone columns, a black metal gate stretching between, and, as if we needed reminding, an arched redwood cap that read "Lindemann Farms." Nicole rolled to a stop at the small guardhouse and a man stepped out. He wore jeans, a gray golf shirt with "Lindemann Farms" in red embroidery on the left chest, and aviator-style sunglasses. He held a clipboard in one hand, a ball point in the other.

"Hello, folks," he said with a relaxed and friendly smile.

"We're here to see Rhea Wilson and Jonathon Lindemann," Nicole said, her own smile high-wattage.

The guard stared for a beat—the Nicole effect—and then said, "Do you have an appointment?"

"We do," she said. "Jake Longly and Nicole Jamison."

He checked his list while clicking the ball point a few times. "Yes, you do." He examined Nicole again. "Welcome to Lindemann Farms."

"Thanks. We're excited to see it."

"Lots to see." He pointed up the paved road beyond the gate. "Head up that way. This road'll bend to the right then you'll see the main buildings. The business offices are just left of the lodge. Someone'll greet you there." He reached inside the shack, pressed a button, and the gate swung open. Nicole entered, giving the guard a wave and another smile.

The property was lush and green with rolling fields and wads of pines and maples and oaks. An eight-foot metal-wire fence, painted flat black so that it seemed to disappear and not distract from the pastoral beauty, embraced the entire property. At least, what we could see of it.

"Nice," Nicole said.

"The perfect place to get your mind right," I said.

"And open your wallet."

The paved road was smooth and flawless. The drives to most farms in this neck of the woods were gravel or dirt or some combination. Many were simply rutted tracks with a weed strip down the middle. Farmers didn't care much about niceties, only function. Money was best spent on tractors, fertilizers, and livestock feed. Here, the only gravel visible lined each side of the drive and was dotted with clusters of red, pink, and white azaleas.

The road veered right and punched into the shade of a thick forest but after a hundred yards, it opened into another clearing that revealed a group of huddled buildings in the distance. Their log construction blended perfectly with the terrain. The largest of the grouping, a two-story slanted-roof affair, appeared to be the lodge, its broad porch holding several rockers and a couple of swings. Homey and country in a sort of upscale Cracker Barrel way. Which reminded me, I was hungry. A bowl of greens and a hunk of cornbread sounded good about now.

A pair of young ladies exited the lodge's front door and waved to us. A blonde and a redhead, both attractive, slim, and attired like the gate guard in jeans and gray Lindemann Farms polos. Nicole stopped. The blonde descended the stairs toward us.

"Welcome," she said. "You can park right there." She pointed to the area sandwiched between the lodge and what appeared to be the offices. It, too, was perfectly paved. No dust or dirt for your Bentley. Not at Lindemann Farms. In fact, a white Bentley convertible sat in the lot, its nose aimed at the office building. Only two other cars were present—a big BMW and a Range Rover.

We climbed out and walked toward the young lady.

"I'm Lorie," she said. "You must be Jake and Nicole."

So we were not only expected but on a first-name basis already. Smart marketing. If you were going to pry money out of folks, offer up that personal touch and make them feel special.

"We are," Nicole said.

"We've been looking forward to your visit."

Of course they were. We being the latest sheep ripe for shearing. I know, I'm not feeling all warm and fuzzy about all this attention, but wasn't it true that we here to be fleeced? Or so they thought, easy marks being the role Ray had assigned us. I flashed on what Tammy had said about them being nice and welcoming. That bothered me on several levels. Tammy never thought anyone was nice, much less welcoming. She judged people by their social status and wealth. Anyone who didn't reside in The Point was immediately suspect. But flash, dash, and cash got her attention. Which is why she never saw their warm hospitality as good marketing, or manipulation, but rather as an open door into an exclusive fraternity of rich folks. Something she wanted to be part of and why she was incensed that their membership rules weren't flexible enough for her to join their little club for free. Or at least at a number she could weasel out of Walter. Didn't they realize she was Tammy Horton, the wife of the best attorney along the Gulf Coast? Surely, they'd come to their senses and embrace her. Something she expected Nicole and I would somehow manage. The missing April Wilkerson wasn't part of Tammy's equation.

Lorie turned and waved a hand. "Let's go inside where it's cooler." She led us up the stairs to where the redhead stood. "This is Robin."

Robin extended a hand and we shook. "Welcome. We're so glad you could make it."

The lobby was cavernous, its log-beamed ceiling soaring twenty feet above us. Oversized sofas and chairs and a few lamp-topped coffee tables rested in comfortable pods on the slate flooring and strategically placed area rugs. One grouping faced a massive floor-to-ceiling stone fireplace that dominated one wall.

"Impressive," I said, getting into character.

"It is," Nicole said. "Much more so than advertised."

"We get that a lot," Robin said. "Mr. Lindemann does everything top drawer."

"You should see the rooms," Lorie said. "Just plain wow."

"Will you be staying with us tonight?" Robin asked.

"No," I said. "We have to head back down to Gulf Shores later today."

"If you change your mind, we have a suite set up for you. You'll love it."

"I can't imagine we wouldn't," Nicole said.

"Can I get you something to drink?" Robin asked. "Coffee, tea, a soft drink?" She smiled. "Something more potent?"

"We're good," Nicole said.

"Rhea should be here soon," Lorie said.

"There she is." Robin nodded.

Rhea Wilson, whom I recognized from TLM's website, pushed through the front door and walked toward us. She wore designer jeans and a lemon yellow silk shirt, untucked. She extended a hand. "Welcome to Lindemann Farms. I'm Rhea Wilson, the Executive Director."

"Nicole," Nicole said as she shook Rhea's hand. "This is Jake."

We shook. Her grip was firm and confident.

"I see you've met Lorie and Robin."

I had to admit I liked the casualness everyone displayed. Rhea's jeans, even if they probably cost a bunch of hundies, spoke to the relaxed vibe, and the fact that first names seemed to be the norm was indeed inviting. See? Marketing.

"Very impressive," Nicole said.

Rhea beamed. "We try."

The first order of business was a tour of the lodge, several of its rooms, Rhea restating that if we wanted to stay the night one would be made available, and one of the outlying cottages, each with a large bedroom, a comfy living area, and a stone fireplace.

"The lodge has sixteen suites, and we have two dozen cottages."

"I assume they're for members only," Nicole said. "No public access."

"True. Our members enjoy privacy. They come to unwind and put the work world behind them for a few days."

"It is peaceful," I said.

We walked back to the lodge. Rhea led us to the Range Rover.

"Let's take a drive around the property. I think you'll like what you see."

Did we ever. The clustered forests, the open land, the paved road that snaked through the acreage were perfectly maintained. I wondered if they'd hired Disney to do it. It was that perfect.

Farther on, the road looped around a large pond, reeds growing along its edges, a blue heron feeding in the shallows. Two covered redwood pavilions, each with a firepit and a collection of sofas and chairs, marked each end.

"This is my favorite spot," Rhea said as she came to a stop near the far pavilion. "I love to come here and read and relax and simply enjoy the solitude."

Who wouldn't? The pond was placid, and the only sounds were the chirps of birds and the rustle of the breeze through the leaves. Made me want to take a nap.

We returned to the lodge where Lorie and Robin awaited with glasses of iced tea. The duo disappeared as we settled around a large burl wood coffee table.

"So, you know Tammy Horton?" Rhea asked.

"We do," I said. "She's my ex."

"Really? She didn't mention that."

"A good thing for you," Nicole said. "She usually rants about Jake." She smiled at me. "Not entirely unjustified."

"You're so kind," I said.

She clasped my hand. "Keeping you in line."

Rhea laughed. "We wish we could have accommodated Tammy, but our rules are our rules. We treat everyone the same."

"Tammy likes discounts," I said, getting my licks in. Sort of. "Particularly free stuff."

Rhea shrugged. "So it seems. Still, she would be a good member. She seems to possess a lot of energy."

Sort of like nuclear fission. Chaotic, explosive, uncontrollable, radioactive.

"Maybe she'll come around," Nicole said.

"Maybe," Rhea said. "What did she tell you about us?"

We ran through what she had said. TLM was a combination of self-help and investing strategies and required a 120K buy-in. That Jonathon Lindemann was an investment guru that made money for his clients and the TLM members.

"That's a good summary," Rhea said. "I guess she was paying attention after all." She raised an eyebrow. "Her focus seemed to be how she could join for free."

"Welcome to Tammy's world," I said.

Rhea expanded on TLM and The Farm, but offered little to what we already knew. Her cell chirped. She lifted it from the coffee table and examined its screen. "Jonathon's finished his Zoom meeting so let's walk over to his office. He can tell you more about us."

Zoom meeting? Jonathon was a techie like me.

CHAPTER 11

JONATHON LINDEMANN WAS exactly as advertised by the website photo Pancake had downloaded. Either it was recent or he didn't age. Maybe he was a vampire. Probably not but I knew he was forty-two yet the man before me looked ten years younger. He carried on the casual theme with jeans and an untucked pale orange polo. His face was angular, his nose Roman, and his smile bright white and high-wattage. He used the latter to welcome us into his office.

"It's so good to meet you," he said after Rhea introduced us. "Welcome to the farm." He waved a hand. "Let's sit over here."

Over here proved to be a cluster of two sofas and three chairs around a rustic wooden coffee table. The spacious office, which seemed to occupy the entire rear half of the administration building's first floor, also contained a large desk, a wall of book cases, a row of filing cabinets, and another massive stone fireplace. Wood-burning, of course. A wrought iron rack held a neat stack of logs. Definitely not needed this time of year. The entire layout mimicked some high-end mountain lodge. Maybe in Aspen, or St. Moritz. Everything I had seen so far, this office, the lodge, the property, the staff, reflected the perfectly crafted TLM image. Designed to wow yet comfort and to make visitors wish to be part of it. Marketing at its finest.

"I know a little about you both," Lindemann said. He looked at me. "I'm a big baseball fan and I remember you well. What an arm."

"Yeah," I said. "Until it wasn't."

"Still, I enjoyed watching you play." He turned to Nicole. "Your moviemaking career seems to be in high gear. I loved *Murderwood*. It's hard for me to imagine someone so attractive, and normal appearing, could have written such a dark story."

"It's based on a real case," Nicole said. "L.A. has a million of them."

He raised an eyebrow. "Can we expect a sequel?"

"Not a sequel, but I am working on another one. It's also based on a real case."

"I'm sure it will a blockbuster too." That Lindemann smile lit up his face and scrunched crow's feet at the corners of his eyes.

"That would be nice," Nicole said. "It helps to have friends in high places."

"Charles Balfour? Your uncle?"

He had done his homework, or someone, probably Rhea, had done it for him.

"He's been very supportive." Nicole shrugged. "Kirk Ford didn't hurt."

"No doubt about that," Rhea said. "He is so hot."

"Pretty is what I tell him," Nicole said. That got a laugh from Rhea. "There're actresses who won't work with him because he steals the scene with his looks."

Lindemann snapped his fingers. "Like that other guy. Back many years ago."

"John Derek," Nicole said. "He couldn't get work for the same reason. I think he and Kirk look a lot alike."

"From what I read, he seems to do okay," Lindemann said. "I see him on TV and in the magazines with a series of beautiful women."

"That's true," Nicole said. "But many so-called serious actresses don't want to be on-screen with him. He's too pretty."

"And here I thought money motivated everyone in Hollywood."

Nicole gave him a brief nod. "Second only to image, which is everything."

Lindemann folded his hands in his lap. "I understand Tammy Horton suggested you come see us."

"She did," I said.

He nodded. "She's a trip."

"Not the word I'd use." I shrugged. "She's my ex."

"Really? I didn't know that."

Yes, he did. No doubt about it. My impression was that not much got past Jonathon Lindemann. Particularly when it came to money and potential investors. My impression was that he laid few cards on the table, carefully guarding his hold cards. Guess that, at least in part, explained his success. Knowledge is power, and power is money. Add to that distraction and manipulation as witnessed by Lorie and Robin and the few other young ladies we had seen during our property tour, and the soup of TLM enticement thickened.

"Well, we're glad you're here," Lindemann continued. "What can I tell you about us?"

"We've read several of your papers and articles," Nicole said. "About planning for success, setting goals, plotting a path to get there, and then actually doing it. Fascinating stuff."

He leaned forward, obviously basking in Nicole's flattery. Maybe basking in Nicole. His gaze did move over her, hesitating here and there.

"That's the gist of what we teach," Lindemann said. "Our goal is to help our members reach their full potential. Personally, professionally, financially."

"Each person has a different set of skills and needs," Rhea said. "Some need to simply see the vision and they can move forward. Self motivators as it were. Others need a bit more hand holding and guidance."

"Once we get their goals and direction lined up," Lindemann said, "we show them how to attain financial success."

Rhea picked it up. "Not only by investing with Jonathon, but we also educate them in sound investing and help them set up a portfolio that will give them sustainable financial growth."

"Exactly," Lindemann said. "It's not simply trusting us to make the proper moves, but also teaching our members how to invest. So they can make intelligent choices themselves."

Rhea nodded. "Of course, the hope is that they stay with us, and most do once they see the returns."

"Which tend to be good," Lindemann said. "We've been lucky, I guess. We've made very few weak choices."

"Jonathon's being modest. He has a knack." Rhea glanced toward him. "For picking good stocks and bonds and IPOs and whatever. That's why we don't charge fees. We take a small percentage of the profits only. Any losses are on us."

Lindemann popped that electric smile again. "Which means we're very careful where we place our clients' money."

They made an effective and well-oiled sales machine. They'd performed this exact conversation, or song and dance act, many times in the past. Offering the gold ring and doing it with style. Showing potential members what's behind the curtain of success. Part of which was Lindemann Farms with its beautiful acreage, classy buildings, attractive young women, and the Bentley parked outside. The trappings of success. Seduction at its best. All wrapped in a casual, low-key sales approach. Easy to see why people with too much money would open their wallets. In my experience, money always wanted more money, as if driven by fear of backtracking to a time when money had been scarce and hard work the norm. TLM offered the promise of using that money to scurry up the financial hill. Of course, guided by the charming and successful Jonathon Lindemann.

"I meant to ask earlier," Rhea said, "but have you attended any of Jonathon's seminars?"

"No," Nicole said. "Not yet."

"We'll have to remedy that," Lindemann said.

"I'll send you a few video files," Rhea said. "Not the same energy as being there, but they'll give you an idea of how they work."

"That would be nice," I said.

"Let me ask you, what interests you the most?" Jonathon said. "Self-help or investment strategies?"

"Actually both," I said.

"Good. We're here to help on both counts."

"Jake needs the self-help for sure," Nicole said.

Lindemann flashed that smile again. "Don't we all." He glanced at his watch. "I have another videoconference in a few minutes with my partners down in Tampa." He shrugged. "We have a property management company down there and it seems as if there's always something that needs attending. It's the bane of my existence." He stood, indicating the visit was over. "We're having an event here on Saturday. Please come as our guests. I think you'll enjoy it, and you can meet some of our members."

"We'd love that," Nicole said.

We stood and shook hands with Lindemann.

"Rhea will make the arrangements." He glanced at her, back to me. "Plan on making a weekend of it. Most of our members do. That'll give you plenty of time to network and get a feel for who we are."

"I'll have to check my schedule," I said.

Nicole bumped her hip against mine. "Jake doesn't have a schedule." She laughed. "We'll be here."

"Excellent," Rhea said. "We'll have a suite set up for you."

CHAPTER 12

"You missed our turn," I said.

"No, I didn't."

I tilted my head to the left. "Gulf Shores is that way."

"Which isn't where we're going."

"We're not?"

"Not yet." She skirted past a slow-moving tractor and accelerated.

"OK, Captain Kirk, where're we going?" I asked.

"Just up the road, Scotty."

"And I forgot my di-lithium crystals."

She glanced at me. "I don't think so. You always have your di-lithium crystals with you."

"I do?"

"I'll point them out later."

I wanted to suggest she turn around, floor it, and get back to her place pronto where we could play Star Trek games. But her focus on the road ahead meant she was on a mission and wouldn't likely be deterred. Even by di-lithium. So, I said, "My guess is that we're headed to Fairhope."

"Clever boy."

Clever boy? I think she was elbowing my ribs, metaphorically, which was fair enough given the fact that there wasn't much else between Magnolia Springs and Mobile Bay except Fairhope. A couple of farm communities but nothing that made an appearance on most maps. We crossed the Fish River, Weeks Bay to our left, and barreled west along U.S. Highway 98.

"Why are we going there?"

"To see a couple of people."

"Chief Warren?"

"My, you're on your game today. Someday you'll make a good P.I."

"If I ever do, shoot me."

She laughed. "Then we'll stop by and see Allison."

That would be Allison Mullins, the owner of Mullins Bakery where all things sugary and buttery ruled supreme. I could almost smell it.

"I could use a cinnamon roll," I said.

"Me, too."

"Maybe we should go see Allison first," I said. "That way my blood sugar won't be low when we see Chief Warren."

She looked my way. "You'd rather be in a cinnamon-roll-induced diabetic coma?"

"I'd be more mellow."

"Jake, if you were any more mellow you'd be comatose."

I should have had a clever comeback. I searched my mental files but came up empty. What I did stumble across was that she had thought this through. Talking with Billie Warren and Allison made sense. If the high rollers descended on Lindemann Farms, they'd definitely also descended on Fairhope. For shopping, restaurants, bars, all the cool things Fairhope had to offer. Magnolia Springs was quiet and sleepy, but Fairhope was a different story.

Finally, something came to mind. "You didn't think I was too mellow last night."

"Nor comatose." She brushed a strand of hair off her face. "Well, maybe after."

We blew past some beautiful farmland and soon rolled into Fairhope. Nicole parked near the entrance to the police department, which meant my cinnamon roll would have to wait. I hate it when she makes executive decisions without consulting me, or my stomach. Inside we found Chief Billie Warren in her office. She looked up as we entered.

"Well, well, look who the cat drug in."

She stood, we shook hands, and then sat.

"What brings you by?" she asked.

"Wanted to say hello," I said.

"Happened to be in the neighborhood, did you?" She raised an eyebrow. "Why don't I believe that?"

"Because you're a good cop," I said.

"Let's have it." She made a come here motion with the fingers of one hand.

"We want to ask you about TLM and Lindemann Farms," Nicole said.

She gave a slow nod. "Okay. In regard to what?"

"We assume you're aware of them."

"Oh, yeah."

"Any issues?"

"What's this about?"

Warren was a cop if nothing else, and from the time we spent with her during the investigation of Emily Patterson's murder, a tough, no-nonsense one. Here we were, snooping around a place that wasn't that far down the road. Maybe a group she'd had trouble with. So, in true cop form, she answered our questions with questions.

"This needs to be kept under wraps for now, but we've been asked to look for a young lady who's gone missing," I said. "Her mother's worried. Her last known location was three weeks ago at Lindemann Farms. Then she went silent, which according to her mother is unusual."

"Any evidence of foul play?" Warren asked.

I shook my head. "None."

"But there could be?"

"All we really know is that she hasn't been seen or heard from and her mother's concerned," Nicole said. "But anything's possible."

Warren considered that for a few seconds. "What do you already know about TLM?"

Nicole ran through what we had learned, including our visit with Rhea Wilson and Jonathon Lindemann. "To be honest, everything seemed above board."

Warren leaned back in her chair. "That's my take too." She glanced toward the window. "They've been plopped down over in Magnolia Springs for the better part of a year. Actually, a little longer. I visited them maybe six months ago. A beautiful piece of property and everyone seemed like nice folks. Nothing smelled hinky to me." She looked back toward us. "Do you think something might've happened to this young lady out there?"

"Not really," I said. "The best bet is she ran off with someone she met there, but we don't have anything to suggest something more sinister."

"Not yet anyway," Nicole said.

Warren gave her a look. "Isn't it always that way? You get nothing until a big old 'yet' pops up and smacks you right in the face." Warren scratched an ear. "Girls moving on from TLM has happened before. At least once that I know of. We had a local girl who worked out there. A very attractive young lady. She met one of the members, a rich guy, an attorney I think, and ended up moving away with him. Over in Florida somewhere if I remember it correctly. Rumor is they got married."

"Anything of concern?" I asked.

"Not that I saw. I talked to her mother just a few weeks ago. I ran into her in town. She said Stephanie, that's the daughter's name, was happy as a clam and looking to start a family."

"What's the mother's name?" I asked.

"Rachel DeLuca. You planning to talk with her?"

"If she will," Nicole said.

"Don't see any reason she wouldn't. She's a nice lady and only lives a couple of blocks from here. I'll get you her address and phone number."

"Thanks," I said. "To be clear, you've had no trouble from the TLM members or heard anything that concerns you?"

"No, on both counts. They come into town and shop and eat and drink and spend a lot of money. I guess you'd say they're good for the local economy. From what I can tell so far, not seasonal like the tourists." Her eyes narrowed slightly. "Why's this girl's mother so worried? I mean enough to hire you guys?"

"Other than the usual mother-daughter stuff, according to the mother, the two are close," I said. Not exactly true based on what Clarice had said, but close enough. "The girl is her only child, the father has passed, and mother and daughter stay in touch almost daily. They did butt heads over TLM. The daughter wanted to join, the mother said no."

"I hear that place is expensive to join," Warren said.

"It is," Nicole said. "But there's a trust fund involved that the mother controls, for now, and won't give the daughter access to it."

"How so?" Warren asked.

"The trust fund kicks to the daughter once she's twenty-five. She's only twenty-two now."

"How much money we talking about here? If you know."

"Fourteen million," I said.

Warren expressed surprise. "That'll get you well in a hurry."

"It will," I said. "The mother now lives down in Jupiter, but before that they lived in Tampa where TLM apparently started. The mother actually introduced her daughter to the program. The mother became disenchanted, the daughter less so. She ended up working at the farm. Then, three weeks ago, she dropped off the radar. The mother went to the farm and asked questions but didn't get any useful answers. Since then all her attempts to contact Lindemann or Rhea Wilson have been unsuccessful. She even went to the sheriff's office but they told her that her daughter was an adult and could come and go as she pleased."

"Which is true," Warren said.

"Still," Nicole said. "A mother's instincts are powerful."

"And sometimes obsessive." Warren shrugged. "Particularly when it's an only child." Warren hesitated as if she expected a response. When none came, she continued. "Magnolia Springs is out of my jurisdiction. It falls under the Sheriff's Department up in Bay Minette. I have a good relationship with them. Let me give them a call and see if they have anything that might help. Or raises a red flag."

"That would help," I said.

"We'll see."

"We're headed over to Mullins Bakery," Nicole said. "Want to join us?"

"Actually, I'm on my way to the gym. As much as I'd love a bear claw, I need the workout more."

Actually, she didn't. Warren was muscular and fit and didn't carry any visible extra weight. She could afford a donut or two, but I knew her passion was pressing steel. And catching bad guys.

CHAPTER 13

OUR WALK FROM the police department down Fairhope Avenue took only a couple of minutes, and when we got within a half a block of Mullins Bakery the aroma of butter and sugar hit me in the face. Talk about marketing. How could anyone resist going inside?

"Now I'm really hungry," Nicole said.

"You're always hungry," I said.

"Look who's talking."

"Smells like something rich and gooey just came out of the oven."

"Whatever it is, I want one."

I nodded. "Maybe two."

"Let's not forget to get some for Pancake."

"How could we? If he found out we were here and didn't grab him a bag of something, actually lots of somethings, we'd never hear the end of it."

"No doubt he'd know," Nicole said. "He'd smell it on us."

"Boy can lock onto food from a mile away," I said.

"Like a cruise missile."

As we approached the door, the aromas intensified.

"We'll load up with enough to require double bagging," Nicole said.

"You know him well."

Allison Mullins stood behind the counter, her back to us. She appeared to be loading something into a flat cardboard box. I caught a glimpse of brown and red. Danishes. Cherry or raspberry, or maybe strawberry.

We walked up to the counter as she turned, a pair of tongs in one hand. A smile erupted on her face.

"Why, hello," she said. "What an unexpected surprise." Then she seemed to lean back slightly. "Is something wrong?"

Which might seem like an odd question but, in fairness, the last time we saw Allison we were wrapping up the investigation of Emily Patterson's murder. Emily, Allison's best friend and coworker and Pancake's sixth-grade sweetheart, had been shot execution style along with Jason Collins, the guy she was seeing at the time. It had been a convoluted case that ran us in circles, part of that circle including Allison.

"Nothing like last time," Nicole said.

"But still something? Right?"

Why did everyone think we were looking into something nefarious? I mean, we were, maybe, or maybe nothing more than a runaway adult, but why was that everyone's immediate go-to? First Bobby Taylor, then Chief Warren, and now Allison. Had we developed a reputation in Fairhope? Maybe a few other places, too. If so, it was Ray's fault. He always got the ball rolling and we ended up on the front lines, the faces people remembered, while Ray remained mostly anonymous.

"We're not sure," I said.

"This doesn't involve another murder, does it?" Allison asked.

"Probably not."

"It's the *probably* that I don't like." She gave a headshake. "Look at me asking all these questions instead of being a gracious hostess."

"Looks like you're busy," Nicole said.

"Big order. A customer's throwing a barbecue tonight and wanted six dozen danishes." She nodded toward four stacked boxes. "Those are apple and cream cheese. These are cherry." She glanced at the clock on the wall. "I've got time. What can I get you?"

"Any leftover danishes?" I asked.

"Plenty. What's your pleasure?"

"Cherry looks good."

"Same for me," Nicole said.

"Good choice. Coffee?" Allison asked.

Nicole nodded. "That would be good. Need any help?"

"No. You guys take a seat and I'll have it right up."

Soon we gathered at a table. The danish was magnificent and I told Allison so.

"It's so good to see you two," Allison said. "But I don't think you drove up here just to see me and have a danish?"

I guess that answered the reputation question.

"We might have," I said.

"But you didn't." She took a sip of coffee. "Let's have it."

"What do you know about Lindemann Farms?" Nicole asked.

Allison's brow furrowed. "In what context?"

"Just in general," I said.

"Not much except that my business has ticked up since they moved in. I think most of the retailers and restaurant owners would agree. From what I hear anyway. Their folks come into town almost daily."

"Any issues?" I asked

Allison cupped her coffee with both hands and looked at me over the rim. "Like what?"

"Like anything," Nicole said. "Any rumors or such."

Allison shook her head. "No. None."

"What about the young girls that work out there? Do you know any of them?"

"Sure. They come in for coffee and goodies all the time."

"Did you meet a girl named April Wilkerson?" I asked.

"Maybe. A girl named April does come in, but I'm not sure what her last name is."

Nicole pulled out her phone and tapped and swiped until she found what she wanted. She extended the phone toward Allison.

"Yeah. That's her." She placed her cup on the table. "What's going on?"

"Her mother's worried about her," I said. "She's been incommunicado for a few weeks. Which is unusual according to her mom."

"When did you last see her?" Nicole asked.

Allison considered. "It's been several weeks, I think. I'm not really sure."

"What about the girls she comes in with? Any names?"

"First only. A girl named Lorie most often. Occasionally one named Robin."

The pair we met out at the Farm. Blonde Lorie and redhead Robin. I didn't offer that but rather asked, "How did they seem while here?"

"Normal. Fun loving, relaxed, giggly. Like young girls."

"Anything unusual?" Nicole asked.

Allison shook her head. "Nothing jumps out." She glanced toward the front door. "From what little I've overheard, they mostly talk about girl stuff. The usual silly things like makeup, clothes, music, and guys of course."

"Of course," Nicole added.

"I think they hope to meet some rich dude who can make their life perfect." She shrugged. "Sometimes I want to grab them and shake them and tell them a nice guy is better than some jerk who happens to have money."

"Did you get the impression that that was April's goal?" Nicole asked.

Allison gave that some thought. "Nothing specific to her but I guess you could say that about several of them. I remember one day, maybe two months ago, they were talking about Stephanie DeLuca. She's a local girl and she worked at the farm. Actually, Stephanie came in here with them a couple of times. Anyway, Stephanie met some hotshot lawyer from Florida. Destin or Fort Walton Beach, I think. Somewhere around there. She got married, the whole deal. They— April, Lorie, and Robin—were jealous of her for sure."

"Jealous?" I asked.

"Envious might be a better word. They wanted to find exactly what Stephanie had."

Hmmm. Was Lindemann Farms a matchmaker? Is that how Jonathon attracted so many pretty young girls? Did he dangle the promise of a rich mate, or a sugar-daddy? Which brought up another thought. What duties were the girls required to perform? Were they simply eye candy to soften up, or more likely harden up, potential clients, or were they expected to do more?

"So, besides the pay, they're looking for other benefits?" Nicole asked.

"That'd be my take." Allison sighed. "I guess I was young and stupid at one time too."

"We all were," Nicole said.

Allison laughed. "So true. I can think of a few do-overs I'd love to have."

Boy, was that ever true. I could think of dozens of do-overs I'd love another shot at. Number one on the list would be Tammy. I should've run away immediately, but young and stupid was young and stupid.

"Other than the members coming in and spending money, and the girls hoping to find the love of their lives, does anything about the Lindemann group raise an eyebrow?" I asked.

"Not really. They seem like normal folks."

"That's our impression," Nicole said.

Allison drained her coffee cup. "I'm surprised Pancake isn't with you. He doing okay?"

"He's fine. He's working on this case."

"Too bad. I'd love to see him. Besides, he was my best customer ever."

"You'd be surprised how many restaurants down in Gulf Shores say the same thing," Nicole said. "Particularly Jake's place."

Yeah, I thought, except he doesn't pay for anything, which technically means he's not a customer. He's more like a large, unruly pet. One that you feed, water, and clean up after.

"I'll load up a bag of goodies for him," Allison said.

"You beat us to it," Nicole said. "We were going to get him some stuff."

"I'll take care of him," Allison said. "So much I'll probably need to double bag it."

It seems Pancake had a reputation in Fairhope too.

CHAPTER 14

RHEA RETURNED TO the lodge and entered the great room. Robin and Lorie sat next to each other on the sofa near the fireplace engaged in an animated discussion.

"Good job," Rhea said. She settled in the wingback chair at one end of the coffee table. "I think you made our guests feel at home."

"They were easy," Lorie said. "Very laid back."

"And so cool," Robin said.

Lorie nodded her agreement. "He was hot."

"She was hotter," Robin said. "Exactly what a Hollywood star should look like."

"She didn't star in her movie," Rhea said. "She wrote it and helped produce it."

"She could have," Lorie said. "Plus she was smart enough to get Kirk Ford to star in it. Major coup."

"The movie was very successful," Rhea said. "No small thanks to him, but even without him it would've been a good movie."

"We haven't seen it," Robin said. She glanced at Lorie.

"Then that's your assignment. Part of your preparation. You'll need to do it before this weekend. I'm sure they'll be back, and I'm going to assign you two to take care of them while they're here."

"Gladly," Robin said. "Do you think they'll join?"

"That remains to be seen. They would be a great addition. So, you girls have your work cut out."

"We'll be ready," Lorie said.

"I know." Rhea glanced at Lorie. "Who knows, this might be your chance to get a Hollywood gig, and I know what that would mean to you."

Lorie leaned forward, elbows on her knees. "I know I've told you this before, we both have, but one of the many things I like about working here is that you, and Jonathon, let us explore options. You make it possible for us to meet people and create connections."

"That's because we know this job isn't your final destination," Rhea said. "You have your own dreams and plans, and we want to help you realize them." She shrugged. "Isn't that what we do here? For all our members? We help them reach their personal goals."

"I know," Robin added. "But the members have money and influence. They're all VIP types."

"So are you," Rhea said. "You weren't selected for your beauty alone, though that helps with the clients for sure, but also for your personalities. Your ability to connect with people and to make them feel good. Special and pampered. That's no easy skill and not one most people possess. It bodes well for your success down the road. Make friends, make connections, and your dreams will materialize."

"I can't imagine not working here," Lorie said. "It's not just fun and rewarding but, I don't know, comfortable is a better word, I guess."

"That's fine for now," Rhea said. "But you're young, smart, and ambitious. You'll want to move on and realize your own success. We truly appreciate what you do for us, and I mean everything you do, no doubt about that, but in the end we want to help you climb your personal ladder. Isn't that the real message behind Jonathon's teachings?"

Robin glanced at Lorie. "Guess we have homework to do."

Lorie stood. "Let's go watch a movie."

Rhea watched the two young ladies leave. She liked them. They had been a welcome addition to the crew. She had a dozen other young women who worked at TLM, either on the road doing PR, here at the Farm, or off on special assignments, but Lorie and Robin were indeed a cut above. They each possessed an innate ability to connect with people, which made them sought-after companions by many of the members

She walked over to the office building where Jonathon sat behind his desk, locked on to his computer screen. "Finished with your meeting?"

"Yeah, and now I'm making trades," he said. "It's been a successful day."

"Aren't they all?" Rhea asked.

"Mostly anyway"

"I don't know how you do it," Rhea said. "Know which stocks and bonds and whatever to move into and which to flee from."

"I wish I had an answer for you. I go more by feel than any of the gurus' metrics. Markets are like wild cats. They can purr and be delightful, or can turn on you in an instant." He tapped his keyboard. "I guess I just have a feel for when they're getting ready to turn." He shut down his computer. "So, what's up?"

"The new couple. Jake and Nicole. What'd you think?"

"They seem like a good fit. I mean, a well-known local athlete and successful restaurant owner, and a stunning and charming and now a big-time movie producer. What's not to like? Or do you know something I don't?"

"Maybe. Jake's father, Ray Longly, is a P.I. He owns Longly Investigations down in Gulf Shores. He has a good reputation from what I could tell."

"Does Jake work for him?" Jonathon asked.

"Not that I could find. Definitely not on the payroll."

"So, what bothers you about that?"

"Not really a bother, just curious. Remember those murders over in Fairhope? It's been a while and I forget exactly when. That couple that was murdered?"

"I do. It rattled the community."

"It seems Jake and Nicole were involved in solving that."

"Really?"

She nodded.

Jonathon cocked his head to one side, raised an eyebrow. "So, maybe he does work for his father?"

"Possible. But I didn't see any evidence of that."

"Let's say he is. What's your concern?"

"More awareness than concern. Isn't that what you pay me for? To be aware?"

"You're way more than aware."

"It's just that with several of the things we have going on, I don't want some P.I. sniffing around our affairs."

Jonathon considered that for a minute. "Forewarned is forearmed."

"My thoughts exactly. I'll see what I can uncover."

"Are they coming this weekend?"

"I think so. I should know for sure tomorrow. In anticipation, I've assigned Lorie and Robin to be their escorts while they're here."

"Good choices. Lorie is particularly good at gathering information."

"I have them watching Nicole's movie. That'll be a good topic to open any conversation and put her at ease. Lorie can do that."

"Flattery is a powerful tool."

"It is." She walked to the door and over her shoulder said, "We'll talk later."

CHAPTER 15

"THE MORE TIME we spend here, the more I like this little village," Nicole said.

"Village?"

"Yeah, Fairhope."

"I thought it was a city," I said.

"Too small."

"Bet the good folks in Fairhope don't feel that way."

She shrugged. "Maybe, but it's still more a village than anything else."

I couldn't wait to hear this rationale. "The difference is?"

"A city is big, sprawling, and usually overpopulated. You know, like Birmingham, Atlanta, L.A. A town is smaller and more manageable."

"And a village?"

"A town that's cozy and cute. Like Fairhope."

We walked in silence for a full half a minute while I gave that some thought. I actually liked it.

"You hate it, don't you?"

"What? Fairhope?"

"No, admitting I'm right."

"It's such a rare occurrence, I don't mind."

"Watch it, buddy." She bumped her hip against mine. "You're cruising and the punishment will be severe."

"What'd you have in mind?"

"Later. Right now, we're working."

See why I hate work? It intrudes on fun, which is always better and it's something I do well. Much more so than work. Just ask Ray.

We left Mullins Bakery, dumped Pancake's massive bag of pastries in the car, walked back up Section St., and turned west down Magnolia, toward Mobile Bay. Immediately the area became residential with homes and mature trees lining the street. After a couple of blocks we came to the home of Rachel DeLuca, Stephanie's mother. Lush trees hugged the two-story white frame house. A brick walkway bisected a well-manicured lawn and led to a covered front porch, complete with a rocker, two-person swing, and an orange cat, who stood, stretched, and greeted us as we climbed the few steps.

"Hey, guy," I said, squatting, extending a hand for the cat to sniff.

Apparently, I was blessed with approval as the cat raised its head, turning it slightly. I scratched behind its ears until it flopped on one side so I could scratch its belly.

"Friendly," Nicole said.

"Sort of like you."

"Meaning?"

Before I could reply, the front door swung open. An attractive brunette stood in the opening. "I see you met Ginger."

I stood. "We did."

"Since Ginger approves, how can I help you?" the woman asked.

"I'm Nicole. This is Jake."

"Rachel," she said.

"We want to talk to you about your daughter," I said.

Her eyes widened. "What? Is something wrong?"

"No," Nicole said. "We're exploring joining the TLM group. Rhea Wilson told us your daughter had been a member and had a positive experience."

Relief fell over Rachel's face. "Oh yes. She's still a member. Her husband is, too." She stepped back. "Come in." She wore black slacks, a blousy gray shirt, and a gracious smile.

As we entered the living room, Rachel asked, "Can I get you some coffee, or anything to drink?"

"We're okay," I said.

Nicole and I sat on the sofa, Rachel in a chair. The home was neat, comfortable, and well decorated.

"We're sorry we didn't call first," I said, "but we were in the area and thought we'd simply drop by."

"No problem. It's a lazy day, and I'm catching up on my reading." She nodded toward the hardback novel that lay on the table next to her. "So, you're interested in TLM. What can I tell you?"

"We're fascinated by Jonathon Lindemann's self-help and financial programs," Nicole said. "From what we hear he does well in the Wall Street and investment world."

"That's an understatement," Rachel said. "He's made a ton of money for Stephanie and James. James Emerick. That's her husband. He's a very successful attorney over in Destin. Perhaps you've heard of him. He's very well known in the area."

We shook our heads.

"Did they meet at TLM?" Nicole asked.

Rachel nodded. "Stephanie worked for TLM doing marketing and PR. She met James at a retreat at the Magnolia Springs farm. That's where she worked."

"Did she like working there?" I asked.

"She loved it. I did too since it meant she was nearby."

"What did her job at TLM entail?" Nicole asked.

"Mostly meeting and greeting VIPs and making them feel comfortable. Stephanie's always been good at that. She's well versed in the TLM program so she also did some lecturing and mentoring."

"I hear that many of the employees travel a good deal," I said.

"Stephanie traveled some. TLM has a strong recruiting and outreach program. They look for new investors and members everywhere. Stephanie went to L.A., New York, West Palm, and once to Europe. London and Paris."

"Exciting life," Nicole said.

"It was. To top it all off, she met James. He's smart, good-looking, and so devoted to her. It was one of those instant romances. In fact, early on it went a little too quickly for me. They were engaged in a couple of months. But once I got to know James, once I saw how perfect they were for each other, all my reservations melted away."

"A fairy tale so to speak," Nicole said.

"Definitely. Now they're planning a family. I'm heading over to see them next weekend."

"Do you belong to TLM?" I asked.

"Not yet. I say that because, at first, after Stephanie began to work there, I looked into it. Rhea and Jonathon pitched the whole membership thing to me. I was tempted, but the price was a little steep." She shrugged. "But now that I see how well they've done for James and Stephanie, I'm reconsidering. Obviously, I don't know all the details, but I do know that James is happy with his returns."

"That's the consensus among the people we've talked to," Nicole said.

"What about you two?" Rachel asked. "Are you married?"

"No, we just hang out together," Nicole said. "But I will say that, like your daughter, our mutual attraction was almost instantaneous." She ruffled my hair. "He's a good guy. When he's not being an ass."

Rachel laughed. "That's a guy thing."

I was smart enough to stay silent, but I did shake my head.

"What do you do?" Rachel asked.

"Jake's an ex-pro baseball player and now owns a bar and restaurant in Gulf Shores. I write and produce screenplays."

"Oh? Anything I might have seen?"

"*Murderwood*," I said.

Her eyes widened and her gaze locked on Nicole. "Really? I saw that. It was wonderful. You wrote that?"

Nicole nodded. "I did."

"It was great. Scary, which is not usually my thing, but I really liked it. Plus, Kirk Ford's my fantasy guy."

Nicole laughed. "He likes that role and he plays it well."

"Why wouldn't he?" Rachel said.

Indeed, why wouldn't he? Kirk had women throwing themselves at him on a daily basis. Hard to ignore that. I'd had a taste of that while playing ball. In every town we traveled to, there were a few bars and clubs we frequented where you could find an overnight companion with ease. It was all part of the game. Truth is, I'm glad I'm beyond all that. It was exhausting if nothing else.

"Do you have any friends at TLM?" I asked. "Anyone else we might talk to?"

"Not really. Not being a member—yet—I don't have any ongoing connections with them."

"Any other young ladies you know of that had positive outcomes?" Nicole asked. "Like Stephanie?"

Rachel gave a soft laugh. "Positive outcome. I like that. Stephanie told me about a couple of other girls she worked with, or maybe heard about, I'm not sure which, but they did well through their work at TLM. One ended up moving to Tampa and working in Jonathon's real estate business. Another was hired by some guy from Dubai to hostess on his private jet. Apparently, she's been all over the world and met some very interesting people. Made me wish I'd had such opportunities when I was a twenty-something." She shrugged. "I probably wouldn't have done anything even if the opportunity arose. I've always been more timid than that."

"You never know," I said.

"True."

"I'd say you did okay," Nicole said. "You live in this great little village." She glanced at me, raised an eyebrow. "Your daughter seems to have found the love of her life. It doesn't get much better."

"No doubts there."

"So you've seen nothing negative with TLM?" I asked.

"Nothing at all." She glanced down and then back up toward us. "When Stephanie first began working there, I had some concerns. I mean, a young attractive woman, hired to do PR by a flashy company—well—you know where my mind went? But in truth, one of the things I learned about TLM is that they want everyone to be successful. Not just the high rollers they recruit, but also their staff. They offer them the benefits of all their programs and seem to push them along a path to success. At least, that was Stephanie's experience."

"Do you know these other girls?" I asked. "The ones you told us about?"

"No." Her brow furrowed. "I'm sure Stephanie told me their names but I can't remember."

"Do you think Stephanie would be willing to talk with us?" Nicole asked.

"I don't see why she wouldn't. If you want, I can call her and tell her that you're going to contact her."

"That would be greatly appreciated," I said.

She smiled. "She'll definitely talk with you since you've been approved by Ginger."

CHAPTER 16

"Am I missing something?" Nicole asked.

"Like what?"

"Pancake said this was a cult. I don't see that."

"What do you see?" I asked,

She glanced at me while blasting around a box truck that had the audacity to go the speed limit. My reflex was to suggest she keep her eyes on the road during such maneuvers but that would be a fool's errand. In her defense, she possessed some sixth sense when it came to traffic, sort of like Luke Skywalker and The Force. Otherwise, we'd have smashed into something long ago. Funny, but after experiencing so many of her wild rides, my heart rate now stayed below 150, and the terrified organ no longer felt as if it were going to jump from my chest. Either I had acclimated to the danger or given up all hope.

We zipped along Highway 59 South, toward Gulf Shores. The sun was low, the shadows long, and the traffic sparse enough for Nicole to play NASCAR.

"Everyone we've talked to seems happy with Jonathon Lindemann and TLM. Members, investors, employees, everyone."

"Except Clarice Wilkerson," I said.

Again, she glanced at me. *Don't do that.* "She could be overreacting and upset that her daughter hasn't kept her in the loop, don't you think?"

"I don't know what I think. Clarice seemed certain that her daughter wouldn't just drop communication and take off to parts unknown."

"Mother-daughter relationships can be tricky." Nicole goosed the car around two others and fell back into the right lane. "We've only heard one side of it. April might see things differently."

"All we have to do is find her and ask."

"That's the trick, isn't it?"

"She's an adult and can disappear if she wants to," I said.

"Which would mean we have no case."

"That gets my vote. I don't want to be involved in Ray's messes anyway."

"Yet here you are." She slowed while a pickup made a left turn and then climbed the RPM scale again. "You kick and whine, but in the end, I think you like it."

"I like you. The rest I tolerate."

"You're such a smooth talker."

"That's me. Old silver-tongued Jake."

"I'll let that one ride." She swung around a slower car. "But I do agree with you."

"About what?"

"Something doesn't feel right. Even if she and her mother have issues, I think she'd at least call, or text, or something."

"Which means Ray does have a case."

"Yes, we do." She glanced at me. "And not the royal we, but rather we as in me and you and Ray and Pancake."

"Can I be excused from class? I don't feel well."

"No skipping school," she said.

"Just this once?"

"Somehow I think you have experience with ditching school."

"It was Pancake's fault. He was bored and said he already knew all that stuff and sitting in class would be a waste of time."

"Were you bored too?"

"Confused might be a better word. Me and algebra never got along."

Nicole laughed. "But you're pretty so it's okay."

I had several clever comebacks and mentally ran through them, but couldn't retrieve one that worked. My dilemma evaporated when my phone buzzed. I tugged it from my pocket and glanced at the screen. Tammy the Insane. Great, just great. She possessed a knack for calling at odd, and annoying, times, which was basically any time. I never wanted to talk to her. Resigned to my fate, I answered and activated the speaker. Nicole loved these calls.

"Well?" she asked without preamble. So Tammy.

"Well—what?"

"Did you meet with Jonathon and Rhea?"

"We did."

"And?"

"And what?"

"Jake, you can be so infuriating. You know why I'm calling."

I glanced at Nicole. "I don't have a clue."

"Is Nicole with you?"

"She is but she's driving."

"Unlike you, she can multitask. Nicole, what did they say?"

"Hi, Tammy. They were very nice and cordial. It's an impressive setup and everyone seems happy. Maybe a little too happy."

"What does that mean?" Tammy asked.

"I don't know. More a feeling than anything specific. Everyone seemed overly invested in showing an upbeat face."

"That's because they're all making money and feeling better about themselves. That's what TLM does. Self-improvement and cash flow. What about me? Did you talk to them about me?"

Nicole glanced in my direction. "We did," she said. "They spoke highly of you."

"They did?" Not waiting for a response, Tammy got right to it. The purpose of her call. "Did they agree to reduce my initiation fee or whatever they call it?"

"I don't think they do that for anyone."

"I'm not just anyone. Neither is Walter. He's the best lawyer in the state and maybe the entire country. He's important. You'd think they'd know that and want me as a member."

"You'd think," I said.

"Shut up, Jake. I don't need your sarcasm."

Good for her. She caught my inflection. That's not all that common with Tammy. She misses a lot and simply plows forward through the convoluted maze of Tammy World.

Nicole smoothed things. "They would love to have you join."

"They would?"

"Rhea said as much."

"Then why won't they let me in?" Tammy's voice took on her patented whine.

"They will," Nicole said. "But, like I said, I don't think they reduce the fee for anyone. It seems written in stone."

Tammy seemed to mull that over. "So your visit was a waste."

"Not really," I said. "We met some nice people."

"Isn't that wonderful for you? But since you didn't get what I needed, it was a waste."

Tammy can be summed up in three words: me, me, me.

Undaunted, Tammy pressed on. "Okay. I guess I need to find another way." She disconnected the call.

"Nice talking to you too," I said to the dark phone.

Nicole laughed. "She's as pure as they come."

"She's pure something. As long it's all about her, she's in, but otherwise, she can't be bothered."

"To think you married her."

"Everyone makes mistakes," I said.

"She does provide a healthy dose of humor though."

"She does? For who?"

Nicole smiled. "Me."

CHAPTER 17

Last night, after NASCARing our way back to Nicole's place, we shared some quality time in the hot tub with a bottle of Patron tequila. As our skin began to prune, a misty rain flared up so we retreated to bed. After that, things descended into a blur, but I do remember parts that were fun. I'm not sure how long it took for sleep to wrestle us into submission, but crawling out of bed this morning proved to be a chore. My head hurt, my eyes burned, and my back felt like I had fallen down a flight of stairs. Nicole has that effect.

She had no such issues and awoke bright-eyed and ready to hit the streets running. I slipped on my jeans, no shirt, and staggered to the kitchen. I stood near the living room windows looking out toward the beach as I worked my way through my first cup of coffee. She slapped my butt and said, "Get dressed. We have work to do."

"We do?"

"We're meeting with Ray and Pancake. Or did you forget?"

"I tried to." Did I ever actually know that we had such a meeting planned? Or did Nicole keep it a secret to spring on me this morning? I had a foggy memory of a conversation about Ray, but that was blurred by tequila so the details remained a mystery. Plus, I try to filter out all things Ray.

"That's what I'm here for," Nicole said. "To remind you of your responsibilities."

I started to say that I didn't have any responsibilities, which was actually true, but instead I opted for, "You're no fun."

"Not what you said last night." Another butt slap. "Now, get moving. We have to feed Pancake."

Were we zoo keepers?

In truth, one of my reasons for existence seemed to be feeding Pancake, something that began when we were kids. We—actually more Pancake than me—would raid his fridge, then mine, and ultimately a neighbor's or two. This was part of our daily routine. Each of the families on the block stocked up with extra provisions just for Pancake. Now, Captain Rocky's was his food trough. Most often he would show up and my manager, Carla, would run point, but on the days he was hunkered down with Ray, like today, I became his food delivery service. Sort of like DoorDash or Grubhub.

Before we left, Nicole reminded me to grab the danishes Allison had bagged up for Pancake. We swung by Captain Rocky's where I powered down two more cups of coffee while we waited for the crew to whip up a bag of breakfast burritos. We then motored to Ray's, where we parked among the stilts that elevated his home above any potential storm surge. Part of life on the Gulf Coast.

Ray and Pancake sat at the deck table. Pancake snatched the bag from my hand before we could even say hello.

"What'd you bring?" he asked. Like he wouldn't know. It was always the same.

"Your burritos," Nicole said. "Got you three so that should cover it."

"We'll see," Pancake said as he unwrapped one.

"We also brought you some treats from Allison," I said. I dropped the bag on the table before him. "A day old but I suspect still okay."

Pancake peered into the bag. "Allison's truly a stellar person. How's she doing?"

"Good," I said. "Business is good too."

Ray put his burrito aside and took a sip of his Dew. "How'd it go yesterday?"

"Excellent," Nicole said. "Everyone was friendly and helpful."

"Any flags?"

"Not really." She glanced at me.

"If anything, I'd say that everyone seemed a bit too friendly," I said. "Like they were trying to sell us on how wonderful they were and how happy everyone connected to TLM was."

"They're trying to get your money," Ray said. "I suspect a soft sell is part of it." He glanced at Nicole. "Did you get the same read?"

"I did. For sure Jonathon and his sidekick, Rhea Wilson, were selling. Very smoothly I might add."

"Like they knew their product was good and we'd be stupid not to see that," I added.

"Exactly," Nicole said. "The two girls we met there, Lorie Cooper and Robin Meade, were definitely onboard. Both young and pretty and very well spoken. They made excellent ambassadors, I'd say."

"Another form of selling," Pancake said. "Particularly if your primary targets are wealthy, mature dudes."

"Sex sells," Nicole said. "Always has."

"Everyone we talked to in Magnolia Springs and over in Fairhope seemed to be happy with them as neighbors," I said. "Bobby Taylor said that other than some increase in traffic whenever TLM hosted an event at the farm, they presented no problems. Even Chief Billie Warren thought they were good neighbors and said that she'd had no issues with them."

"How's she doing?" Ray asked.

"Seems good," I said. "Even more pumped than before. We stopped by and talked with Allison, but you know that." I nodded toward the bag of pastries. "She said they were good customers and sure helped the local economy."

"Allison said she knows April," Nicole said. Ray and Pancake both raised an eyebrow. "She would come in from time to time with Lorie and Robin."

"And?" Pancake asked.

"Nothing really. She said they were friendly, happy, and talked about girl stuff."

"And how they hoped to meet Mr. Right at TLM," I said.

"Like Stephanie DeLuca," Nicole said. "She apparently hung out with Lorie, Robin, and April some. At least they came into Allison's bakery together a few times. Stephanie apparently found the love of her life at TLM."

"We talked with Stephanie's mother, Rachel DeLuca," I said. "She lives near downtown Fairhope. She was delighted with TLM and said it made money for her daughter Stephanie and her new husband."

"Who is he?" Pancake asked.

"James Emerick. According to Rachel, he's a hotshot attorney over in Destin, and a TLM member. She seemed overjoyed that her daughter married him."

Pancake began working his laptop.

"She said that TLM had been good for the couple," Nicole continued. "Made them a bunch of money. Her take was that Jonathon Lindemann was a financial genius."

"'Guru' she called him," I added.

"That's what we've found so far," Ray said. "He does know how to pick stocks, bonds, properties, those kinds of things." A sip of Dew. "When's the last time Allison saw April?"

I glanced at Nicole. "Three weeks, a month, something like that." Nicole nodded.

"Which parallels the last time anyone saw her," I said.

"James Emerick," Pancake said. He read from his computer screen. "He graduated with honors from Vanderbilt Law School and opened his office a month later. He owns the firm and has three associates. He also owns his office building over in Destin. Four floors, eight offices, current value about one-point-two million. His investment portfolio is thick and broad. He's only thirty but already has a net worth upwards of four mil."

How did he find this stuff so quickly? I knew the answer to that. He was a freaking computer whiz, and possessed the nose of a blood-hound, but it still amazed me. He could dig up more in a minute than I could in a month even though I'm a techie. I still wasn't sure exactly what a browser was. I'm better at resting, snoozing, and relaxing than I am at browsing.

"No wonder Stephanie DeLuca's mom was thrilled," Nicole said. "Maybe we'll head over and talk with her."

"Good idea," Ray said. "She apparently knows April, so she might offer some useful intel."

"We have a couple of days before the big shindig at Lindemann Farms," I said. "Plenty of time to fly over to Destin and have a chat with her."

"Fly?" Nicole asked. She punched my shoulder. "I keep my tires firmly on the ground."

I shrugged, thinking, *Two out of four anyway.* I refrained from saying that.

"Tell them what you found on Jonathon Lindemann," Ray said to Pancake.

Pancake shoved the last of his second burrito into his mouth and spoke around it. "His TLM gig and his real estate business down in

Tampa rake in the cash, but it's his investment firm that goes deep. He services not only the TLM members but also has thirty-three other clients listed. Looks like he does make money for everyone and so far he looks clean."

"No painting outside the lines?" I asked.

"The only thing that's possibly off kilter so far is that he has a chunk of cash in several offshore accounts, which is not all that unusual for folks moving big money around."

"Doesn't that offer the ability to hide money and avoid taxes?" Nicole asked.

"Not as easy as it once was, but still doable," Pancake said.

"What's your next step?" I asked.

Pancake retrieved a cherry danish from the bag and took a bite. "Hmm. God, I've missed these." He swiped his mouth with a wadded napkin. "I'm going to finish off these pastries and then dig deeper into his offshore accounts and a few of his bigger investors and see where it leads."

CHAPTER 18

"You okay?" Rhea Wilson asked as she entered Jonathon's office.

"Fine," Jonathon said. "Why'd you ask?"

"You seem stressed."

"I do?" He tapped the keyboard.

"Your shoulders are tense, your jaw clenched. You know, stressed."

He swiveled his chair toward her. "One of the properties down in Tampa's having roof issues. It seems a few leaks have appeared."

"A few?" Rhea asked.

"Several units flooded."

"Not surprised with the rain they've had the past couple of days." She dropped into the chair that faced him. "I just saw on the Weather Channel that's it's clearing so that should help."

"Still got to fix it."

"Want me to handle it?"

"Already done. It'll cost a bundle though."

"The joys of property ownership."

Jonathon leaned back in his chair. "Tell me you have good news."

"I do. I think so anyway."

He moved a stack of papers aside. "I assume it's about Jake Longly and Nicole."

"That case they worked on over in Fairhope. The victims were Emily Patterson and Jason Collins. She, Emily, grew up with Jake down in Gulf Shores. Seems his involvement was more as a friend. His father, Ray, was part of the team, but from what I could find, Jake and Nicole were there for support more than anything else."

"You sure?"

"As sure as I can be without really digging," Rhea said.

"Which might raise someone's curiosity."

"Like maybe the local cops. But I think it was just what it seems. An old childhood friend gets murdered and they came to support family and friends."

"Sounds reasonable."

"Emily was working through a divorce and her attorney was Walter Horton, Tammy's current husband, and as you know Jake is Tammy's ex. So there's also that connection."

"What I hear is that you don't see any red flags," Jonathon said.

"Jake's father, Ray Longly, and his partner, Tommy Jeffers, were involved in the investigation, but mostly it was Chief Warren. I don't think that Jake was actively involved."

Jonathon nodded.

"The word on the street is that he and his father don't see eye to eye, which makes it even less likely."

"Good. Those two, Jake and Nicole, could be great assets."

"Jake's major league career gives him good name recognition around here and adds a certain cache. Nicole might be even better because of her Hollywood connection. She's definitely part of the community and has a hit movie and rumors of another one underway. Not to mention her uncle is Charles Balfour and he's nothing to sneeze at."

"You think? He's mega."

"Which might get us a pipeline to all that easy money in LA."

"And beef up our supporting cast here at the farm."

"Exactly." Rhea stood.

"What else you have on for today?"

"Remember those two girls I told you about? The sisters?"

"Yeah."

"I'm heading over to South Alabama to chat with them. They have an apartment just off campus."

"Sisters could be a good hook."

"Absolutely. I already have a couple of people in mind for them."

"If you can get them onboard," Jonathon said.

"From my research, it should be an easy sell."

"I take it they're already in the game?"

"They are."

"Love to hear that."

CHAPTER 19

DESTIN, FLORIDA, OCCUPIED a prime place on the Florida Panhandle in an area known as the Emerald Coast. Its name is often uttered right along with nearby Fort Walton Beach, with folks saying "Destin–Fort Walton" as if they were one and the same. In many respects that's true since the similarities far outweigh the differences. Both were bustling with tourists and populated with condos and second homes for people living inland or in faraway states. Good vacation spots with solid rental income. Each had sugary, white, sun-drenched beaches and a host of water-view restaurants and bars.

I liked both towns, preferring Destin a bit more, but since I lived in Gulf Shores, also blessed with sun, sand, and bars, including mine, I rarely wandered that far east. It was only eighty miles but during tourist season the drive could take three hours. Not my idea of fun when I could simply walk out on Captain Rocky's deck and have the same views and, in my biased opinion, better food and drink.

Nicole blasted through Pensacola, Navarre, and Fort Walton Beach before skidding into Destin. We quickly located the home of Stephanie DeLuca in a desirable neighborhood in Destin Harbor. The large white, gray-roofed, north-facing, two-story home was fronted by an inviting circular drive flanked by flowering shrubs and several palm trees. Very classy.

"You made good time," Stephanie said as she opened half of the double front door and let us inside.

"We always make good time," I said.

"Jake's a wimp," Nicole said. "He can't handle my driving."

"Jim says the same about me. But a girl's got to get to the outlet mall early."

Stephanie, petite and trim, wore designer jeans and a pale blue silk tee. She led us into a massive living room where a wall of windows looked out over the harbor. A sturdy power boat in the forty-foot range hugged a wooden dock beyond a sparkling swimming pool. She asked if we wanted anything to drink. We declined and sat on a deep, plush sofa, facing Stephanie across a low coffee table.

"Thanks for seeing us," Nicole said.

"Glad to do so. Mom vouched for you, and more importantly, Ginger did too, so all's good. She said you seemed like a normal couple."

"One of us anyway," Nicole said. "Jake still needs some training."

Stephanie glanced my way. "Don't they all?"

"I can dress myself," I said. "And I'm toilet trained."

"We measure progress in small steps," Nicole said.

Stephanie seemed amused with that. "Mom said you were thinking about signing on with TLM and wanted my take on it."

"That's right," I said.

"I wouldn't be here—" she waved a hand— "were it not for Jonathon and Rhea. I met Jim at TLM."

"He's an attorney, right?"

"He is."

"We understand that he was a TLM member and you worked up at the Farm," Nicole said.

"Jim had met Jonathon through a mutual friend. He attended one of his seminars down in Tampa and then a couple of retreats up in Magnolia Springs. He was impressed with the entire program. Self-improvement and, even more so, the financial side."

"That's the consensus from the people we've talked to," I said.

"No doubt Jonathon has a handle on life and success," Stephanie said. "Even as an employee, I learned a lot about being self-sufficient, confident, pursuing dreams. Rhea helped me create my own life plan. Finish college, law school, hang out a shingle. I had it all planned and there's no doubt in my mind that I was on the right track." She shrugged. "Then I met Jim."

"And things changed," Nicole said.

"Did they ever. We're trying to start a family so all that law school stuff is on hold right now. Not completely. I'm taking some online college courses and only have a few credit hours left to get my degree."

"Then law school?" I asked.

"That's the part on the back burner. Jim and I decided that kids would come first."

"We're most interested in the financial side of TLM," I said. "The hundred and twenty thousand buy-in is not pocket change and we want to make sure it's worth the investment."

"It is a big number, but as Jonathon and Rhea say it makes sure the members are committed to the program. For sure, without marrying Jim I would never have been able to afford it. Jim has said more than once that it was the best investment he ever made. Jonathon has done well for us."

"He does seem to have a gift," Nicole said.

"It's almost magical," Stephanie said. "He understands the market, stocks and bonds, real estate, you name it. I don't know how he does it, but he does. I have little concept of any of that. Jim understands it better but Jonathon is the guru."

That word again.

"How did you end up at TLM?" Nicole asked.

"They recruited me." Her gaze shot downward, then back up. "I was in my junior year of college. I attended a TLM seminar on campus and it was as impressive as all get-out. I mean, Jonathon had the attendees in the palm of his hand. He not only excited everyone with his vision for living a successful life but also he gave us a bunch of practical tips on investing and money management."

"What kind of advice?" I asked.

"Number one was to avoid debt. Pay off things before you buy more. He said debt interest was a killer and, like empty sugar calories, wasteful. He said not to chase the current deals on stocks and bonds but stay with the tried and true. Once you have some savings you could get more adventurous, but early on a degree of caution was best."

That coming from who I viewed as a scam artist? On some level anyway. But, to me, this felt like sound advice. More or less how I approached things. No doubt Jonathon Lindemann talked a good game and from what Pancake had uncovered so far, that seemed to be the case.

Was I wrong about him?

"Anyway," Stephanie continued, "a few months later I went to another seminar. Then, Rhea came to visit me."

Stephanie glanced downward, and another hesitation followed, as if she were trying to organize her thoughts or carefully choose her words. Was she hiding something? Was there something about TLM, or Rhea, or Jonathon that made her uncomfortable? It felt that way, but was I over-reading it?

Stephanie lifted her gaze back to us. "She said she had a job for me. My response was that I was in school and didn't have the time, but she said I could continue school and work in between. On weekends and holidays, that sort of thing. She also said that they could help me finish my degree remotely from Magnolia Springs. Either way they would help pay for it. An education stipend is what she called it. Plus room and board and a generous salary on the days I worked."

"An amazing offer," Nicole said.

"It was, and I took it. Turns out that it was a smart decision. I had fun, learned a lot, and got a chunk of my college paid for by them."

"What did they expect in return?" I asked.

Yet another brief but uncomfortable hesitation. "That I do a good job for them and carve out a successful path for myself. Of course, they hoped I'd eventually join TLM."

"But that wasn't required?"

Stephanie shook her head. "No."

"What did you do there?" Nicole asked.

Stephanie shifted in her chair and tossed another glance down and to her left. "Lots of things really. Mainly marketing and PR. I entertained clients and helped Rhea arrange social events and the seminars."

"Any travel involved?" I asked

"That was one of the real perks. I went to San Francisco, L.A., New York, Chicago. All very high-end events."

"Sounds like the perfect job," Nicole said.

"It was. I met people I'd never have met. Rich and important people. And, of course, Jim. That alone made it all worthwhile."

"I guess it's safe to say you had nothing but a positive experience at TLM," Nicole said.

"Oh yes," Stephanie said. "I even referred a few friends, ones I thought would fit in, to Rhea."

"Which means?" I asked

She shrugged. "Pretty, smart, good with people."

"Like you?" Nicole asked.

"Oh. That's not what I meant." She gave a headshake. "I wasn't talking about me."

"But it fits," I said. "From where I sit anyway."

"That's a nice thing to say."

"Do you know Lorie Cooper?" I asked.

"I do. She's a sweetheart. Is she still at TLM?"

"She is. So are a couple of other girls I think you know. Robin Meade and April Wilkerson?"

Stephanie's face lit up. "Yes I do. How are they?"

"The same. Still working at TLM and enjoying it."

"I miss those days hanging out with them. We had fun. It was like a little sorority. Of course, I wouldn't take anything for my life now. Finding Jim and marrying him changed everything. For the better, but I do miss my friends. Please tell them I said hello and that they have an open invitation to come visit anytime."

"We'll do that," Nicole said.

"Do you or did you ever have any concerns about TLM?" I asked. "Anything you didn't like, or thought was maybe not right?"

"Like what?"

"Anything."

"None. I'd do it again in a heartbeat." She glanced toward the pool. "It was work and not all fun and games." She looked back at me. "But it was a very exciting time. Meeting people, traveling, just being able to hang out with Jonathon and Rhea and learn from them. In some respects it was even better than college life and that's saying something."

As we blasted back toward Gulf Shores, I mentally ran through the conversation with Stephanie. Along with holding on as Nicole tacked through traffic. Stephanie's enthusiasm for TLM and Jonathon and Rhea was real, but I had an uncomfortable feeling that there was more to the story. What, I wasn't sure, but something seemed off kilter.

"She's hiding something," Nicole said.

"You sensed that too?"

"I did."

"What do you think it is?" I asked.

"I don't know but for sure there were things she didn't want to get into."

"How are we going to find that out? Without blowing up our cover story?"

She passed a slow truck on the right, her tires kicking up some dust, the car rocking slightly.

"We'll be there Saturday. Maybe we can uncover something then. Carefully."

Carefully being the operative word.

CHAPTER 20

STURDY PINES AND elegant oaks dotted the campus of the University of South Alabama, which snugged against the small town of Wheelerville, a few miles west of Mobile. Rhea Wilson's drive from Magnolia Springs took only a half hour. She arrived twenty minutes early for her meeting with Shane and Sara Hutton, students, sisters, and hopefully new TLM employees. She swung by their apartment complex, The Oaks, just south of campus to make sure it was as easy to find as her GPS suggested. Four three-story structures, each with twelve units, red brick base topped with gray siding. The sisters' apartment, D-1, first floor, left end, faced a pool complex that sported a rock waterfall and several palm trees. It looked like a nice place and Rhea estimated it probably ran around $2,500 per month. Even split two ways that was a chunk of change, and coupled with partying, drinking, and, based on their Facebook postings, the trendy clothing the sisters relished, meant they could use an extra income stream. Didn't most college-aged girls?

She remembered her own school years. Tight money, even tighter hours with classes, studying, and partying, something she had excelled at. She wished someone had offered her the proposition she had for the Hutton sisters. Would she have taken them up on it? Probably, but maybe not. Back then, she had been more naive and cautious and didn't really understand how the world worked. Hadn't yet grasped the power of money and sex. She now had a firm grasp of those tools.

Rhea exited the campus and rolled through downtown Wheelerville, a town she'd never visited, to get the lay of the land. Not much to it but it seemed pleasant enough. A few restaurants, Italian, Japanese, and Cajun that she saw, a couple of bars, and clusters of industrial buildings. Typical of towns this size, little traffic impeded her path. Wheelerville served the college crowd's basic needs, but she suspected that for fun and hookups they ventured east into Mobile where restaurants and watering holes were plentiful.

Back at the apartment building, she pressed the doorbell button next to the dark green front door. Almost immediately it swung open revealing a tall young woman with fashionably short cropped dark hair and bright green eyes.

"Rhea Wilson?" the girl said.

"I am."

"I'm Shane."

They shook hands and then Shane stepped back, welcoming Rhea inside. A carbon copy of Shane rose from the living room sofa.

"This is my sister, Sara," Shane said.

"Nice to meet you." Sara nodded

"I've been looking forward to meeting you both," Rhea said.

Shane waved Rhea to the chair opposite the sofa. She sat.

"Can I get you anything?" Shane asked. "Water, soft drink?"

Rhea shook her head. "I'm good."

As the sisters settled on the sofa, Rhea studied them. She had seen photos and knew they were beautiful but they were more impressive in person. They carried themselves well, free of silly giggles or overt nervousness, and with an air of confidence and assuredness. Rhea prided herself in being able to read people, to understand body language, facial expressions, and word choice. Shane and Sara seemed curious, laced with a hint of caution. Sara clasped her hands in her lap, Shane entwined her legs in an obviously protective posture.

Rhea considered these minor tells of their apprehension completely understandable. She had given them just enough information to pique their interest and get her in the door. She had offered only that she had a job for them. One that wouldn't interfere with their school and where they could make good money. Very good money was how she had put it. If you're going to set a hook, do so deeply. She had spoken only with Shane, who had asked what the job entailed, but Rhea deflected the question by saying it included hostessing for parties and gatherings for their rich clients. The details needed her face-to-face sales pitch. Another area in which she excelled.

Her first impression was that these two would do well at TLM. They certainly fit the desired profile. Their neat, clean, well-appointed apartment underscored that assessment. Not typical for college kids, it was clutter free and matched their demeanor and attire. Each wore tailored jeans, Shane an untucked black shirt, sleeves rolled to her elbows, Sara a spaghetti-strapped camisole, peach.

Rhea settled in the chair, letting them sense that this was a relaxed chat. No hard sell, no deception, no pressure. Shane's shoulders relaxed, even if Sara remained on alert.

"How's school going?" Rhea asked.

"Fine," Sara said. "It's school. Classes and studying."

"And hopefully a little fun?" Rhea said.

Shane laughed. "We manage."

"Good. These are the best years of your life. Whether you realize that or not, they are. You will forever look back on these years as times of learning, of adventure, of exploration." She gave a half shrug. "I know I do."

"We're curious about what you told me," Shane said. "You said it was a job of some sorts."

"Which we don't really understand," Sara added.

"That's why I'm here," Rhea said. "To explain everything. Let me start by saying thanks for seeing me." When neither of the sisters responded, she continued. "I'll begin by explaining who we are and what TLM is all about. It's a program for self-improvement and teaching people how to navigate financial success." Rhea smiled. "Doesn't that sound highfalutin?"

The girls returned the smile in unison.

"Jonathon Lindemann is the founder and the creator of TLM, The Lindemann Method. I'm his executive VP. We work to help people improve their well-being. Happiness, success, and life stability are our goals. We also help them become financially secure. Or in many cases more so. Most of our members already have some degree of success. Business types, professionals, entrepreneurs, and the like. Most of them work too hard for their money and sacrifice their family, friends, and personal wellness chasing the gold ring, which is the road to total burnout and ultimately loss of what they worked for."

"Sounds like college," Shane said.

"That's a good analogy. I bet you know people who work too hard at it. Not because they aren't smart enough but because they aren't well organized or are not confident enough in their own abilities. They spend four hours on something they could do in half the time. The ones that cram for tests the night before rather than doing it step-by-step."

Sara glanced at Shane. "We have a few friends like that."

"But I suspect you two aren't that way."

"We do okay," Shane said.

"I know," Rhea said. "I do my research. Your GPAs are excellent."

"You researched us?" Shane asked.

"I did. As I should. What kind of recruiter would I be if I didn't analyze potential candidates? And my analysis says you two would be perfect for the position I'm offering."

"Which is?" Sara asked. "I mean, we aren't rich, or successful, or any of those things you mentioned."

"That presents no problems," Rhea said. "We aren't talking about you as investors but rather as employees."

Shane leaned back and crossed her legs. "We're in school. We don't have time for a job."

"Does fifty to a hundred thousand a year interest you?"

"What?" A look of suspicion crossed Shane's face. "For doing what?"

"Serving as hostesses, entertaining clients, and the like."

Now concern settled on Sara's face. "What exactly does 'entertaining' mean?"

"We schmooze and pamper our clients, and potential clients. Mostly at our farm in Magnolia Springs, sometimes elsewhere. You would be the face of TLM at these gatherings."

"Eye candy?" Shane asked.

"To some extent that's true, but the job is much more. We do employ young women who are physically attractive, but they must also be smart, well spoken, educated, and classy."

Sara couldn't suppress a quick laugh. "You think we're classy?"

"I do. Since you both made an A in the public speaking class you took, I know you're good communicators and would represent TLM well."

The two girls looked at her but said nothing.

"Our events tend to be on the weekends so they wouldn't interfere with your classes. You might want to travel with some of our clients or to one of our retreats. Mostly these are down in the Tampa area, so not too far, but they are really everywhere. Even in Europe and Asia. Such travel isn't a requirement, but most of our girls really like that. Top drawer, all expenses paid, always fun trips."

"You'd pay us for that?" Sara asked, her skepticism apparent.

"Handsomely. We're offering each of you two thousand a month plus extra for your weekends at the farm, special events, and travel. In addition, we will help you invest that money and create your own portfolio."

"That's a lot of money," Shane said.

"We think you're worth it."

"Are you sure it wouldn't interfere with school?" Sara asked.

"I'm sure. You'll only be over at the farm on the weekends you're working and maybe you'll take a week off here and there for travel, which again is completely optional. That said, we have a couple of girls your age who we helped facilitate their classes virtually. They live at the farm full-time. Room and board is also covered."

"What's this farm you're talking about?"

Good. The hook was digging deeper.

"It's wonderful. Not really a farm, actually far from it, it's more like a high-end resort than anything else. We call it Lindemann Farms and it's on two hundred beautiful acres in Magnolia Springs. We have a lodge, a world-class restaurant, and elegant accommodations, not only for the members but for the staff as well. You'll have your own private quarters while you're at the farm."

Sara's skepticism bled over to Shane. "What's the catch?"

One minute after meeting the pair, she knew Shane would be the one to convince. Whatever she decided would drag Sara along in her wake. Sara might be more skeptical, but Shane was the dominant one.

Rhea shook her head. "No catch. We need hostesses who are attractive and smart and can present a professional and cultured face. Girls like you."

"I'm not sure we'd be considered cultured," Sara said.

"Of course you are. You're bright and charming and present yourselves well." Rhea leaned forward. "Don't get me wrong, it's a real job. You'd be required to learn about our members and clients so you can be engaging, interesting, and carry on intelligent conversations. Our members are successful, well educated, and cultured. Your main job would be to make them feel at home and comfortable."

"I see," Shane said.

"And I'm sure you could use the money and the connections."

"What connections?"

That's it. Swallow the bait.

"Like I told you, our clients are wealthy and successful. Several of our girls have developed relationships along the way. Even marriages."

Shane's chin rose slightly. "And mistresses?"

Rhea nodded. "I won't deny that some of the girls have followed that path. It's their choice. I can tell you that each and every one that went that route was happy. Traveling the country, the world, with a guy worth eight or nine figures. Doing and seeing things they never imagined. Two now live on yachts along the French Riviera, another in Gstaad, Switzerland, one in Singapore, one in New York City, two others in L.A. All over really. Whether those relationships evolve into something more permanent or not is up to the fates, I guess."

"Is that what we're expected to do?" Shane asked. "Entertain, and maybe have sex, with these guys?"

"That's entirely up to you. We have no restrictions on that, but it's not really required. Plus, not all of our clients are men."

"Sounds sketchy," Shane said.

"In what way?" Rhea asked.

"You offer us insane pay for smiling, looking pretty, and making small talk. You tell us that others that have done the same are now concubines."

"Concubines," Rhea said. "I like that word. But it doesn't fit here. You will be in control. You will decide what you do or don't do. All we ask is that you represent TLM in a positive light."

Shane raised an eyebrow. "But you wouldn't mind if we slept with some of your clients?"

"Again, that's completely up to you. But is that really much different than playing the sugar baby game?"

The trump card.

Both girls reacted as if joined at the hip. Head up, shoulders back, eyes wide.

"Yes," Rhea said. "I know about it. Again, part of my research." Shane started to speak but Rhea raised a hand. "I looked into the guys each of you is seeing. They're married, of course, which is typical, but they seem to be nice and stable. That reflects well on your personal choices."

Shane sagged, glanced at her sister. "Like taking money for sex?"

"If you want to look at it that way. I prefer to see it as a business arrangement. One that is mutually beneficial. Your choices in partners show me that you make sound decisions. That's a gift and a big plus as far as we're concerned."

The sisters gave her blank stares, as if not sure what to say.

"Look," Rhea continued, "I did the same thing back when I was in school." A lie but one she had told many times to other girls. "My belief is that if I wanted to trade companionship for money, it should be a lot of money laced with a lot of perks. Travel, clothing, jewelry, even stock certificates. You'd be amazed what some rich guys will do to have an attractive young lady on their arm."

"So sex is involved?" Sara asked.

"Only if you want. If not, no problem." Rhea sighed. "The truth is that we need hostesses and in exchange we're offering you money, self-help, career and financial advice, as well as the opportunity to meet many successful people. Networking at its best. What type of relationships you establish are completely up to you."

Sara looked at Shane. "What do you think?"

Shane shrugged. "I'm not sure what to think. Part of me says it's an amazing opportunity while the other part tells me it's too good to be true and to pump the brakes. I need to digest all of this."

"Good idea," Rhea said. "We only want you if you're committed to the program."

"Can we call you in a few days?" Shane asked. "After we've had time to discuss it?"

"I have a better idea. We're having a gathering at The Farm this Saturday. Be our guests. We'll provide you rooms in our lodge, and food and drink and fun. You can meet some of our clients, get a feel for how we do things. No strings attached. We'll even pay each of you five hundred just for attending."

The girls exchanged a long glance.

"That might be fun," Shane said.

The hook had been set and the reel was spinning.

CHAPTER 21

OUR THIRD-FLOOR SUITE was magnificent, which wasn't a surprise given the luxurious nature of Lindemann Farms. The exterior might be upscale ranch-style but the rooms screamed high-end resort. The corner suite Lorie directed us to had a living area, a separate bedroom with a king bed, and a massive bathroom, which I noticed had a marble vanity with two sinks, a four-shower-headed glass-enclosed stall, and plush towels. I saw fun in my future.

"Wow," Nicole said. "This is so nice."

"One of our best rooms," Lorie said. She walked to the living room window and waved a hand. "You have a great view of the property."

Panoramic would be a better word. The window looked over the entry area and out toward the fields and trees of the farm. I noticed the window along the adjacent wall faced the office building. Jonathon Lindemann stood beneath a maple tree in the small parking lot that stretched between the lodge and the office building, chatting with a tall, well-dressed man. Next to them rested a black Bentley, driver's door open, the man's hand resting on the doorframe. They seemed to be sharing something humorous. They shook hands, the man climbed in the car, backed out, and drove away. Jonathon watched him leave, then reached inside his own white Bentley, lifted out a briefcase, and walked toward the office entry.

Lorie drew my attention back to her, saying, "You guys get settled and then if you want, I'll meet you downstairs for lunch."

"I'm starving," Nicole said.

No news there.

"You're in the right place. Chef Michael makes the most incredible food." Lorie patted her flat belly. "I'm amazed I haven't gained a ton since I've been here. Fortunately, we have several hiking and jogging trails on the property so I can run off the calories."

Lorie left us to unpack, which took all of three minutes. We each had only a shoulder bag.

I lay down on the bed. "Comfy." I patted the bed next to me. "Come see."

"Get up, Bucko. We can check out the bed later, but right now I need food. Besides, we aren't on vacation. We're working."

"Doesn't mean we can't have fun."

"Oh, we will. Just not right now."

"Is that a promise?" I asked.

"A threat."

Okay, now we're talking.

We had seen the dining room during our last visit. It had been empty then, but now several tables were taken. I noticed Rhea Wilson sitting with a woman at a four-top near the massive stone fireplace. No fire this time of year. She nodded to us, raised a finger as if to say give me a minute, and then continued her conversation. Lorie seated us at a table near the windows. Robin appeared.

"Hello," Robin said. "Great to see you again." She sat.

A waitress appeared. Lorie introduced us to Beth, a cute brunette with a warm smile.

"Welcome," Beth said. "You're new here?"

"We are," I said.

"I suggest going lite for lunch," Beth said. "The food for the party tonight is over the top."

"Isn't it always," Lorie said.

"Hard to argue with that," Beth agreed. She took our orders, and following her advice we settled on salads and sweet tea all the way around.

Robin asked, "All settled in?"

"We are and the room is amazing," Nicole said.

"It's one of our best," Robin said.

"You're VIPs," Lorie added. "Jonathon and Rhea want you to enjoy your stay with us."

Of course they did. Plus, they wanted in our pockets. I wondered what they'd think if they knew our real reason for being here. We'd probably get tossed off the VIP list and downgraded to a basement dungeon. Or be escorted to the entry gate and kicked in the butt.

"I'm sure we will," Nicole said.

"I've been here a year and I still can't believe how cool everything is," Robin said. "Even our room."

"We're roommates," Lorie said.

"Where is your room?" I asked. "Here in the lodge?"

"There's a building over behind the office building," Robin said. "Maybe fifty yards beyond. All us girls live there."

"It's in a wooded area," Lorie added. "Very peaceful and quiet. And Robin's right, the rooms are wonderful."

"Much better than my apartment in college," Robin said.

"Where'd you go?" I asked.

"Southern Miss over in Hattiesburg."

"Did you two know each other before you came here?" Nicole asked.

Lorie shook her head. "No. I'm from Birmingham and went to UAB. Well, for two years. Then I got this job and put school on hold."

"Do you plan to go back?" Nicole asked.

"Absolutely. But this was too good to pass up. I mean, good money, a great place to work, and all the wonderful people you meet. I can get back to school later and have some money in the bank to pay for it."

I saw Rhea approaching. When she reached us she said, "I'm so glad you could make it."

"How could we not?" Nicole said. "This place is amazing. Thanks so much for inviting us."

"The pleasure is ours." Rhea glanced at her watch. "I'd join you but unfortunately I have a meeting right now. We'll sit down and chat later. You're in good hands so relax and enjoy your lunch."

"She's so nice," Robin said as she watched Rhea head toward the front door. "She looks out for us. Actually, everyone."

"Oh, I almost forgot," Nicole said. "We were in Fairhope the other day and visited Mullins Bakery. Allison told us to tell you girls hello."

"We love her," Lorie said.

Robin gave an enthusiastic nod. "What we really love are the pastries she makes." She glanced at Lorie. "Seems like we're there all the time."

"At least once a week," Lorie said. "How did our names come up?"

"We told her we were looking into TLM. She said a lot of folks from the farm come over to Fairhope and stopped by her place. She remembered you girls."

"What'd she say about TLM?" Robin asked.

"She loves having the farm nearby. She said everyone seemed nice and it was good for business."

"I bet that's true. There's not much around here, just farms and more farms, so everyone goes over to Fairhope for fun. Good restaurants and bars, and Page and Palette, my favorite bookstore ever."

"She said you guys were always with a couple of the other girls, but she hasn't seen them in a while," I said.

"I think she said their names were Stephanie and April," Nicole added. "Are they still at TLM?"

Lorie shook her head. "April is but Stephanie got lucky."

"Oh?" I asked.

Robin picked it up. "Stephanie met this big-time lawyer, got married, and moved down to the coast."

"Destin," Lorie said.

"And April?" Nicole asked. "Did she meet a guy, too?"

"Maybe," Lorie said. "You never know with that girl. She's down in the Tampa/St. Pete area right now."

"There was a big party down there," Robin said. "When was that?"

"A couple of weeks ago," Lorie said. "No, three weeks."

"Lorie and I were down for the party," Robin said. "Only for the weekend. We came back here to work, but April stayed for some trip or something." She gave a slight shake of her head. "I forget what she said."

"Party cruising," Lorie said. "On Andrew's yacht."

"That's right," Robin said. "Now I remember. I think she also had some recruiting trip lined up. I don't remember where."

"I think I heard something about Las Vegas and L.A.," Lorie said. "But I might be wrong." She shrugged. "Regardless, she's been gone a while."

Three weeks, I thought. Exactly how long it's been since she talked to her mother.

"I miss her," Robin said. "She's so much fun."

"She'll have tales to tell when she gets back," Lorie said.

"Totally," Robin agreed.

"Who's Andrew?" I asked.

"Andrew Heche," Robin said. "He's a friend of Jonathon's and has a great party house. Massive and on the water. With a pool as big as a lake."

"And a yacht that defies description," Lorie added. "Huge and over the top."

Robin nodded her agreement. "If you guys join TLM, you'll see. We have parties down there all the time."

"Is that part of your job here?" Nicole asked. "Parties on estates and yachts?"

Robin gave another nod. This one more enthusiastic. "That's one of the best parts of this job. That and the trips."

"Those are always fun and you meet some very impressive guys," Lorie said. "Hopefully we can get as lucky as some of the other girls who've worked her." Lorie gave a soft laugh. "I mean I can think of worse things than hooking up with a gazillionaire and flying around the world."

So it might seem, I thought. Unless things aren't that way at all. Sure, Stephanie DeLuca hit the jackpot, but did April Wilkerson? Was she cruising around on some endless party or did she also find her one true love and ride off into the sunset? If so, why didn't she tell her mother? How long does it take to call or send a text? Or was she in a situation where such communication wasn't possible? Imprisoned on a boat or in a basement or trafficked to the other side of the world.

Listen to me. I'm starting to think like Ray and Pancake, and Nicole. April is fine. She's having fun and simply tweaking her mother as payback for not giving her the money April thought she was entitled to. Nothing more than a mother-daughter spat.

Yeah, that makes the most sense.

CHAPTER 22

NICOLE AND ROBIN followed a pine needle–covered trail into the woods behind the TLM office building. As they entered the shade, the temperature dropped a good ten degrees and the aroma of the pines thickened. Jake had stayed behind "to relax and rest" but in truth to chat with some of the staff. One of Jake's gifts was schmoozing and the hope was that someone would part with some useful information. Lorie begged off the walk saying she needed to help with the setup for the party and to greet the members who would begin flowing in soon. So, off Robin and Nicole went.

"That's where we live," Robin said.

She indicated a wooden structure that matched the lodge's construction in style and substance. Its two stories consisted of six units up and six down, each with a spacious patio or deck. Two young women sat on one of the decks. Robin waved to them as she and Nicole strolled deeper into the woods.

"This is my favorite part of the farm," Robin said. "I love the trees, and the shade."

"It's wonderful," Nicole said.

"I walk here almost every day. There're several paths that wind all over the property. Gives a lot of variety."

Nicole saw one trail veering off to the right and fifty yards later another that angled left. They continued forward until the trees thinned and an open field of flowers and various tall grasses appeared. They stepped into the bright sunlight, and Nicole saw that a trail cut a serpentine path through the waist-high grass.

"Isn't this beautiful?" Robin asked. Not waiting for an answer she said, "Every time I walk here I feel like Julie Andrews. Like I should dance and break into 'The Hills Are Alive with the Sound Of Music.'"

"Go ahead," Nicole said.

Robin laughed and began to spin and sing the song. The first stanza anyway. She wobbled to a stop. "Whew. That makes me dizzy."

"You have a good voice. Did you ever sing?"

"In the shower. And some karaoke." She laughed. "If I'm drunk enough."

They crossed the field, walked another hundred yards through more trees, and finally reached the pond Nicole had seen the other day when Rhea showed her and Jake around.

Robin picked up a pebble and skimmed it across the water. Three bounces. Pretty good. Nicole followed suit.

"I can see why you like it here," Nicole said. "But I bet it was hard to leave college."

Robin tossed another stone. "It was. I had some really great friends there so it wasn't easy."

"Do you keep in touch with them?"

Robin stared at the water for a beat, a pebble in her hand. "Yeah. Not as much as I should though."

"What made you decide to leave college and come here?"

"This." Robin waved a hand. "And the opportunity to learn about myself, finances, which I had no clue about, and to make some connections."

"Like a boyfriend?" Nicole asked.

"That would be great. One that's young and charming and rich." She laughed. "It could happen."

"It sounds like it has. For your friend Stephanie, and maybe April."

"And a few others I know of."

"Any luck so far?" Nicole asked. She got four bounces off her next pebble. "Anyone on the line, so to speak?"

"Not now. There was a guy, maybe six months ago. He lived in Nashville. He took me up there a couple times and once to New York. Another time to Miami. All very amazing. A world I didn't know really existed outside of movies. The best hotels, the best restaurants."

"But?" Nicole said

"His business took him to London for a year and I guess he wasn't ready for that commitment."

"You would have gone?"

"Absolutely. He was a great guy." She picked up another rock and examined it, turning it over and over in her hand. "Maybe he'll come back."

"You still stay in touch with him?"

Robin stared at the water. "Some. I hear from him about once a month. Nothing very promising though. Just hello and how are you."

Nicole tossed another rock. Only two bounces this time. "How did you end up here? I mean, how did you meet Jonathon and Rhea?"

"They found me. While I was at Southern Miss, Rhea came to Hattiesburg and offered me a job. Just like that."

"You didn't know her before?"

Robin shook her head. "I'd never heard of her or TLM or anything."

"How did she pick you then?"

Robin looked away. She worked a rock with her fingers, obviously buying time, searching for the right answer.

Interesting. It reminded Nicole of Stephanie's hesitations when asked similar questions.

"I don't know."

"You don't know or you don't want to talk about it?" Nicole asked.

Robin stared at her. She started to speak, stopped, started again. "It's embarrassing."

"How so?"

"You'd think badly of me," Robin said.

"So it's about sex," Nicole said.

"How'd you . . ."

"Relax," Nicole said. "I grew up in Hollywood. A place that's built on sex. Virtually every business deal has a little sex involved."

Robin tossed the rock she held toward the middle of the pond, making no attempt to skim it. It hit with a soft plop and she watched the expanding circles bloom from the spot where it entered. She sighed. "I had a boyfriend." She glanced at Nicole. "An older one. He helped pay for my school, and some other things."

"A sugar-daddy."

"You know about those?" Robin asked.

"I do."

"He was a bank VP, married with two kids. Fifty years old, but handsome and kind."

"Like most sugar-baby, sugar-daddy arrangements."

Another sigh. "That's awful, isn't it?"

"No, it's not. It's actually very common."

"Still."

"Still nothing. Like I said, I spent my childhood and young adult life in Hollywood. The casting couch, the kept women, and men for that matter, the whole exchange between power and sex is on full display in Tinseltown. It was so common that it was expected. Part of life in the industry."

"I suppose that's true," Robin said.

"It is. So, I assume Rhea knew about your arrangement and that's why she reached out to you and made the offer."

Robin nodded. "That's what she said."

"How did she know that?"

Robin gave that some thought. "You know, I'm not sure."

"Were you on one of those sugar baby sites online? Is that how you found your bank VP?"

"It was. At first, I was simply curious. Some girl I didn't really know was talking about it in a bar we college kids hung out in. She said she had done it and in fact had two guys she saw regularly and made a lot of money. I was surprised that she talked about it so openly, but she seemed fine with it and she looked like any other college girl. I explored several of those sites and ultimately put up my own profile and that's how I met him."

"That's probably how Rhea found you."

Robin looked toward her feet but said nothing.

"What about Lorie?" Nicole asked. "Did she play the same game?"

Robin looked up. "I'd rather not say."

"Which means she did."

Robin nodded.

"Was she on the same sugar baby site as you?"

"A different one."

Interesting. Were Jonathon and Rhea mining these sites for girls who were more than just pretty faces? Girls who weren't shy about hopping in bed for cash and benefits. Not those on the various prostitution sites. From what Nicole had seen so far, those wouldn't meet TLM standards. But if you needed to offer such benefits to your members, what better way than finding girls who were in school or employed, going about a seemingly normal life, but who had a history of using sex for benefits? In this case it would benefit both the girl and TLM. If that was true, it was a clever marketing approach. Diabolical and unseemly, but clever nonetheless.

"Is that expected from you here?" Nicole asked. "Do Jonathon and Rhea encourage you to entertain the members and clients?"

"Not really."

"That's a qualified no." When Robin didn't reply, Nicole continued. "If Rhea found you both through online sugar baby sites, then she wants you to do the same here. Doesn't that make sense?"

"I feel uncomfortable talking about it."

"There's no need to," Nicole said. "You're not doing anything thousands of others haven't done. It's part of life." Nicole laid a hand on her arm. "Besides, this is between you and me. I'm just curious."

"If you mean is that in our employment contract, then no."

"I wouldn't expect it would be, but is it an implied duty?"

"They don't discourage it and don't frown on it. So, yeah, it's okay if we hook up with the members."

"Like your London guy?"

"When he first hit on me I wasn't sure about it. I mean, I liked him and given any other circumstance I would've jumped at the chance. Working here actually gave me some reservations. The whole thing about not mixing work and pleasure because sometimes those things blow up. I've seen it. Hell, I've done it."

"Oh?"

"A summer job I had right before I started college. I had just turned eighteen and got a sales position in a clothing store. The manager was a guy twice my age, and married. We had a thing for a couple of months, but then he got possessive and finally his wife caught on. I don't think she knew for sure but she definitely suspected. She kept showing up at odd times. It became very uncomfortable, so I quit and found another job." She shrugged. "Lesson learned."

"Until you got to college," Nicole said. "And here."

"I saw that most of the other girls were doing it, hooking up with members, and they seemed happy. Lorie said it was all cool and casual and not to worry so much and just have fun. And enjoy the benefits. So, when that guy asked me to go to Miami with him, I said yes and the rest is history you might say." She tossed another rock. "Mostly I'm okay with it but at times I do feel uncomfortable."

Nicole could see that. Why wouldn't she feel uncomfortable with her decision? Of course, she would never tell Robin that.

"Don't," Nicole said. "It's all very natural. If you met this guy in a bar, Mr. London, and hooked up with him, would you be fine with that?"

"Sure."

"So the fact that you met him here changes that in some way? Is that what you're saying?"

"I don't know. It just feels different."

"Because you feel they expect you to, right?"

Robin stared at her. "You do understand."

"I do. Look, you're young, smart, and beautiful, so why shouldn't you have fun and explore options and see the world? You have time to be an adult later."

That definitely brightened Robin's mood. The desired effect.

"I like you," Robin said. "You're so cool."

"As are you."

CHAPTER 23

WHILE NICOLE AND Robin went for a walk, and Lorie was off tending to her duties, I further explored the lodge in hopes of meeting some of the members who were now trickling in for the evening's festivities. In fact, as I walked through the lobby, Rhea intercepted me and introduced me to a middle-aged guy named Will Buckley. He owned several car dealerships in Atlanta. He had dark hair, graying at the temples, and wore jeans and green polo, his handshake firm.

"Will's been a member for some time," Rhea said. "What? Three years?"

"That's right," Will said. He waved a hand. "Long before you guys built this palace." He looked at me. "What about you?"

"I'm not a member yet," I said. "I'm exploring the opportunity."

"It's a good deal." He glanced at Rhea. "She and Jonathon've made me a bunch of money. Plus, I get to hang out here whenever I want."

"Jake's an ex-baseball player," Rhea said.

Will's eyes lit up. "Jake Longly. I knew it sounded familiar. You were a pitcher."

"That's right."

"Well, we need to sit and talk baseball. I love the game. I'm a big Braves fan."

"I'd like that," I said.

He glanced at his watch and said, "I need to get settled in my room and make a handful of calls, but after that I'll find you and we can have a drink."

He left. Rhea said she had to go oversee the party prep, but added she'd send Lorie down to keep me company. I assured her I was fine on my own, so she left, and once again I was free to explore.

I wandered through the lobby and into the dining room. It was undergoing a transformation. Before, during lunch, it had looked like a restaurant with four-tops everywhere. Now, larger twelve-tops littered the area, each draped with a white tablecloth. Better for community dining and networking.

Lorie and another young girl entered, pushing a cart with slim white vases filled with flowers.

"Hey," Lorie said. "Rhea said you were down here. Are Robin and Nicole back yet?"

"Not yet."

"Sorry I'm tied up with this," Lorie said.

"No problem."

"Can I get you anything?"

"I'm good. Just exploring."

"Explore away. I'll be finished soon and I'll come find you."

She and the other girl began arranging the vases on each table. I walked to the wall of double French doors that lined one side of the dining room and looked out toward an expansive flagstone patio that extended almost the entire width of the lodge. I stepped outside. Two oak trees rose from its far side, their broad limbs shading the entire area.

At one end, several staff members circled a long buffet table, stacking plates on one end and arranging half a dozen metallic food warmers in a regimented line as if waiting for duty. Beyond the table, a large stainless-steel grill and smoker arrangement pumped white smoke into the air along with the smell of bar-b-q. My stomach growled.

Toward the opposite end of the patio, I saw an unlit firepit with surrounding Adirondack chairs as well as clusters of comfy chairs and sofas. I walked that way. More French doors opened into a very cool bar with even more comfy-looking chairs and sofas. Behind a long carved-wood bar, backed by shelves of liquor, a man stood, tugging bottles of wine from a cardboard case and lining them along one of the shelves. He obviously heard me come in and glanced my way.

"Welcome," he said. "Can I get you anything?"

"I'm just exploring. You look busy and I don't want to interfere."

"No problem." He leaned on the bar. "If it's too early for alcohol, I've got some coffee, soft drinks, even milk." He gave a soft laugh.

I sat at the bar. "Never too early for alcohol."

"You got that right. I'm Peter."

"Jake." We shook hands.

"I know who you are," Peter said. "I remember when you pitched."

"A long time ago now."

"Not that long. What's your poison?"

"What the hell. I'll have a Maker's Mark on the rocks."

"You got it."

Peter filled a glass with ice, poured an overly generous amount of whiskey, and slid it toward me. "To your health."

I tilted my glass toward him and took a sip. "Back at you."

He reached under the bar and into an ice bin. He snatched a Corona and twisted the cap off. "Hell, might as well get the evening started." He took a slug.

"How many are you expecting for this shindig?" I asked.

"Probably forty or fifty. Thereabouts."

"You worked here long?"

"Since it opened just over a year ago. Before that I was down in Tampa. I bartended at a restaurant down that way."

"What brought you here?"

"Jonathon. He and his crew came to the restaurant all the time. It was his favorite. We talked a lot. When he decided to open this place, he asked me to head up the bar."

"You like it?"

"I love it." Another swallow of beer. "He's easy to work for and the members are good people for the most part."

"The beauty of a private club," I said. "My bar can get a little rowdy at times."

"Captain Rocky's."

I couldn't hide my surprise. "How'd you know that?"

"I've actually been there. Nice place. Besides, part of my job here is to know all the members and everything I can about them. They like that personal touch. Since you're a prospective member, the same holds true. Rhea gave me all your info to make sure you and Nicole feel at home."

Of course she did. I would've been surprised if she hadn't. Wasn't this entire ordeal a form of seduction? Wine and dine and rifle through your wallet? Peter the bartender was part of the cast yet he still seemed like a good guy. Hell, I'd hire him if he took the job this seriously. It's not easy to keep names and information for so many people straight. People you might not see for months at a time. It was a gift to be able to do that. Apparently, Peter possessed that skill.

Actually, I did too. Knowing and schmoozing people at Captain Rocky's was my main duty. Carla did the rest. The boring business part. I was good with names and faces so it worked out.

"The entire staff here seems very nice," I said.

"And easy on the eyes," Peter said with a wink.

"I can't argue with that."

"What can I say, the members like the young and the beautiful."

"Don't we all," I said.

"I think you did well." He saw the question in my eyes. "I saw you guys when you were here for lunch the other day."

"No doubt she's well above my pay grade but I'm not complaining."

"Nor should you." Another gulp of beer. "One of the perks of owning a bar, or being a bartender, is the young ladies you meet." He raised a eyebrow. "And spend quality time with."

That is so true. Before Nicole came along, my entire social world revolved around Captain Rocky's and the female patrons who wandered in. Pancake too. Of course, he still does. Do I miss those days? Not really. None could compare with Nicole so why reminisce?

"Isn't that the case," I said. "Of course, my place is open to the public so we get all types. I imagine here, in a private setting, you're restricted a bit."

"With the members and guests, you bet. But the staff? That's a different story."

"Oh?"

"Working together day after day, here in a relatively isolated environment, it'd be surprising if folks didn't bump against each other every now and then."

"No problems from the top with that?"

He shook his head. "Not really. Jonathon and Rhea are fairly relaxed on all that. As long as it doesn't create drama or other problems."

"What about the members?" I asked. "And the staff?"

"Again, not advertised, but not really frowned on. You could even say it's expected. Isn't that one of the benefits of being rich? You get pampered in every way."

Reminded me of my days in Major League Baseball. We were definitely pampered.

"I assume the girls know that when they sign on? That they might need to do some pampering."

Peter seemed to consider that for a minute. "Probably. But it's not really that way. The girls that work here, most of them anyway, are not only here to make good money, and they do, but also to find Mr. Right. Someone who can show them the glitter and glam and fairy-tale life that comes with money."

"And since they're young and adventurous, it's an opportunity."

"Exactly," Peter said. "In fact, a few of the girls that worked here did exactly that. Met some dude and took off around the world or even got married to a member and moved on to a happy life." He finished his beer. "Even if not, they could do much worse than spend time here having fun, and traveling, and doing all the things that come with working for TLM."

"There you are."

I looked up. Will Buckley walked in.

"Mr. Buckley," Peter said. "Welcome."

"Peter." He nodded. "The usual."

"Johnnie Walker Blue coming up."

Johnnie Walker Scotch comes in various label colors, and quality. Red, black, and up the line is blue. It retails for around $400 a bottle. Will Buckley had good taste. Expensive anyway. In contrast, my Maker's Mark is around $35 a bottle. I felt pedestrian.

After Peter poured his drink, and Will took a sip, Will asked, "So what's the topic of the day?"

"Talking about the staff here," I said.

"Mostly the ladies," Peter added.

"Ah yes. One of the main reasons I come here so often. Good whiskey and quality companionship. What's not to like?"

Indeed. Alcohol and "quality companionship" can definitely generate a memorable weekend, but what struck me was how open and casual it seemed. As if everyone knew and no one cared. Here I was, a stranger, openly talking about hookups between staff and members, and staff and staff, and neither Peter nor Will seemed the least bit reluctant to discuss it. Like it was an open secret. Or maybe, it wasn't so secret. Was TLM a dating service, a prostitution ring, or both? I had the impression that whatever label you chose, TLM was definitely full service. Maybe, or perhaps I was being cynical again. One thing for sure, when I was younger and if I wasn't playing baseball, I'd have jumped at the chance to tend bar here.

CHAPTER 24

PETER AND WILL, my new buddies, and I were into our second, or was it third, round and had continued our discussions of the easy sex to be found at TLM before moving on to football, which I enjoyed, and fishing, which I didn't understand and thought was a boring waste of time, when Nicole and Robin came in.

"Why'd I know I'd find you here?" Nicole said.

"Because you know me."

Nicole's damp tee shirt clung to her body and her slightly flushed face and wonderful legs glistened with perspiration. She looked exceptionally sexy, even for her. Will apparently thought so too, his gaze devouring her. I was accustomed to such looks, but with lecherous old Will, I wanted to throw a baseball at his face, maybe his family jewels. That'd cool him off a bit.

I introduced Nicole to Peter and Will. Robin, of course, knew Will, who she hugged, saying, "It's so good to see you again."

"You too," Will said. "I was hoping you'd be working this weekend."

I noticed that when Robin broke the embrace, she remained snuggled up to Will, his arm casually over her shoulder, her hand flattened against his chest. She looked up at him.

"I need to go clean up and then help Lorie," Robin said. She broke the embrace. "But I'll see you later."

"Yes, you will," Will said.

She slipped from his embrace and they shared a look. Well, well, there's a story there. Not really surprising given our earlier conversation about Will and his escapades with the staff here at TLM. He and Robin definitely had a history, and from the exchanged glances, a future.

After Robin left, Peter offered Nicole something from the bar. Sure, why not? She asked for a margarita.

"You're about the prettiest thing I've ever seen," Will said to Nicole. "I take it you and this dude are together?"

"Yeah," Nicole said. "Like gum on a shoe, he's hard to shake." She punched my arm. "But he's fun after a couple of drinks."

Will laughed. "Isn't that the case with all guys? Fun after a couple and trouble after a half a dozen."

"I don't know," Nicole said. "After Jake has that many, he's defenseless, and I can have my way with him."

I started to say she could do that alcohol or not, but she already knew that so I said nothing.

"Darling, I don't think you need alcohol to seduce old Jake or anyone else. As pretty as your are, I suspect you could do whatever you wanted." He took a sip of his drink. "Hell, I'd volunteer."

My new buddy Will not only humped the help, he was also flirting with my girlfriend. That's "Will the Snake" to you. He seemed less amusing now than he had earlier. Where was a baseball when you needed it?

"That's very kind of you," Nicole said, and then as if to brush Will off, she said to Peter, "You make a mean margarita."

"Better than the ones at Captain Rocky's?" Peter asked.

"You know about Jake's place?"

"Like I told Jake earlier, I've even been there."

"Well, at the risk of insulting your mixology skills, I'll have to go with Captain Rocky's." She nudged me with an elbow. "Of course, I have to say that."

"No offense taken," Peter said. "I'll work on it."

Nicole raised her glass toward him. "I'll be your tester."

"Sounds like a plan."

The conversation turned to the business end of TLM, Will saying he loved being involved and was very happy with their investment strategy. He heartily recommended that Nicole and I join, saying, "If you want to retire early, that is."

I thought about that. I was more or less retired. Sure, I owned a business, but I didn't really do anything, except meet and greet and hang out with Nicole and Pancake. Whether that qualifies as a job or not is open to debate, but I felt retired and I liked it.

Nicole drained her margarita.

"Want another?" Peter asked.

"Later. Right now, I need to go shower and get ready for tonight."

"I'll go with you," I said. "We can shower together and save water."

Nicole shook her head. "Jake is so environmentally conscious."

That's me, Jake the conservationist.

I'm not sure how much water we actually saved since the shower was rather extended, but isn't it the thought that counts?

Afterwards, I slipped on some sweatpants and stretched out on the bed. Nicole sat on the edge brushing her hair.

"What'd you learn today with all your roaming around?" she asked.

"TLM is more than it seems. It's not only a self-help cult and a moneymaking machine, it's a brothel."

She stopped brushing and stared at me. "How'd you come to that conclusion?"

I told her of my conversations with Peter and Will and how it seemed to me that the girls were more than simply staff and eye candy but were also expected to service the members. "At least that's the feeling I get."

"I agree," Nicole said.

"You do?" She nodded. "Here I thought I might be too harsh in my assessment."

Nicole gave her hair a few more brushes, tossed the brush aside, and crawled up on the bed, lying next to me. "What if I told you that both Lorie and Robin had been involved in a sugar-baby, sugar-daddy arrangement before being recruited by TLM?"

I raised up on one elbow and looked at her. "Really? How'd you uncover that?"

"Robin told me she had a sugar-daddy while she was in college. She said several girls she knew did the same thing. She posted on one of those websites that tout such things and met a married bank VP. She said it more than paid for her apartment and tuition. According to her, Lorie had done the same."

"Are you thinking Rhea and Jonathon search those sites for workers?"

"It's a possibility."

"We need to get Pancake on this," I said.

"My thoughts exactly. I'll give him a call."

Nicole grabbed her iPhone from the bedside table and dialed Pancake, her phone on speaker.

"Talk to me." Pancake's voice came toward us. As did the sound of other voices and laughter in the background.

"Are you at Captain Rocky's?" Nicole asked.

"Gotta eat sometime."

"Page one or page two?" I asked.

The thing is, Pancake orders by the page, not the item. Yes, he can devour an entire page of food. I'd be amazed if I hadn't seen it a thousand times.

"Sort of mixing and matching today," Pancake said. "Chili and tacos and fried shrimp and key lime pie go well together. Did you know you're almost out of jumbo shrimp?"

"Was that before or after you arrived?" I asked.

"You're a funny guy. But since you asked, after. I only had a couple of dozen so you were almost out anyway. I think you should stay on top of your inventory a little better."

Right. Like I was able to do that. "That's Carla's job."

"She ordered a bunch more so looks like I'll be set for lunch tomorrow."

"Lucky you."

"So what do you need?" Pancake asked.

"We need you to look into something," Nicole said.

"I got my laptop right here next to my nachos so fire away."

"What do you know about sugar baby sites?"

"A bit. I did some peeking in that direction for a case we had a couple of years ago. I assume this is connected to April Wilkerson and not just Jake being creepy."

"No more creepy than usual," Nicole said. "But he's charmingly creepy."

"Can we get to business now?" I said.

"The two young ladies we met here, Lorie Cooper and Robin Meade, were involved in that world before they landed at TLM," Nicole said.

"Interesting," Pancake said. "You're thinking TLM might seek out young women that way?"

"If not, it's one hell of a coincidence," I said. "Plus, to me it seems the girls who work here aren't merely hostesses and PR staffers. I think they are here to entertain."

"Never heard that story before," Pancake said. "Bunch of rich dudes and a covey of young women, they gotta do something to pass the time." Then to someone else, apparently his waitress, "Thanks, darling." Back to us: "Just got me another cheeseburger. On the house."

"Oh, one more thing," Nicole said. "Check out a guy named Andrew Heche. He's down in the Tampa/St. Pete area and a friend of Jonathon's. Apparently, April and the two girls we just told you about, Lorie and Robin, were down at his place for a party. They came back, April stayed."

"Oh?" I said.

"Oh?" Pancake said.

"You didn't mention that," I said.

"Because you were pestering me in the shower."

Pestering?

"That's more than I need to know," Pancake said, "but thanks for sharing. Why did April stay behind?"

"Part of her job. More parties and some deal on this Andrew's yacht."

"When was this?" I asked.

"Three weeks ago."

"About when she went missing, or at least incommunicado," Pancake said. "I don't like it."

"It might be nothing," Nicole said.

"Or it might be something," I said.

"She could have hung around for a party or some other event and then split for parts unknown," Nicole said. "Maybe she met someone and took off. That seems to be common among the TLM staff."

"I'll get on this as soon as I finish filling up," Pancake said. He disconnected the call.

The problem there is that Pancake was not fillable, like a landfill with no bottom. Or maybe that big abyss in the Pacific Ocean. What was that called? Oh yeah, the Mariana Trench. That's perfect. Pancake is the Mariana Trench. I loved the analogy. I told Nicole that. She wasn't overly impressed with my poetic nature.

"What's his monthly food tab?" Nicole asked.

"I don't know. We never kept one. I was afraid to know."

"Smart move."

"I don't like that whole thing with April," I said.

"At least it gives us a last known location." She shrugged. "And it wasn't here."

"But, if Andrew and Jonathon are friends, there're still connected dots."

"Pancake will dig it out," I said. "He always does."

"Between cheeseburgers."

"What time do the festivities begin tonight?" I asked.

"Seven. Let's go a little early so I can help Peter work on his margarita skills."

CHAPTER 25

NICOLE FINISHED BRAIDING her hair, fastening the tip with a black nylon loop. She examined her work in the mirror. Satisfied, she tucked her peach silk shirt into her jeans and adjusted its collar. She turned to Jake, who lay on the bed, one knee bent, his iPad propped against his thigh. Jake also wore jeans topped with a dark green polo. She liked that color on him. She sat on the foot of the bed.

"What're you reading?" she asked

"A trashy novel."

Jake only read paperback thrillers and only paper and ink, never on his iPad. "No you're not."

He looked at her over the top of the device. "I could be."

"Not likely."

"I'm checking out sugar baby sites. There're a ton of them and they have such cute names. Find-a-Daddy, Rich Daddy Hot Baby, Be My Daddy, and, my favorite, Sugar Hookup."

"Did you stumble on anybody we know?" Nicole asked.

"You mean like Lorie or Robin, or even better April Wilkerson?"

"Yeah."

"No. I'm just skimming, trying to get a feel for this world. I'll leave the deep diving to Pancake."

"Good idea." She tapped his leg. "Let's go."

Jake closed his iPad cover and tossed it on the bed. He rolled to a sitting position and began slipping on his sandals.

"Here's the plan," she said. "I'll chat up the girls and you do the same with the guy members we meet. Maybe we'll dig up something useful."

"Divide and conquer."

"Obviously, our focus is to gather information on April but we'll need to be careful. I can't shake the feeling that her disappearance is tied to her duties here, or her connections with some of the members."

"Like being kidnapped and whisked to a remote island? Or maybe sold into sex slavery?" Jake asked.

"I wouldn't dismiss either of those," Nicole said. "But it's just as likely, maybe even more so, that she met some rich dude and disappeared of her own free will. And didn't tell mommy as an act of defiance."

"I still don't like that part." Jake stood. "You ready to go?"

"Try to avoid ruffling feathers," Nicole said.

"I never ruffle feathers."

"Sure you do. You just don't realize it."

"When is the last time I ruffled anyone's feathers?" Jake asked.

"That's a long discussion and we don't have the time. Today try to keep your eyes and ears open and your mouth shut." She smiled.

"My mouth?"

"It often gets you in more trouble than it helps. Particularly during an investigation."

"I need to ask questions."

"All I'm saying is use that little nugget of common sense you possess."

"You sound like Ray. I think he's rubbing off on you."

Nicole clasped Jake's hand as they descended the stairs into the lobby and turned toward the bar. Inside, an older couple sat at a corner table, while a younger duo stood at the bar. Peter the bartender slid a pair of margaritas toward them and they walked away, the girl smiling and checking out Jake as they passed. Nicole knew that men stared at her and that Jake was cool with it, and that women did the same with Jake and she was cool with that too. One of the many things that made their relationship so comfortable. She had been in liaisons where jealousy and insecurity had reared their green-eyed heads, making things untenable—on the guy's part, never hers, as she didn't do jealousy. She had walked away every time.

"I see you're working on your margarita skills," Nicole said to Peter as she and Jake slid up on barstools.

Peter swiped the bar top with a towel. "After you threw down the challenge, why wouldn't I?"

"Let's see how you're doing."

"Coming right up." He poured the lime green liquid from a plastic bottle labeled in black marker as "Marg Mix," obviously his own concoction, into a blender. He added tequila, packed it with ice, and whirred it to life. He looked at Jake. "Maker's rocks?"

"You got it."

Once the blender did its work, he poured the margarita into a salt-rimmed glass and handed it to Nicole.

Nicole took a sip. "Oh yeah, much better. What'd you do differently?"

"A tad more lime juice and a little less sugar."

"I like it," Nicole said. "Clean and fresh."

Rhea and Robin appeared followed by two young ladies who looked alike. Sisters?

Rhea solved the mystery. "This is Shane and Sara Hutton. They're our guests this weekend. This is Nicole and Jake."

"Nice to meet you," one of the sisters said.

"Who's who?" Nicole asked.

"I'm Shane."

"I'm Sara," her sister said.

Shane was half an inch taller, a couple of pounds slimmer, and her hair a shade lighter than her sister, but other than those minor differences, Nicole couldn't distinguish one from the other.

"Let's head out to the patio," Robin said. "We can grab a drink and enjoy this wonderful weather."

Before they could move, Rhea grabbed Jake's arm. "I'm going to steal him for a few minutes. There's someone I want him to meet."

"We'll head on out," Robin said. "Come find us after you're done."

Nicole followed Robin, Shane, and Sara to the patio.

The sun hung just above the distant tree line and painted everything a warm orange. At the far end of the massive patio, a smoker manned by two young men pumped aromatic smoke into the air. A couple stood nearby, plates in hand, each gnawing on a rib bone. Only a half a dozen of the twenty or so patio tables were occupied, the party not yet in full swing. Nicole and the girls settled at a teak table beneath one of the massive oak trees.

Beth Hodges, who had been Nicole's and Jake's waitress at lunch, walked up. She looked at Nicole. "I see Peter took care of you." She indicated Nicole's glass. "What about you ladies?"

"The margaritas are excellent," Nicole said.

"Works for me," Sara said.

Shane agreed, Robin declined. Beth headed toward the bar.

"Nicole is a big-time moviemaker," Robin said to Shane and Sara.

"Not exactly," Nicole said.

"*Murderwood* was a hit," Robin said.

Shane looked at Nicole. "You made *Murderwood*?"

"I wrote it. My uncle made it."

"Charles Balfour is your uncle?" Sara asked.

"He is."

"That's so cool," Sara said. She nodded to her sister. "We loved it."

Shane nodded. "Dark but very good."

Nicole saw Rhea from the corner of her eye. She raised a finger to grab Robin's attention and then motioned her that way.

"Looks like work calls," Robin said. "Can you girls carry on without me for a few?"

"We'll be right here," Nicole said.

Robin stood and followed Rhea inside.

"How did you get Kirk Ford to star in it?" Sara asked.

"He's a longtime friend, and he and Uncle Charles have done a lot of work together in the past."

"Yeah, I'd say," Shane said. "Like *Space Quest*. We're obsessed with that series."

"Is he as hot in person as he is on the screen?" Sara asked.

"More so," Nicole said. "Kirk's a good-looking dude for sure."

"Did you ever date him?" Shane asked.

"Not really. We had dinner a couple of times but mostly we're friends. He's not my type."

"What?" Sara asked. "He's everybody's type."

"And that's the problem," Nicole said. "Kirk's a player. A big-time player."

Shane raised an eyebrow. "He could play with me."

Nicole laughed. "Given the chance, I'm sure he would."

"Not likely." Shane gave a headshake. "I can't compete with all those Hollywood beauties."

"That's mostly smoke and mirrors," Nicole said. "Makeup and lighting. You, both of you, are as pretty as anyone in Hollywood."

"You're just being kind," Sara said.

"Trust me, it's a fact."

The margaritas arrived, along with a bowl of warmed nuts. "Anything else?" Beth asked. That garnered three headshakes. "I'll check back later."

"I've always wanted to be an actress," Shane said. "Actually, both of us have fantasized about it. We did take a couple of drama classes in high school and did some community theater stuff."

"That's a good start," Nicole said. "Every chop you learn will make you better."

"That's about as far as we went," Sara said. "I mean, doesn't every little girl want to be a movie star?"

"That's true," Nicole said. "But the reality is very different from the image. Moviemaking is a lot of long hours and hard work. I made a couple, many years ago, and discovered it wasn't for me."

"Why?" Sara asked.

"Boring. On a movie set every little thing takes forever so there's a lot of sitting round. Besides, I was mostly eye candy. The girl in the bikini with a couple of lines. Nothing very inspiring." Nicole popped a nut in her mouth. "I prefer the writing."

"I'm surprised someone as pretty as you wasn't a big success."

"Pretty girls are everywhere out in L.A. If you have the right look, no acting is required. Which is fine, just not for me. To be a serious actress requires study and hard work. Again, the writing attracted me more."

"I'd love it, I think," Shane said.

"If you're serious about it, I can introduce you to the right people," Nicole said.

"Really?" Sara asked.

Nicole nodded. "Through my uncle, and now with my movie, I know a lot of people in the industry."

"And Kirk Ford," Shane said.

"And Kirk Ford," Nicole said.

"Are you a member here?" Sara asked.

Nicole shook her head. "No. Jake and I are exploring the possibility though. What about you guys?"

"I wish," Shane said. "We're students so we don't have the financial clout for that."

"But Rhea said you were guests," Nicole said.

"She offered us a job and invited us for the weekend to see how we liked it."

Interesting. These girls were being actively recruited by TLM. They certainly fit the mold of the girls Nicole had met so far.

"Doing what?" Nicole asked.

"PR and hostessing," Shane said. "Something like that."

"Probably what Robin is doing," Sara added.

"Does that mean your school will be put on hold?"

Shane shook her head. "That's one of the cool things about the job. Rhea said it would only be part-time and mostly on weekends so we can simply drive over when we work."

"We go to South Alabama," Sara said. "It's not that far."

"Oh," Shane said. "And there could be some travel. I imagine we'd miss a few classes." She shrugged. "But the pay will more than make up for that."

"It's pays well, then?" Nicole asked.

"Amazingly so." Sara glanced toward the lodge's rear door. "She said from fifty to a hundred thousand a year."

"Plus staying here when we work and all the travel is paid for," Sara added.

"Very generous," Nicole said.

Too generous for smiling and chatting. Didn't they see that? She wanted to shake some sense into both of them but that would definitely blow their cover.

"Better than that diner we worked at last year," Sara said, glancing toward her sister. "That was a lot of work for very little money. I mean, it helped with the bills, but it wasn't an easy job."

"It was a greasy spoon," Sara added. "Good food if you like fried everything covered with gravy. It was on the highway so a lot of truckers stopped in. They can be a little handsy."

"And crude," Shane added. She gave a headshake. "Some of the offers I got were seriously freaky."

"Totally." Sara laughed. "Like inviting you into their truck cab would be tempting."

"Sounds like working here would be a definite upgrade," Nicole said.

"Totally," Sara said.

"Did you apply for the job here or did they seek you out?" Nicole asked.

Shane hesitated, glanced at her sister. "Rhea recruited us, I guess you'd say."

"How did that happen?" Nicole asked. "Did you put your resume up on one of those job sites or something?"

Shane gave that some thought before she responded by shaking her head and saying, "You know, I'm not sure how she found us."

Shane would not make a good poker player. Nicole instantly knew she was lying. It was all over her face. Were these two involved in the sugar baby world like Lorie and Robin? If so, that would be too big a coincidence to be one. It would be a conspiracy. But how to approach that? What was the next best question? One that would get an answer without making them uncomfortable or, worse, silencing them? Nicole turned options over in her mind, not able to come up with a good one.

Didn't matter as she never got the chance. Rhea walked up.

"Having fun?" Rhea asked.

"We are," Sara said.

"Let me show you girls around," Rhea said. She looked at Nicole. "You're welcome to join us, but I think you've already seen everything."

"I'm good right here," Nicole said. "I'm going to finish my margarita and then go find Jake."

Rhea nodded. "I think I saw him in the bar."

"Exactly where I expected him to be."

CHAPTER 26

THE PERSON SHE wanted me to meet was a mid-fifties guy, a good five inches shorter than my six-three. Graying brown hair and intelligent blue eyes, he was deeply tanned, indicating he spent more time outside than in an office. She introduced him as Gordon Buchanan, a "longtime and close friend" of Jonathon's, adding that he had been one of the very first members of TLM. Rhea then excused herself and flitted off to deal with some issue for the party. Buchanan and I grabbed barstools.

"I wanted to meet you because I'm a huge baseball fan," Buchanan said. "I remember you well. You had game."

"Thanks. It was a fun few years."

"Rhea said you own a bar down on the Gulf."

"It's a cool place," Peter the bartender said as he slid another Maker's on the rocks toward me. "What can I get you, Mr. Buchanan?"

"I'll have one of those." He nodded toward my drink.

"What do you do?" I asked.

"Move money around." He grinned. "I manage a hedge fund, some real estate holdings, and a couple of other things."

"You and Jonathon go back a few years?"

"Since we were in our twenties. Over the years we've done a number of deals together."

Peter placed Buchanan's drink on a bar napkin, gray with "TLM" in a bold red diagonal script on it. "There you go." A couple approached the other end of the bar and Peter moved that way.

"I hear you're thinking about joining TLM," Buchanan said.

"I am."

"I couldn't recommend it more." He took a sip of bourbon. "If you like to make money."

"Doesn't everyone?"

"That's a fact. Most folks don't know how though."

"I understand Jonathon does," I said.

"Oh yeah. I'm pretty good with numbers and understanding the market and bonds and other funds, but Jonathon has a knack. It's almost like magic. He seems to know when to hold them and when to fold them."

"Like a true gambler."

"Except it's almost like he's playing with loaded dice. He's that good. He sure as hell has taught me a lot, and made me a bunch of money."

"Not to mention the self-help classes he offers," I said.

"I'm afraid I'm beyond redemption there, but many of our members sing his praises in that arena."

"Where do you live?" I asked.

"Near Tampa."

"When did you fly in?"

"I drove." Another nip at his bourbon. "I just bought a new Ferrari GTS. This offered a good opportunity to get it on the road."

"In traffic."

He nodded. "Unfortunately, that's true. The damn thing has seven hundred and eighty-nine horsepower, and I bet I didn't use a dozen of them." He laughed. "Felt like I was holding back a team of eager thoroughbreds."

"I know someone who could use them. Probably all of them."

"Who?"

"My girlfriend, Nicole. She likes to drive fast."

"Woman after my own heart. I'd like to meet her."

"You will, I'm sure. She's here with me this weekend."

"So, how much do you already know about TLM?"

I ran through a thumbnail of what little we did know. TLM will fix what ails you and make you rich. If actually true, that's a strong pitch.

"It's true," Buchanan said. "In all the years I've been working with Jonathon, I've never seen—or even heard—of him losing money. We did some risky stuff when we were younger, but it always worked out."

"What kinds of risky things?"

He drained his glass and signaled to Peter he'd have another. Then to me, "You ready for a refill?"

"Sure, why not."

"That's my philosophy." He raised two fingers toward Peter. "We bought a couple of condo projects, maybe ten years ago, and did a full-on rehab and upgrade. Sunk a lot more money than intended, but it paid off. Comps in the area skyrocketed and we made out like bandits. Then there were a handful of IPOs that I wasn't enthralled with because I felt they could've tanked but Jonathon believed in them and as usual he was right. We got well on every single one of them."

"You're saying I should hook my wagon to the TLM program?"

Our drinks appeared on the bar.

"Couldn't recommend it more." He lifted his glass. "To your future wealth."

We sat quietly for a moment, then Buchanan said, "And that doesn't count the benefits."

"Which are?"

"Look around. You'll see a bevy of young ladies you'd want to spend quality time with. Best of all, there's a constant turnover so there're always new fish."

Fish? I wondered what the young ladies would say to that? But then I had to admit, everyone we had met seemed to know the score.

"If your girlfriend would let you," he said. "Or didn't know."

"She wouldn't, and she would."

He laughed. "I get it."

Lorie came into the bar, saw us, and headed our way.

"Gordon," she said. "It's so great to see you again." She hugged him.

He returned her embrace and then pushed her back a step, looked her up and down. "Prettiest girl in the room as always."

Lorie looked at me. "Gordon's big on flattery."

"Just telling the truth," he said. "Don't you agree, Jake?"

"How could I not?"

"I've got to run but will I see you later?" Lorie asked Gordon.

He flashed her a knowing look. "Definitely."

After she left, Buchanan said, "She's something else."

"Sounds like you guys have a history," I said.

"We've had our moments, you might say. She's smart, fun, and very easy on the eyes." He took a slug of bourbon. "We spent a week in the Bahamas once. A memorable week. I have a place down there. You'll have to come down sometime. With your girlfriend, or if you can shake away, I promise it'll be epic."

Nicole appeared.

Buchanan did a double take. His eyes widened. "My, my. You certainly don't need any help from me."

"Help with what?" Nicole asked.

"Nothing," he said. "Guy talk."

Nicole slapped me on the butt. "Jake's good at guy talk. Just don't believe everything he says."

"Mr. Buchanan has a new Ferrari," I said.

Now Nicole's eyes lit up. "You do?"

"I do. But call me Gordon."

He never asked me to call him Gordon.

"My dream car," Nicole said.

"Want to see it?"

"Absolutely."

We walked out to the parking area near the administration offices. The Ferrari was red, of course, with tan interior and it was spectacular.

"Makes my Mercedes look pedestrian," Nicole said.

"It runs like a scalded cat," my new first-name-basis friend Gordon said.

"I bet." Nicole ran a hand along the car's sleek front fender. "It even feels fast."

"Want to take it for a spin?"

"Really?"

"Let's go." He opened the driver's door and Nicole slid in. He walked around to the passenger door and opened it. "We'll be back in a hot minute."

Nicole cranked the car to life, the engine rumbling as only a Ferrari can. She revved it a bit, slipped it into gear, and they were off.

I watched as the car turned toward the drive and Nicole hit the afterburners. She was in her element.

"I see you met Gordon."

I turned as Jonathon walked up. "Interesting guy."

"We've been friends for years. In fact, he's probably my best friend."

"That's what he said."

"I hope he sung our praises."

"He did."

"Enough to make you want to sign on?"

"Let's say we're moving in that direction."

"Good. You'd be a welcome member and I think you'd quickly realize the benefits."

Like money and a never-ending string of young women. Sort of like my baseball days.

"I've got a couple of calls to make before the party heats up." He glanced at his watch. "I'll find you later and we can talk more."

"Sounds good."

He headed back toward his office.

I heard the Ferrari's engine whining from the distance, closing fast. Nicole was pushing it. A flash of red and she came to a stop exactly where the car had been sitting before. They climbed out.

"Wow. That was incredible," Nicole said. "I want one."

Of course she did.

Nicole hooked her arm in mine. "Will you buy me one, daddy?"

That drew a chuckle from Gordon.

"As soon as I rob a bank," I said.

"I can vouch for the fact that she can sure as hell drive," Gordon said.

"It's one of her gifts," I said.

"Come on," Gordon said. "I'll buy you some drinks."

"We'll be there in a second," I said.

"Don't dally or you'll fall behind." Gordon gave a wave and headed inside.

We walked toward the far end of the circular drive that fronted the lodge, out of earshot. I pulled out my cell phone and called Pancake, putting it on speaker. "I got another name for you. Gordon Buchanan. From Tampa and a good friend of Jonathon's"

"The name has come up in my research," Pancake said. "Along with that other guy you mentioned, Andrew Heche. Not much on either yet, but I'll dig a little deeper."

"Anything on those sugar-baby, sugar-daddy sites yet?" I asked.

"You looking to replace Nicole?"

"Right," Nicole said. "He can't even handle me much less one of these young dollies. Besides, he promised to pull a bank job and buy me a Ferrari."

Pancake grunted. "You'd be dangerous. Or should I say, more dangerous."

"Can't be too much of that," Nicole, said.

"Are you two finished?" I asked.

"Probably not," Pancake said. "Truth is I haven't gotten much done on those sites yet. I've been chasing down Lindemann's and TLM's money. Ain't easy. He's got accounts and moves money all over the world and keeps it pretty well disguised. But I'm making progress."

"Such as?"

"Let me keep sniffing and then maybe I'll have something sorted out later."

"When you get back to the sugar baby stuff," Nicole said, "remember to check if Lorie Cooper, Robin Meade, or April pop up anywhere. And add Shane and Sara Sutton to your list. They're sisters and students at South Alabama and are being actively recruited to work here."

"You got it." Pancake disconnected the call.

CHAPTER 27

APRIL WILKERSON WASN'T happy. She hadn't been for a week now. The past three days had been a series of arguments with Andrew about calling her mother to let her know where she was and that she was okay. Sure, she didn't have her cell any longer, and they were god knows how far from civilization, but Andrew had a cell, which he refused to let her touch. It was for business and business only, he had said. April didn't see how one quick call to her mother would harm his business. I mean, really? He countered with claiming there wasn't any service this far out anyway.

Okay, fine, but she knew he had a satellite phone, again for business only. Also, didn't boats have radios or something? Didn't they have to call ship to shore at some time? Andrew had said those channels were for emergency use only. She complained, but he said talking to mommy didn't constitute a crisis. It could wait.

He could be such a dick sometimes.

She bickered with him about the call but didn't really get irate. Didn't throw a foot-stomping tantrum or anything close. What good would it do? Besides, part of her felt it might do her mother good to worry about her for a few days. Rather than remaining wrapped up in herself and her latest boy toy, Sean. What a creep.

Now, she watched Andrew as he stood near the starboard railing of his yacht, an eighty-five-foot beauty named *After Hours*. He held the satellite phone to his ear and spoke toward the water so she couldn't hear what he was saying. She guessed it was business or some emergency since he was using his precious satellite phone. The one she couldn't touch.

They had just finished a wonderful meal on the rear deck and were waiting for desert. The staff busied themselves with clearing the table, Paulo, the sous chef and head waiter, asking her if she needed anything while the soufflés were prepared.

"Maybe some coffee, Paulo."

"Coming up."

Andrew glanced her way and now seemed to have a new wrinkle to his brow. Was he angry or was he having trouble hearing whoever he was talking to?

The past two weeks had been a whirlwind. More so than any other trip she'd taken since joining TLM. Most previous trips were for a couple of days and involved a little bit of smiling and small talk, and occasionally a trip to the lavish bedroom with some rich guy who worked with Andrew and Jonathon. Or at least invested with them. She didn't have a problem with that even if the sex mostly left something to be desired. That was also true of Andrew, but since he was footing the bill for everything, how could she complain? The pay was good, the benefits amazing, and now it seemed that Andrew had a special interest in her. As if he had selected her for his companion. For how long? She had no idea but knew the ride would be first class all the way. Andrew did nothing half-assed as far she could see. She could think of worse ways to pass time.

She had intended to call her mom from the Mobile airport while she waited for her flight to Tampa. But Rhea had been late in dropping her off, and then check-in and security had been a slow and painful process. Something about them being understaffed. Not something she believed. She saw a lot of folks with airline uniforms, mostly standing around and doing little. The bottom line was that she never had time to call. Besides, she was still pissed at her mother. Why couldn't she simply give her what was hers and then she wouldn't need a job? Any job. Not the old one at that dinky-ass bar in Orange Beach, and not this new one at Lindemann Farms.

When she landed, a limo picked her up and whisked her to Andrew's massive Spanish-style home on the water near St. Petersburg. It wasn't her first visit there for some party, far from it, but it never failed to impress anew. It had twelve bedrooms and even more bathrooms for christ sakes. This time she had been settled in Andrew's enormous master quarters rather than one of the other suites. The rules were clear from the beginning. She was to be his plaything for however long this lasted. Again, she could think of worse things.

Lorie and Robin had flown down for yet another of Andrew's epic weekend parties. They left on the following Monday, but at Andrew's insistence, April remained. A relaxed five days followed where she sunned by the expansive pool or lounged in a chair shaded by palm trees. The food was exquisite, and the endless stream of staff was attentive to her every need. The shopping trip in Tampa ran up a bill of several thousand and garnered her a pair of dazzling outfits she had already worn to classy dinners.

Losing her cell phone on the second day was the only bump. She searched for the next two days, trying to remember where she had last had it, sure it was in the bedroom, on the nightstand. She even had Andrew call her number, but no chiming was heard anywhere in the house. Then on the fifth day, they boarded *After Hours* and left the skyline of Tampa behind.

Most of the next ten days were at sea, though they did stop briefly in Belize City, Playa del Carmen, and Cancun for shopping or a meal or simply to play tourist. She forgot about her phone.

But now, with the last two days being in open water, no land in sight, she felt uncomfortable. She wasn't sure why but it seemed that Andrew had become more distant and had many more calls, most employing his satellite phone. He always made sure she couldn't eavesdrop, but during a couple of them what she overheard sounded like financial negotiations of some sort. One seemed to be about changing some meeting time and location, which irritated Andrew. The upshot was that for the last two days, Andrew had not been in a good mood.

His current call was the fourth, maybe the fifth, today.

Andrew ended his call, slipped his phone in the pocket of the loose white pants he wore, and returned to the table. He was smiling and to Paulo he said, "Some cognac would be good. The Louis the Thirteenth."

"Must be good news," Paulo said. "Will you have some also?" he asked April.

Before she could answer, Andrew said, "Absolutely."

Paulo left.

"I take it you got good news from your call?" April asked

"I did. The buyer finally met my price and all is good."

"What are you selling?"

"Nothing much. Just some equipment I no longer need."

Typical Andrew answer. Vague and noncommittal. In his defense, though, April imagined that negotiations among men at Andrew's level weren't for public consumption. Surely not for the hired help, which April felt more like with each day that rolled by. Something had changed between them. Maybe he was simply stressed by some difficult negotiation. If so, all that must have been resolved because right now, as he looked at her across the table, he seemed more like his old self. Relaxed and happy. She could roll with that.

The cognac arrived. April had had cognac before but didn't really care for it. A little too harsh. She took a sip. This was totally different.

"Wow," she said. "This is good."

Andrew tipped his snifter toward her. "The best." He took a sip. "At two thousand a bottle it better be."

"Two thousand?" April peered at the golden liquid. "So this is what? A hundred dollars in this glass?"

Andrew shrugged. "Maybe a little more. Enjoy."

Paulo returned and placed a Grand Marnier soufflé in front of each of them. He spoon cracked the top and poured a generous amount of crème anglaise sauce in each. "*Bon appetit.*" He walked away.

April dug in. It was heavenly. They ate quietly for a few minutes, sipping the cognac between bites.

"I'm sorry," April said.

He looked up. "For what?"

"For being a pain."

"You haven't been. If anyone has, it's been me. This deal has driven me crazy the past couple of days."

"I should have been there to smooth things."

"You were. Or have you forgotten about last night?"

No, she hadn't forgotten. Last night he had been different. He had been aggressive, even domineering. Something new for him. As if he was fucking and not making love. She wasn't complaining, she actually liked it, but it was different.

"I'll never forget that. But I'm sorry about badgering you over calling my mom. It's my fault I lost my phone and that I didn't call her before we left. I should have, but part of me really didn't want to talk to her. All I do is get mad at her so sometimes it's better to not engage." She sighed. "Anyway, I'm sure it will turn up."

"If it doesn't, I'll buy you a new one."

"You don't have to do that," April said.

"I want to." He reached over and cupped her chin. "You're very special."

She felt her face flush and her breath catch. First his aggression last night, now his romantic side. What was going on? Whatever it was, she loved it.

"You're so sweet."

"We're headed in and tomorrow we'll dock in Tampa. Then you can call your mother."

She dropped her spoon and stood. She circled the table and climbed in his lap, straddling him, kissing his neck. "You're amazing."

He laughed. "I am, aren't I?"

CHAPTER 28

THE PARTY PROVED amazing. Jonathon, Rhea, and the entire TLM crew created a relaxed, yet elegant, atmosphere with the perfect mix of business and pleasure. I had never been around so many millionaires at one time. Well, except for the locker room when I played Major League Baseball. Virtually everyone on the team had a seven-figure net worth. Of course, most of them pissed it away on houses, cars, sex, and drugs. I bought a bar instead. Looking back, a smart move.

Nicole and I met a bunch of interesting folks. All enthusiastically onboard with TLM. We even met a guy from Miami who was a billionaire. With a big B. I had to admit I was a bit intimidated. Couldn't billionaires buy anything and anyone? Even cops and judges? Weren't they more or less bulletproof? This guy, Simon Leclerc, was small, thin, mousy, and had a whine to his voice. Not so scary. But the billions trumped all that.

He was nice and friendly and fervently touted TLM. He said Jonathon had made him a "chunk of change." A chunk for him was probably seven figures. I wondered how he knew since even a cool million wouldn't make a blip on his portfolio's bottom line. But I guess if you made that much money you had to pay attention to cash flow.

Jonathon and Rhea had a strong marketing program. Fill the room with rich and happy folks and the rest simply flows. There was no hard sell, but the pressure was palpable. Many flattered me with my baseball career and Nicole with her looks and movie success. If I had a buck for every time someone said we'd be great assets for TLM, I'd have enough money to join, or maybe to feed Pancake. Not completely, but it would've made a dent in his tab.

Around midnight, the party began to wind down. Many of the guests headed to their rooms, while some congregated in the bar. Nicole and I, along with Robin, Shane, and Sara, grabbed seats around one of the two firepits on the patio. The other one also blazed but was unoccupied.

Beth took our drink orders and headed toward the bar. Did she work every day, and night? Had she been on duty for the past twelve hours, or did she have some downtime between lunch and now? She certainly didn't appear tired, or stressed, or anything but friendly and energetic. That was probably in the TLM manual.

Through the windows that looked into the bar, I noticed Lorie snuggled against Gordon Buchanan. He had one arm around her and a drink in his other hand. She laughed at something he said. Gordon was a real charmer. Or was he shooting "fish" in a barrel? As if to confirm the thoughts that formed in my head, they turned and headed toward the lobby. Where the stairs led to the upstairs suites. Circle of life at TLM.

"I'm sorry Lorie's tied up and not here with us," Robin said.

Was she ever. Maybe literally. Gordon Buchanan had more money than many small cities, a red Ferrari, and could afford to be as weird and kinky as he wanted to be. Particularly with the hired help. Maybe I was being too cynical but I had a growing feeling that TLM provided any and all distractions for its members, including young and willing entertainment.

"Don't you hate it when work interferes with fun?" Shane said.

Our drinks arrived.

"Did everyone have a good time at the party?" Robin asked.

"We did," Nicole said. "Impressively done and we met several interesting people."

"I hope interesting enough for you to join."

"We just might," I said.

"Jonathon and Rhea would welcome that," Robin said, then to Shane and Sara, "What about you girls? Having fun?"

"It's amazing," Sara said. "I don't think I've ever been around so many successful people."

"They were all so friendly," Shane added.

"Could you see yourselves working here?" Robin asked.

Shane nodded enthusiastically. "Absolutely."

"You'd love it," Robin said. "All us girls do. It's sort of like a little sorority. We look after each other."

Until one of you goes missing, I thought.

"What do you like best about it?" Sara asked.

"There's so much," Robin said. "I get to work here in this amazing place." She waved a hand. "A place I could never afford to stay at, but here it's all free. The work is fairly easy. These parties can be hectic but mostly it's low key and fun."

"Are you here often?" Shane asked. "For work?"

"I more or less live here now. I do have an apartment with a roommate down on the Gulf, but I spend less time there than I do here."

"Do all the girls do that?" Sara asked. "We have school to consider."

"That's not a problem. Lorie and I do more than just PR and parties. We've worked with Rhea on marketing strategies and programs for the past year. Before, I was in school, like you, and that worked fine. I'd be here a couple of weekends a month. And Jonathon and Rhea even helped pay for my school."

"She told us the same thing," Shane said. "I wasn't sure that was true or not."

"It is. They want you educated and cultured and happy and successful. Part of the job here is building your own future. It's part of the TLM way. Anyway, for the last year Lorie and I have been more involved in the day-to-day stuff so we are here more often than not. Rhea is a dream to work with. She's so smart."

"Sounds too good to be true," Sara said,

"It does, doesn't it?" Robin said. "But it's all true and I love it here."

"Do you travel much?" Nicole asked.

"As much as I want. It's part of marketing and recruitment." She glanced at Shane, then Sara. "But it's not all work. TLM has frequent retreats just for the members and staff. This is a recruiting weekend." She glanced at Nicole. "The hope is to attract new members." Back to Shane and Sara. "But the retreats are for fun. As Rhea says, they're for bonding and stress reduction, which makes for better communication among all of us. During those, we are treated more like guests and have few work duties."

"Awesome," Shane said.

"Where do these retreats usually take place?" I asked.

"Let's see, we went to the Bahamas once. Another time to Aspen, during ski season. Once to New Orleans, which was insanely fun. But I have to say my favorite is when we go down to Tampa. You met Gordon Buchanan," she said. Nicole and I nodded. "He has a great home down there. But best of all, he has this friend, also a TLM member, Andrew Heche. I think he and Mr. Buchanan and Jonathon do a lot of business together. Anyway, he has a home on the Gulf near St. Pete. *Home* doesn't do it justice. It's more like a boutique hotel. I have no idea how many rooms it is, but it's laid out like a Spanish castle. Totally amazing."

"Sounds dreamy," Shane said.

"He has a huge yacht and we take that out for day cruises and parties."

"All that's part of the job?" Sara asked.

"It is. I mean, you don't have to go on the retreats, but why wouldn't you? Four or five days of fun and it really does bring the staff and the members more closely together."

I wondered about how close members and staff came together on these adventures. Actually, from what I had seen, I knew the answer. I wanted to pump Robin for details but couldn't think of a way to do so comfortably. I did notice the excitement in the eyes of the sisters. No doubt they were sold and would sign on before the weekend was over.

"I don't know what your goals are," Robin said, "but if you two are looking for a special guy, some of these retreats are perfect. Most are for all members but some are restricted to the single members. It's sort of crazy then. But in a good way. Mr. Heche seems to be a matchmaker. He's made some amazing introductions. I know several girls found a successful guy and moved on. One now lives on a huge estate in Switzerland."

"Where in Switzerland?" Nicole asked.

Robin considered that. "I can't remember for sure. Maybe Lucern. Or Gstaad. I can't remember. I never met her. She was before my time, but I've heard she's very happy."

"I could go for that," Shane said. She glanced at her sister. "There aren't those kinds of choices where we live."

"Not even close," Sara added.

"My advice would be to find a good guy, not necessarily a rich one," Nicole said.

"Like Jake?" Robin said with a smile.

Nicole laid a hand on my arm. "Exactly."

That's me—the perfect boyfriend.

"Well, we have both here at TLM," Robin said.

CHAPTER 29

AROUND ONE A.M., Shane and Sara began to fade, eyelids drooping, shoulders down. Finally, Shane said, "I need to go crash."

"Right with you," Sara said. They stood.

"I'd better too," Robin added. "It'll be a busy day tomorrow."

The three girls left. Nicole and I remained seated near the firepit. The night was cool but with little breeze so the flames warmed the air.

"Want a nightcap?" I asked.

"Maybe a cognac?" Nicole said.

I walked into the bar where Peter was putting things away and shutting down for the night.

"How about a couple of cognacs before you fold your tent?" I asked.

"You got it."

I carried the two snifters back outside, handed one to Nicole, and sat. She took a sip.

"Excellent," she said.

We enjoyed the warming burn of the cognac for a few minutes.

"I like this place," Nicole said.

"It is special."

"I should get Uncle Charles to buy it."

"He could afford it," I said. "It would be a good place for a retreat. Maybe a cool filming location."

"Much cheaper away from Hollywood, for sure."

"Unions?"

"Yep," Nicole said. "They drive up the budget and the bullshit."

I saw Lorie exit the back door of the bar. She appeared tired and slightly disheveled, still wearing the clothes she had worn to the party. I guessed she had completed her duties with Gordon Buchanan. She turned toward the parking area, the building where she lived beyond.

"Lorie," I said.

She jerked to a stop and turned toward us. "Oh. I didn't see you."

"We're enjoying the fire," Nicole said. "Join us."

Lorie hesitated, glanced toward the trail that led to her condo, then said, "Sure."

"Want a cognac?" I asked.

"You know, that would be nice."

I walked inside where Peter was wiping down the bar, most of the lights now off.

"Maybe one more?" I asked.

"No problem." He poured the drink and handed it to me. "I'm out of here, but if you need more or anything else, help yourself. I believe you know your way around a bar."

"I think this will do it, but thanks."

Back on the patio, I handed Lorie her drink.

She took a sip. "That's nice. I take it you two are night owls."

"Sometimes," Nicole said. "Especially with a place like this. I want to soak it all in."

"It is special, isn't it?" Lorie asked.

"We were just talking about how it would make a good filming locale," I said.

"Do I get a part?" Lorie asked with a slight smile.

"You do," Nicole said.

"Cool. I'd love to do some acting."

"Why don't you?" Nicole asked.

"I wouldn't know where to start." She took a sip of cognac.

"Acting lessons, community theater, build a foundation and see if it's really for you. Trust me, it appears more glamorous than it is."

"If I had the time, I just might." She sighed. "This place keeps me busy." She cocked her head slightly. "Not that I'm complaining. I do love it here."

"Easy place to like," I said.

"You should join," Lorie said. "Then you can come here whenever you want."

"That's a big perk," Nicole said. "TLM seems to have a bunch of those."

"Robin told us about the retreats for members and employees," I said. "Those sound incredible."

"Oh my god, are they ever. I've been all over. Even the Bahamas. But the best ones are down in Tampa. Mr. Buchanan and his friend Andrew Heche have places down there that simply boggle your mind. Especially Andrew."

That name again. Andrew Heche. I wondered where he sat in the hierarchy of TLM. Obviously near the top if he was tight with Gordon and Jonathon.

"That's what Robin told us," Nicole said.

"Andrew's place is great for parties or just to chill by his pool. It doesn't hurt that it's right on the beach. Plus he has a crazy cool yacht."

"How many times have you been there?" I asked.

"I don't know. Five or six."

"With Gordon Buchanan?" Nicole asked.

Lorie's shoulders elevated and a hint of discomfort fell across her face.

Nicole reached over and touched her arm. "No judgment here. It's obvious you and he have a connection."

Lorie nodded. "He's nice. And, actually, a cool guy. I like spending time with him."

"Can I be straight up with you?" Nicole asked.

"Sure."

"Is that part of your job here? Again, no judgment, but is spending quality time with members and prospective members encouraged?"

Lorie stared at her and then me. She blinked but didn't respond.

"Look," Nicole said, "Robin told us she had been in the sugar baby world before she came here. She said this was similar but better. A higher class of people and, who knows, the opportunity to meet someone who can give you a lucky life."

Lorie stared at the flames, obviously gathering her thoughts. "That sounds awful, doesn't it?"

"Not really," Nicole said. "I grew up in Hollywood where the casting couch still operates. Sometimes it works out for the girls who go that route, sometimes it doesn't, but in the end, it's their choice."

Lorie swirled her cognac, took a sip, and leaned back in her chair. "Yes, I did do that back when I was in school. I had two men I saw regularly. Both were married. For some reason that seemed safer. They wouldn't likely talk or make trouble. It helped pay the bills and they were both good guys."

"That's what Robin said about her situation back then."

"At first, I felt uncomfortable with the whole arrangement. I mean, it felt like prostitution. I believe most people would agree that it was. But ultimately, I rationalized it, I guess, by considering it simply a mutually beneficial arrangement."

"Which it was," I said. "Nothing wrong with that."

Lorie shrugged but said nothing.

"How'd you get into that world?"

She gave a soft laugh. "It's actually pretty funny. I met this guy in a bar. He was married but handsome and charming and, well, I ended up going to a hotel with him. A nice hotel. He was *of means* as they say. Anyway, we had a fun night and the next morning as we had room service coffee, he said he wanted to make it a regular thing. I wasn't sure since he was married and all. He said he wanted to help me with my college. I asked how." She gave a headshake. "Was I ever naive! He said he could help with my tuition and books and spending money and my apartment. I wasn't sure what to do. But he pulled out five crisp hundred-dollar bills and that was that. At first, I refused but he said not to get all freaky. That's the word he used. *Freaky*. He reminded me that we had ended up in his room by mutual consent, not by some pay for play arrangement. Which was true since we hadn't arranged a money for sex thing but rather he and I had simply hooked up." She looked at Nicole. "Rationalization at its finest, huh?"

"Not on your end," Nicole said. "He might've had an agenda from the beginning but you simply ran into a good guy and took it to the next level."

She gave a slight nod. "That's what I told myself. Anyway, he said he liked me and wanted to help and wanted to see more of me." She pushed her hair back from her forehead. "That made sense to me. He had the means and I could use the help, and like I said, he was a fun guy." She looked a me, then Nicole. "That's how it started."

"You said you saw a couple of guys," Nicole said.

"Yeah. That relationship lasted about six months and then he moved on. I was down for a while. Like I had been rejected. Needless to say, my finances took a hit. I had worked odd jobs here and there but when he came into the picture that wasn't necessary. I guess I got used to his help. I didn't want to go back to waitressing or pouring coffee at Starbucks so I joined one of those sugar sites and met a couple of other guys that way. I ended it with them when I came here. It's hard to believe but that was over a year ago."

"Did Rhea know about your past when she hired you?" I asked.

"I don't think I should talk about that," Lorie said.

"It's a completely private conversation."

She hesitated, then nodded. "She said it was a good thing that I had experience."

Well, well. Experience in the money-for-sex world was an asset in Rhea's mind. No surprise since everything I had heard since arriving here smelled that way, but hearing it stated out loud made it very real.

I could tell that Lorie was becoming uncomfortable with the conversation. She became fidgety and her eyes darted from place to place. Nicole obviously felt it too and broke the tension.

"Your current situation sounds like a great gig," Nicole said. "A comfortable place to live, good pay, and the chance to meet some very interesting people. Who really cares about the rest of it?"

"Do you really mean that?" Lorie asked.

"Absolutely. You're young and adventurous. Why not enjoy the ride?"

Lorie exhaled a slow breath as if releasing a bubble of tension. "I'm still wrestling with it but I'm glad you understand. I like you guys, so that means a lot."

"We like you too," I said. "What do you see down the road?"

"Best-case scenario is to meet the right guy. Maybe someone like you." She smiled at me. "Not just rich but a good dude."

That's me. The good dude.

"Others have, from what I understand," Nicole said.

"That's true. Stephanie Deluca for sure, and now, hopefully, April."

"When did you see them last?" I asked.

"Stephanie was months ago when she and her new husband came back for a weekend. April and Robin and I were together at Andrew's place down in St. Pete, just a few weeks ago. After the weekend, Robin and I came back here, but April stayed. She said Andrew was going to introduce her to someone he felt she'd like. Apparently, she did because I heard she took off somewhere with him."

That confirmed what Robin had said earlier.

"Any idea who or where?" Nicole asked.

Lorie shook her head. "I never heard the guy's name, but the rumor is that they are somewhere in Europe. At least I think so but I don't know for sure."

"Who told you that?" I asked.

"Rhea."

CHAPTER 30

APRIL AWOKE, HER legs tangled in the sheet, her face buried in her pillow. Momentarily disoriented, she rolled over searching the darkness for something recognizable. Her eyes adjusted and she saw the ornate bedside lamp and the open door to the bathroom. The master suite of *After Hours*. No light pushed against the curtained window. What time was it? She glanced to her left. No Andrew. She raised up on one elbow so she could see the clock on the nightstand. The digital face showed a pale blue 4:33.

She fell back on the pillow. Her head didn't necessarily hurt, no throbbing or aching, but definitely felt full and fuzzy. Her neck and shoulders felt stiff with a low-level ache. She replayed last night. Champagne, cognac, and a couple of hits of weed. Then Andrew. He had once again been aggressive, maybe even more so. Was this the new Andrew? Did this mean he felt more comfortable with her and could be himself in bed? Or was he growing tired of her? Or angry with her harping about calling her mother?

She wasn't stupid. She knew she wasn't the first and probably wouldn't be the last woman to go on such a junket with him. He had said they were docking today and she could call her mother. Would that alleviate any stress she had caused him? Or would he put her back on a plane to Mobile and on to the farm? A week ago she would've welcomed that but now, after spending more time with Andrew, she wasn't so sure. Could there be a future here or was she simply the next trinket to be discarded when boredom set in?

She guessed she would know soon enough.

She yawned and stretched.

Where was Andrew?

She felt the low rumble of the engines soften. They were slowing. Andrew had said they'd reach shore this morning, but at this early hour? She rolled out of bed and walked to the window. She parted the curtains. Nothing but black, no city lights. Maybe Tampa was off the yacht's other side.

She decided she might as well get up, shower, and get ready to go ashore.

The hot water eased the tension across her back. She could stand there for hours but felt an urgency to check on Andrew. He was an early riser, but during the time she had been with him, he had never been up at this hour. Maybe it was a business thing or maybe he was simply preparing to dock. Wouldn't the crew take care of that?

She finished bathing, toweled herself dry, and slipped on fresh underwear. She dug a pair of jeans from the drawer and pulled them on along with a black long-sleeved pullover, scrunching the sleeves up to her elbows. As she applied a little makeup, she heard the engine noise decline sharply and sensed the boat slowing more quickly. Were they at the dock already? She hurried to complete her makeup.

She took a last look in the mirror, and satisfied with what she saw, returned to the window and looked out. No city, no dock, but rather another yacht. Close, maybe two hundred feet away, its stern aimed toward her. Both vessels were at a standstill and rose and fell gently on the calm sea. The other boat's white and blue script indicated it was called *El Jugador*. A small skiff came around the port side and eased toward *After Hours*. What the hell?

She heard the door open behind her and she turned that way.

"Good, you're up and dressed," Andrew said. "That'll save us time."

"What's going on?"

"You're going over to another boat."

"What? Why?"

"Because I said so."

She tensed at the harshness of his voice. "I don't understand."

"You're going to meet my dear friend Victor Mendoza."

"Who is that?"

"Remember I told you I had made a deal to sell some equipment I no longer needed?"

Her heart thumped so hard she was sure he could hear it. Her vision blurred with tears. A lump formed in her throat making a response impossible.

"You're the equipment," Andrew said.

"What does that mean?"

"You now belong to Victor. Or should I say Victor's boss?"

This wasn't real. It couldn't be. *He had sold her?*

Andrew continued. "Pack up your shit if you want to take it. But it doesn't matter because you won't really need it."

She swallowed the lump. "No. I won't do it."

"Actually, you will." He pushed open the door. Two young, hard-looking Hispanic males stood in the opening. "You want to do this the easy way or make it hard?"

CHAPTER 31

NICOLE AND I stirred around seven. She rolled over and nestled her head in the crook of my arm. Neither of us spoke or moved further as if by mutual consent more sleep might be in order. We had been up late, after all.

I ran through all we had learned yesterday. Before I had suspected, but since last night I was sure that a sugar baby connection between many of the girls and TLM was real. As sure as I could be without hard evidence. Robin and Lorie for sure had come from that background and I'd bet anything there were others. Nicole had said she felt that sisters Shane and Sara had a similar history but she never got an opportunity to confirm that. Still, she held that belief and I knew Nicole was good at reading people. Could Robin and Lorie merely be a coincidence? Sure, but if you tossed in the sisters, that was too much and made such a connection even more likely.

The other thing I was sure of, even more sure than the sugar baby connection, was that the duties assigned to the young women at TLM put sex on the menu. Both Lorie and Robin had essentially confirmed that.

Hopefully, Pancake had uncovered something that sealed that deal on both counts.

"We need to talk with Pancake," I said.

"Then get your butt up and let's go."

"You're holding me down."

"You wish." She rolled away and sat up.

"Wouldn't it be rude to simply leave?" I asked.

"Let's shower and get dressed and then we can see if either Jonathon or Rhea is up and around."

We found Jonathon and Rhea at a table in the dining room, coffee at hand, a stack of papers before Rhea.

"You guys are up early," Rhea said.

"It's a bad habit," Nicole said.

"But a successful one," Jonathon said. "I think there's a correlation between less sleep and success. Those of us who need less have a leg up on the sleepyheads."

That actually made sense. Nicole never needed much, and for sure Ray and Pancake didn't. I didn't either, but the difference was that they had jobs, Ray and Pancake the P.I. stuff and Nicole the screenplay business. I didn't really have a job so less sleep meant more time to do nothing. Something I took pride in and excelled at.

"That's an interesting concept," Nicole said. "I like it."

"How about some coffee and breakfast?" Rhea asked.

"Actually, we're going to hit the road and get back down to Gulf Shores."

"Is something wrong?" Jonathon asked.

"No," I said. "I just have a stack of paperwork to get through and I hate doing it on Mondays."

"See? Early risers work more and are more successful."

"Jake works too much," Nicole said with a straight face. "I keep telling him to delegate responsibility and he'll have more time for fun."

"I hope you enjoyed your time here with us," Rhea said.

"Marvelous," I said. "This is truly a special place."

"Did we convince you that joining TLM is a smart move?" Jonathon asked.

"You did," Nicole said. "We'll talk it over and be in touch."

"Good," Jonathon said.

Rhea stood. "I'll walk you out."

"I can do that."

The voice came from behind us and I turned to see Lorie approach. She looked fresh and wide awake with no sign of the late night she had had.

Lorie continued. "You have work to do." She nodded toward the papers on the table.

Nicole and I retrieved our bags from our room and along with Lorie walked out to Nicole's SL.

"Thanks for everything," I said. "You're a great hostess."

"That's my job."

"Maybe, but you were above and beyond the call of duty."

"That's very kind." She glanced back toward the entrance to the lodge, hesitated before she spoke, as if she didn't want to be overheard. "That stuff we talked about last night. My past and what I do for TLM now. Please don't say anything."

Nicole stepped forward and laid a hand on Lorie's shoulder. "You don't need to worry. That was a private conversation and just between us."

Lorie nodded, relieved. "Thanks."

Nicole gave her shoulder a squeeze. "I meant what I said last night. This is a good job and you have nothing to feel ashamed about. But if it's ever not, if you ever have problems or concerns, don't hesitate to give me a call."

"I will. I promise." Her gaze dropped toward the ground for a second and then back up. "Who knows, maybe you'll join us and I'll see you here soon."

We hugged her and then headed out the gates toward the highway back to Gulf Shores. I called Pancake to see where he was and if he had uncovered anything new. He did have news and, shock of shocks, he and Ray were at Captain Rocky's. No surprise Pancake was there, he practically lived there, but Ray hates my place. He avoids it like it's a toxic waste site, yet now he's there with Pancake. Maybe it's me and not Captain Rocky's he's avoiding.

"Stop by Alison's and bring me a bag of stuff," Pancake said.

I guess half of the entire Captain Rocky's menu for breakfast wasn't enough. "It's Sunday so I don't think she's open."

"People got to eat on the Lord's Day too."

His logic was hard to a argue with. "Unfortunately, we're down the road headed your way."

"Nicole knows how to make a U-turn."

More logic.

"Order another omelet. You'll be fine."

"Already had one and a half of Ray's. Maybe some nachos will do. And a breakfast burrito."

"Sounds good," I said.

"Ain't pastries though."

CHAPTER 32

LAST NIGHT AFTER they had ferried her from ship to ship, April had been taken to this small room by the same two Hispanic men she had confronted on Andrew's yacht. She asked what was happening, but the two men simply stared at her and told her to stay inside her quarters for now. They closed the door and walked away.

Immediately, she felt more than heard the engine's rumble to life followed by a gentle rolling as the vessel moved over the Gulf's swells. She pulled aside the curtain that covered the porthole window and peered out, seeing only blackness. Then the yacht swung left, and Andrew's yacht, *After Hours*, came into view, its image receding, dropping a faintly moonlit wake on the surface of the black water. She felt as if her sole lifeline had been severed. If Andrew Heche, the guy who sold her to—who?—was her savior, how deep of a hell had she descended into? All she really knew was that in the last half hour, two ships had come together in the dark of night; she had been moved from one to the other; and now each went on its way, leaving her confined to this cabin. An icy dread settled over her.

She collapsed on the uncomfortable bed and cried so hard she hurt. Her neck, shoulder, and stomach muscles knotted with painful cramps. Finally, exhaustion pulled her into sleep.

Her sleep was brief and fitful and for the second time this morning she awakened disoriented and momentarily confused. Nothing was immediately recognizable. Definitely not Andrew's suite onboard *After Hours*. The vibration of the engines and the light pushing against the blue porthole curtain brought everything back. The harsh way Andrew had treated her, her transfer here on a fast-moving and jarring skiff, her confinement and exhausted sleep.

What the hell was happening? Who were these guys? Where were they taking her? How could Andrew do this? Did he actually *sell her*? Tears gathered in her eyes and a panic bubble expanded in her chest. She couldn't breathe.

Unlike *After Hours*, there was nothing plush about these quarters, which were claustrophobic with a bed attached to one wall, a small desk and chair along the other, and the single curtained porthole. More a prison cell than a stateroom. She sat on the thin, firm mattress and stared at the door. Who was out there? What did they want? What were they going to do to her?

Andrew had been crystal clear that he had sold her. How could he do that? More importantly, to who and why? What did this unknown person have in store for her? What was his name? Victor something. What kind of a man bought women in the dead of night?

The scenarios that swirled in her mind weren't pleasant. She had seen those TV shows and read stories about kidnappings and sex trafficking. Is that what this was? She fought to chase such thoughts away, with little success.

A wave of helplessness swept over her and she broke, sobbing so hard her stomach knotted yet again. Nausea and dizziness followed. She lay back on the bed and attempted to regain control. Still the sobs came. Finally, after what seemed an eternity, they receded from sheer exhaustion more than anything else. The muscles of her stomach, and arms and legs, ached and an invisible weight compressed her chest.

She stared at the ceiling and ran through the past two weeks. Andrew had been kind, fun, even loving. Was that a ruse to keep her calm and complacent? Was their sex simply him using her for pleasure before he passed her on to someone else? Sampling the goods? Why didn't she see it coming? Was he that good or was she that naive?

Her cell phone? She suddenly realized she hadn't lost it. Andrew had taken it and hidden or destroyed it. He didn't want anyone, particularly her mother, knowing where she was and who she was with. Better that she disappear with no trace and no trail back to him. At least not one he couldn't cover.

She rummaged through every conversation she and Andrew had had, every thing they had done, the parties, the gatherings, the meals, the sex, looking for some clue she had missed that could have exposed his evil. She found nothing. She had read that true sociopaths could sell themselves better than anyone. That they never showed fear, or anxiety, and were able to cover their true thoughts with charm. Andrew definitely had charm.

Another realization emerged. Jonathon and Rhea were involved. No doubt. This was planned, and carefully so. She had purchased her own plane ticket from Mobile to Tampa. Rhea said she'd get reimbursed later, but what that really did was show she had left on her own—on her own dime so to speak.

What about Robin and Lorie? They could attest that she had been with them at Andrew's. Or were they in on it? God, she prayed not. If so, she was truly fucked. Was that why she was sent down a couple of days before them? Anyone looking for her would only know that she left TLM and flew to Tampa and had paid her own way. If she then disappeared, everyone at TLM could feign innocence. If Jonathon and Rhea and Lorie and Robin all confirmed that, as would the airlines, how would anyone even know where to look for her?

The door opened. She abruptly sat up. Two young women stood in the doorway. Both attractive, one blonde, the other brunette. They entered.

"Are you okay?" the brunette asked.

"What's going on?" April said.

The brunette said, "I'm Emanuella Carlo. This is Roberta Winslow." She indicated the blonde.

"I'm April. April Wilkerson."

"Here," Roberta said. She handed April a paper bag. "I'm sure you're starving so we brought you something."

April looked inside and found a wrapped egg sandwich. She unwrapped it and took a bite. "Thanks."

"Where are you from?" Roberta asked.

"What?"

"Where did they grab you?" Emanuella asked.

"Out on the water. Near Tampa I think." She looked at the two girls. "At least I was told we were returning there. Then we stopped in the middle of nowhere, and I was taken from another boat to here."

The two girls exchanged a glance. Roberta nodded. "That's sort of what happened to us. Near Houston. That's where we live."

"I see," April said. "What's going on?"

"You won't like it," Roberta said.

April swiped tears from her eyes. "I already don't like it. Tell me."

Emanuella sat next to her. "Where to start?"

Roberta dragged the chair around so that it faced April and sat down. She leaned forward, resting her elbows on her knees. "We're college roommates. At the University of Houston. We were down in Galveston for a few days of fun. We met a guy in a bar. He seemed rich and fun. He took us to another place where we danced and drank too much. He said he knew of a very cool party on a yacht up near Kemah and Clear Lake."

"He said he'd bring us back to our car later, and since Clear Lake isn't far from Galveston we figured why not?" Emanuella said. "I felt uncomfortable as soon as I got onboard. The boat was much smaller than this one and a lot classier."

"There was no party," Roberta said. "In fact we were the only women onboard. The crew was a half a dozen young and hard-looking men. It didn't take long to discover we couldn't leave."

"Almost as soon as we got onboard," Emanuella said, "the yacht left the harbor. In minutes we were out in the bay and headed into the Gulf."

"An hour later we met this boat. Middle of nowhere, dark of night. We were moved to this ship and have been here since."

"That was three days ago," Roberta added.

"Did they—harm you?" April asked.

Emanuella glanced at Roberta, then squeezed April's hands. "Not the crew. We're apparently off limits to them. But the owner, Victor Mendoza, is another story."

April's throat tightened. She couldn't speak.

"I'm sorry," Roberta said. "But you need to know that." She sighed. "I can tell you firsthand that he'll like you. He likes blondes with blue eyes." She dropped her gaze to the floor. "At least he sure liked me."

"Also Chloe," Emanuella said. "She's blonde too." She sighed. "First time in my life I'm glad I'm a brunette."

Roberta obviously saw the question in April's eyes. "She's here. They picked her up in New Orleans. The day after we ended up here."

"She and Roberta are the ones Victor calls for the most," Emanuella said. "He's insatiable. Several times a day."

"Fuck," April said. "What am I going to do?"

"Nothing," Roberta said. "There's nothing you can do. The good news is I think Chloe was with him last night so maybe he'll sleep in. For a few hours anyway."

That proved untrue. The door opened and a man entered. Tall, lean, dark hair, dark eyes, thick mustache, and a face that hadn't seen a razor in a few days.

"Welcome, April," he said. "I see you've met Emanuella and Roberta." Then to the two girls, "Leave. April and I need to get acquainted."

CHAPTER 33

THE SUNDAY MORNING traffic was nonexistent, so Nicole set some kind of time-trial record from Magnolia Springs to Gulf Shores. At least she didn't pass anyone on the right, so we arrived at Captain Rocky's with my heartbeat only hovering about 120. Carla greeted us as soon as we entered.

"He's going for the record today," Carla said. "Go talk with him so he'll slow his pace and the kitchen can catch up."

Carla knew that wouldn't help. Nothing slowed Pancake's food consumption. I think he even eats in his sleep.

"We got here as quickly as we could," I said.

"Next time drive faster."

"Nicole was driving."

"Oh."

Yeah, oh. No one flies faster than Nicole except maybe an F-14 Tomcat, or a cruise missile.

"Ray's here," Carla continued. "What'd you do wrong?"

"Why would you think I did something wrong?"

"Playing the odds. Want me to make you guys breakfast burritos? Pancake just ordered his third."

"Sounds good," Nicole said.

We joined Ray and Pancake at my table on the deck. The Gulf lay calm and the sun was beginning its daily warming of the beach, already filling with sun worshipers. My staff had deployed the yellow Captain Rocky's umbrellas and three of them shaded several early beachgoers.

"What's up?" I asked.

"No pastries?" Pancake asked.

"Sorry," Nicole said. "We were well down the road by the time you asked."

"Guess you'll have to have another burrito instead," I said.

"Already on the way."

"I know. Carla told us."

"You keeping a tab now?" Pancake asked.

He knew better than that. "The math required to do that is too complex for me."

Pancake leaned back, crossed his arms over his chest. "Simple math is too complex for you."

"But he's pretty," Nicole said.

And so it begins.

Libby, my latest addition to the waitressing corp and Pancake's current fascination, poured Nicole and me coffee. Pancake gave her a wink and she returned a smile as she walked away. Carla appeared with three burritos.

"Anything else?" Carla asked.

"Banana pancakes," Pancake said.

"You had some earlier."

"That was then, this is now. Add some pineapple and toss on a handful of pecans."

"Will that do it?" Carla asked.

Pancake took a huge bite out of his burrito. "I'll think on it and let you know."

"It's what I live for," Carla said. She gave Pancake's shoulder a friendly punch and walked away.

"Tell them what you found," Ray said to Pancake.

"There're a lot of those sugar baby sites. Most are shaky at best, but several seem legitimate. As legitimate as any could be." Another bite of burrito. "I found Lorie Cooper on one out of Birmingham where she used to live. It's called Find-A-Daddy. Isn't that cute? Her profile was taken down a year ago."

"That fits what she told us," Nicole said.

"If it was taken down, how did you find it?" I asked.

"Everything on the internet is archived somewhere if you know where to look. Nothing ever truly disappears. But on this site, they keep the old profiles and just don't display them. It seems that many people walk away from the site but then return. Makes it easy to re-up." Another bite of burrito. "Is it just me or are these things getting better?" The question was rhetorical, so no one answered. Pancake continued. "It looks like she only hooked up with a couple of guys. Both from the Birmingham area. One of those guys has since left the site, but the other one's still active. I found Robin Meade on another site out of Biloxi. It's called Sugar Hookup and is larger and covers much of the Gulf Coast. She too dropped off around a year ago. She'd had four relationships over the three years she was active. Same kind of deal as Lorie. Each older, two married, but a couple single. Pretty vanilla stuff."

"Okay," I said. "We more or less knew that would be the case. What else did you find?"

"The two girls you asked about? Sisters Shane and Sara Hutton? They, like Robin, are listed on the Sugar Hookup site. They live just off campus in Wheelerville. Each of them has a single guy they see. Single as in just one. Both are married."

"That's what we thought," Nicole said. "We never got a chance to talk to them one-on-one and neither ever said anything, but our take was that they had also been in that world." Nicole shrugged. "Nothing specific. Just a feeling."

"Your instincts were right," Ray said. "But it gets better." He nodded to Pancake.

"Stephanie DeLuca."

"Really?" Nicole said. "That I didn't see."

I hadn't either. But then again, why not? She was beautiful and worked for TLM. Even met her husband there. Did he know about her past? Maybe. She was at TLM and it would seem logical that her husband, the hotshot attorney, would know that the girls on staff were—what's the word?—available. It was increasingly looking that way for sure.

"Same group as Robin, Shane, and Sara. She wasn't very active."

"Of all the girls we've met," I said. "Stephanie seemed the most normal. That's not the right word, maybe the most straight and narrow."

"No doubt," Nicole said. "To me this sort of seals the deal. TLM culls girls from the sugar baby world. Three girls either work or have worked there and two others are prospective employees. Way too many for coincidence."

"It gets better," Ray said.

Before he could continue, Pancake's banana, pineapple, and pecan pancakes arrived. They looked amazing. Pancake began dismantling them as if he hadn't eaten in days. It had actually only been a few minutes, but that's what the big guy does. Sherman's March to the Sea came to mind.

"You should put these on the menu," Pancake said.

"Maybe we will," I said. The "we" meaning Carla of course.

"It's what I'd do." He forked pancake into his mouth. "Ready for the punch line?" More pancake. "April Wilkerson did the same thing."

Nicole stopped, her burrito only inches from her mouth. She lowered it to her plate. "Really?"

Pancake nodded. "Her profile was up on yet another site. You ready for this? It's called Rich Daddy Hot Baby."

"They can't be accused of false advertising," I said.

"Her profile's still active," Pancake said. "It hasn't been used since she joined TLM, but it is still up. The last guy she saw was from right next door in Orange Beach. Dude named Tony Amato. Interesting guy with a wife, four kids, and some loose mob connections."

"Mob as in Mafia?" I asked.

"Not the big ones in New York or New Jersey but a local outfit involved in some shady stuff. Car thefts, money laundering, some small-time drug dealing. No murders I could find."

"This is amazing," I said.

"But what does it tell us?" Nicole asked. "So TLM recruits girls with a history of hooking up with rich guys. From what we've seen, TLM, in the interest of promotion, wants them to do the same, and these girls did so of their own free will."

That was true. So what if they simply moved their activity to a new program presumably with a better clientele? It seemed a win-win situation. "Which means that April might simply have found the guy she hoped she would and took off."

"Without telling her mother?" Ray asked.

"She's mad at her," Nicole said. "This could simply be that she's having a little spat with mommy, nothing more sinister. Or maybe she intended to call or text and let her know but never got the chance before she took off to Europe or South America or out to sea on a yacht. Maybe she'll contact her next week."

Ray eyed her. "Do you believe that?"

Nicole shook her head. "Not really. I'm simply saying it's possible."

"If so, we have no case," Ray said. "Which is fine so long as she's safe."

"I still have a few more things to look into," Pancake said. "I was working on Jonathon Lindemann's and TLM's money trail when I got sidetracked on this sugar baby stuff. I'll get back to it and see what I can find."

"We need to go chat with this Amato guy," Ray said.

"We can handle that," Nicole said.

Of course we could. I was hoping for a day off to simply goof around. Basically, get back to my normal routine.

"Not this guy," Pancake said. "Ray and I'll handle him. He probably doesn't play nice, which could make for a fun day."

"For you." Nicole pouted. "We never get to have fun."

"Sure we do," I said.

"Not that kind of fun. I mean work fun."

I started to say that work and fun never belonged in the same sentence but was interrupted by the chirp of Nicole's phone. She answered and listened for a good half minute.

"Okay, when and where?" Another pause. "That works but let's meet at Captain Rocky's in Gulf Shores. That's Jake's place and we can talk privately." Pause. "Great. See you then." She disconnected the call and looked at me. "That was Lorie. She wants to talk."

CHAPTER 34

TONY AMATO LIVED in a nice house in a nice neighborhood. An expansive Tudor style in a cul-de-sac that butted against swampy open land. The front yard was manicured with perfect grass and thick shrubs and well-maintained flower beds. It seemed to try too hard to be a normal house for a normal guy. Tony wasn't that.

The double garage door stood open, and Tony was bent into the back cargo area of a silver Lincoln Escalade. As Pancake pulled his black Chevy dual-cab pickup into the drive, Tony straightened and turned their way. Thick and stocky, he wore khakis and a two-tone brown bowling shirt, no logo, no embroidered name. Pancake and Ray climbed out.

"Mr. Amato?" Ray said.

"Who's asking?" Tony squared his shoulders, his chest expanding. His body language said that Tony didn't back down, or avoid confrontation, rather he charged straight ahead. Exactly as Pancake's research on him had suggested. His record was fairly clean, probably more so than it should be. Only two charges, both later dropped, for bar fights. In one, the other dude ended up in the hospital with a broken arm and a blow-out fracture of his left orbit. Tony must have a good right hand. The guy dropping assault charges from his hospital bed meant Tony had the clout and the connections to make big-time indictments evaporate.

"I'm Ray Longly. This is Tommy Jeffers, but you can call him Pancake."

Tony seemed to take inventory of them both before settling his gaze on Pancake. "Football?"

Score one for Tony.

"That's right," Pancake said. "We need to ask you a couple of questions."

"About what?"

A woman stepped through the door that connected the garage to the house and peered out over a white Mercedes. "Tony? Is everything all right?"

"It's fine. Go on back inside. I'll handle it."

"Should I call the guys?" she asked.

The guys? Pancake pictured a group of hard-nosed dudes with fire-arm lumps beneath leather jackets.

"No. They'll be here in a minute anyway."

The door clicked shut as she retreated back inside.

"We need to ask you about a girl I think you know."

"Who might that be?" A slight crease of concern wrinkled Tony's forehead.

"April Wilkerson," Pancake said.

The creases deepened, but Tony didn't flinch. "Never heard of her."

"We aren't here to cause you any trouble," Ray said. "But we know that's not true."

"Who are you guys?"

"Private investigators," Pancake said. "April's gone missing. Her mother hired us to find her."

"What do you mean *missing*?"

"Just that. She dropped off the radar about three weeks ago, and according to her mother that's not like her."

Tony digested that for a beat. "Wish I could help, but I don't see how."

Pancake stepped closer to Tony, looked down on him. "This is private and not something we wish to expose. We know you met her just over a year ago on the Rich Daddy Hot Baby website."

Tony recoiled. "How did you . . ."

"Relax," Ray said. "We aren't going to blow your cover. We don't care how you run your life. Our agenda is to find April. When did you last see her?"

Tony glanced back toward the door where his wife had stood earlier. "This doesn't go any further?"

"Not on our end," Pancake said.

Tony nodded. "I haven't really seen her in nearly a year. Since she hooked up with that TLM group. Well, maybe a couple of times after that, but for sure not in the past six months."

"Any issues?" Ray asked.

"Between us? No." He shook his head to emphasize his denial.

"What about with TLM?" Pancake asked.

"Not that I know. She seemed enthralled with the program."

"And you?"

Tony opened his hands. "What can I say? She tried to sell that deal to me, but I don't do that kind of stuff."

"What stuff do you do?" Ray asked.

"I own a construction company. I don't have the time or the inclination to hook up with some cult."

"Is that how you saw TLM?"

"Look, I don't know much about it. April was all wound up with it and thought that Jonathon what's-his-name was some kind of self-help guru and financial genius. Isn't that what most cults do? Dazzle the unsuspecting?" He raised one shoulder. "I've heard that story before."

"Did you and April talk about TLM?"

"Not really. Once she realized I was a no-go, she dropped it and we just took care of business." He offered a half smile. "If you know what I mean."

"How was your relationship with her?" Pancake asked.

"It wasn't a relationship. It was a business arrangement."

"Okay. How was your business arrangement going?"

"I like her. She's a nice girl and a lot of fun. We had some good times. Even spent some fun times together."

"She was at FSU in Tallahassee," Ray said. "That's a bit of a hike from here."

"Not that much. I was often down that way for business or she'd come up this way. Sometimes we'd meet in between. Either way, I'd get her a room for the weekend, a few days, whatever. Then she moved up to Orange Beach and worked in some bar. That definitely made things easier. Until she took off to Magnolia Springs."

"Any problems between you two?" Pancake said.

Tony's eyes narrowed. "I don't like your insinuation here."

"None intended. What we're trying to accomplish here isn't blame. We want to know where she might've run off to."

"You don't think something happened to her?" Tony asked.

"Do you?"

"God, I hope not."

To Pancake, Tony's prayer seemed sincere. Like, despite his writing this off as a business arrangement, he was more invested. "You liked her, didn't you?"

Another glance toward his house. "I love my wife. You can take that to the bank. But this was . . . different. Sure, it started out as merely a sexual thing, but April is a smart, funny young lady. Easy to talk to and be with. I enjoy her company. Do I like her? Very much. I was sorry it ended."

"As we stand here right now," Ray said, "you haven't talked with her in several months and have no idea where she might be. Is that correct?"

"It is. Whether you believe me or not, it pains me that she's missing, and my hope of hope is that nothing has happened to her."

"She never shared any concerns she might have had with TLM or anyone in that world?"

"No."

"Did she have any issues with other guys she saw?" Ray asked. "Or old boyfriends? That sort of thing?"

"Not that I know." He glanced toward his shoes and hesitated, as if recalling something. "And I think I would've known. She asked for my advice on lots of things. You know, life stuff. When she was down or stressed out, she'd call and we'd talk. Sort of like I was a father or uncle figure. I think if anyone had spooked her, she would've told me and asked for my help."

"And you would have helped her?" Pancake asked.

Tony almost smirked. "I would've fixed it."

CHAPTER 35

NICOLE IMMEDIATELY SENSED Lorie's nervousness. She knew Jake had, too. As soon as Lorie entered Captain Rocky's, she scanned the room before seeing them and approaching Jake's corner table. When Lorie reached them, she fidgeted with her purse strap and examined the other deck tables. Most were unoccupied and those that were revealed people talking and laughing, absorbed in their own worlds.

"It's OK," Nicole said. "Please sit down, relax."

Lorie sat, but Nicole saw no signs that the tension in Lorie's shoulders had dissipated. She hugged her purse to her chest.

Before meeting Lorie, they had decided that Nicole would handle most of the conversation and ask most of the questions. If there were any. That depended on what Lorie wanted to talk about. No doubt it was important or why go to all this trouble? Her calling and arranging this meeting and then driving down to Gulf Shores meant that whatever she had in mind was secretive and required a face-to-face conversation.

The hope was that Lorie would openly talk with both of them, but if Nicole sensed she was shutting down or hesitating, they had devised a signal so she could let Jake know to excuse himself and leave the two of them alone. That might not be necessary, but just in case.

When Nicole outlined the plan to Jake, he had said that with all this pre-planning she'd have made a good Boy Scout.

"I was a Brownie," she had said. "That's as high up the totem pole as I went."

"Did you earn a bunch of merit badges?"

"I did."

"Was one for conducting interrogations?" Jake asked.

"This isn't an interrogation. We simply need to hear what she has to say."

"And ask questions," Jake said.

"Which is not the same as an interrogation."

"It isn't?"

"Look, consider this a spy game with a secret signal."

Now, Nicole touched Lorie's arm. An almost imperceptible recoil. "Are you OK?"

Lorie took a deep breath and let it leak slowly, as if attempting to calm herself. "I don't know."

"You're safe here," Jake said. "Anything said here stays here."

"I know," Lorie said. "But they have a way of finding things out."

"You mean Jonathon and Rhea?" Nicole asked.

Lorie nodded.

"Where do they think you are now?" Jake asked.

"I told them I was coming down to visit a friend. Just in case someone saw me, I also told Rhea I'd swing by, and if you guys were here, I'd see how you were doing."

"What'd she say to that?"

"She thought it was a great idea. Good marketing was how she put it."

"Smart move on your part," Nicole said. "Let's eat something. I think that'll help."

"Maybe that'll unknot my stomach."

"Perhaps a margarita too," Jake said.

"I could use that," Lorie said.

Jake waved to Carla who came their way. He introduced her to Lorie. They ordered fish tacos and margaritas. Small talk about the party and how much they loved the farm and how pleasant everyone was followed. Nicole was buying time, waiting for their drinks to arrive, and for Lorie to calm down. The margaritas showed up and after Lorie took a couple of quick sips, Nicole jumped in.

"What did you want to talk about?"

"You said that if I ever felt uncomfortable or had any issues that I should call. That you might be able to help."

"That's true. What's going on? You're wound up tight."

Lorie's eyes glistened. She picked up her napkin and dabbed them. "What we talked about the other night. All that sugar baby stuff and how TLM might simply be an ungraded version."

"I remember," Nicole said.

"Well, that's exactly what it is." She looked at Jake and then back to Nicole. "We're expected to take care of members and guests."

"Take care of their personal needs?" Jake asked.

Lorie nodded. "The weekend parties, the trips, the retreats down near Tampa all involve us sleeping with guys. Some we know and some we don't."

"Know as in Gordon Buchanan?" Jake asked.

"Especially Gordon. He's very close with Jonathon and Rhea. He likes me, so I have the pleasure of sleeping with him every time he's at the farm. I've been down to his place in Tampa several times. Usually a weekend, but once for over a week. He has parties and I take care of things."

"What things?" Nicole asked.

"I fuck whoever he tells me to." Her eyes screwed down tight, fighting back tears. Then a burst of laughter escaped. "Wow. I can't believe

I finally said that out loud." She exhaled a heavy breath. "It actually feels good. Like a weight's been lifted off my chest."

"Venting does help," Nicole said. "Say whatever you have to say. We're here to listen and to help."

"Can you really help?"

"Maybe," Jake said. "Whatever you need, we'll sure give it a try."

The food arrived and they began to eat. Lorie only nibbled but did devour her margarita.

"What do you want?" Nicole asked.

Lorie forked her fingers through her hair. "I don't know. I think I just want out."

"Then leave," Jake said.

"And do what?"

"Whatever you want."

Lorie nodded. "I know I could simply walk away, but if I'm being honest, the money they pay me, the benefits of being in that world, the amazing travel, the wealth, the powerful people, and the possibility of meeting some rich guy and being set for life make it hard to walk away."

Nicole waited her out, letting Lorie gather her thoughts.

"I feel dirty. I feel ashamed. I feel lost as if I'm no longer me. And I feel scared."

"Scared?" Nicole said. "Of what?"

"I don't know. It's just a feeling."

"Based on what?" Jake asked.

Lori's gaze dropped to her lap, then she looked back up. "Maybe six months ago, I went down to Gordon's place with a girl named Mia Santos. She worked at TLM too. There was a party with lots of alcohol and sex. Mia and I both ended up in Gordon's bed for the night. A first for me. I think for Mia too. Anyway, the next day we went over to St. Pete for a weekend cruise party on Andrew's boat. Three days of insanity on the high seas." She took a breath and let it out slowly. "Anyway, in the end, Mia stayed with Andrew and I came back to the farm." A more ragged breath. "I never saw or heard from her again."

"Did you think something happened to her?"

"I was told that Andrew introduced her to some guy from Saudi Arabia and she left with him."

"Who'd you hear that from?" Jake asked.

"Rhea."

Nicole shared a look with Jake.

"But you don't believe that's true?" Nicole asked.

"I don't know. I mean, it's possible and it's happened before. I remember a girl going off with a Saudi guy right after I went to work at TLM. I never really met her, so I don't remember her name. I heard that another girl went off to Switzerland with some jet setter and another to Singapore with a businessman from there. So, I guess that girl going off to Saudi Arabia could've happened."

"Isn't that part of the TLM program?" Nicole asked. "We were told a lot of the girls ended up finding love and happiness. Isn't that the party line?"

"It is and, like I said before, that's one of the things they dangle as perks. They have a track record to lean on. I mean, Stephanie DeLuca met her husband through TLM, and I know they're happy."

"So maybe that's what happened with your friend Mia and the other girls."

"Maybe."

"But?" Nicole asked, sensing there was more to come.

"April. Her disappearance doesn't feel right."

"In what way?" Jake asked.

"I can't remember if I told you this before or not . . . my brain's scrambled . . . but she, Robin, and I went down to Gordon's place for a weekend of the usual craziness. We partied on his estate and took a day trip on Andrew's boat. April decided to stay and hang out with Andrew. Robin and I came back. I haven't heard one word from April since."

"Do you think something's wrong?" Jake asked.

"I don't know. Maybe I'm making too much of it. I mean, she could be anywhere and having a great time with Andrew." She exhaled a deep breath. "But it's exactly what happened with Mia. Off with Andrew and then never heard from again." She gazed toward the beach. "Maybe I'm just being squirrelly about all this."

"Are you?" Nicole asked.

Lorie looked at her. "My head says yes, but my gut says no."

Nicole gave Jake another look and he returned a slight nod, knowing exactly what she was thinking.

"Can we trust you?" Nicole asked her.

"What does that mean?"

"Can we trust you to not say anything about what I'm going to tell you?"

Her eyes narrowed, brow wrinkled. "What's going on?"

"First, can we trust you?"

"Yes."

"We aren't looking to join TLM," Nicole said. She now had Lorie's full attention. "We're private investigators. We work for Ray, Jake's dad. He's a P.I. and very good at it. He was hired by April's mother to find her. She hasn't heard from her in over three weeks either."

"Don't say that." Lorie's eyes welled with tears. "Did something happen to her?"

"We don't know," Jake said. "But, like you, and her mother, we're concerned."

Lorie's chin raised, crinkled, trembled. "If something did happen, Andrew Heche is behind it. I feel that in my bones."

"Why him?" Nicole asked.

"He's creepy. I know April liked him, but I think he's an arrogant prick. He has dark clouds behind his eyes. I was never comfortable with him."

"Anything specific?"

She shook her head. "It's more a feeling. But he gave me looks and found ways to get close, to touch me all the time. He knew I was with Gordon, but he seemed to always fish for an opportunity. Plus, he was the last person I saw Mia with."

"We'll check him out," Jake said.

A good move on Jake's part, Nicole thought. Lorie had no need to know that Heche was already on their radar, or better, Pancake's radar. Making his name seem casual, no big deal, wouldn't pile any more anxiety on Lorie's already stress-filled plate. She had more than enough going on in her head, and right now she needed to be as cool and calm as possible.

"In the meantime, don't tell anyone about this conversation," Nicole added.

"Don't worry. If Jonathon and Rhea knew about this they'd have a fit." She looked at Nicole. "Be careful with your snooping. Jonathon and Rhea have a long reach and a lot of power."

"Based on?" Jake asked.

Lorie fell silent for a full half a minute then sighed, as if making a decision. "They have videos."

"What kind of videos?" Nicole asked, knowing the answer.

"Compromising videos. Of people who stay at the lodge."

"Which they can use for leverage," Jake said.

"I assume so."

"Were you aware of that? When you were entertaining members at the farm?"

"No." She shook her head for emphasis. "I had no idea until I discovered those videos."

"How did find them?" Nicole asked.

"One day Jonathon and Rhea were over in Fairhope for lunch with a member. I had to do some paperwork and was in Jonathon's office. He had left a cabinet drawer open. One that he always locked up. I was curious so I looked inside. There was a metal box filled with I'd guess a hundred DVDs. I looked at a few of them. I was on two of them that I saw. Robin and April too. And several other girls. Including Stephanie DeLuca."

"Having sex?" Nicole asked.

Tears welled in her eyes and slid down her cheeks. She used her napkin to wipe them away, sniffed. "Yes. With a lot of very powerful people."

"Such as?" Jake asked.

"Each of the DVDs was labeled in Jonathon's handwriting. The name of the guy and the girl, and the date—I guess so he'd know who was with who and what video they were on. The guys were all members and prospective members. I had met most of them, so I knew who they were. A couple of the ones I saw included Gordon Buchanan and Andrew Heche."

"I thought those three were close friends?" Nicole asked.

"They are." She gave a snorting laugh. "I guess Jonathon wanted leverage over his friends."

"Plus, they're each in business with him," Jake said. "That would give him negotiating power and perhaps protection if they ever got in a legal dispute."

"Did you tell anyone about this?" Nicole asked. "Any of the other girls?"

"No. I didn't want to risk that sort of gossip getting back to Jonathon and Rhea. If it did, they'd know it was me. I do a lot of business work for them. They trust me, so I have access to the office much more than any of the other girls."

Nicole liked Lorie and now realized she was a clever girl. Even under the circumstances, she kept her head screwed on straight and kept what she knew buried. "What did you do after you found the videos?"

"My first reaction was to take them and destroy them, but I knew I couldn't. Few people have access to Jonathon's office and he knew I was in there that day, so I was too scared to do that. Besides, the DVDs had to be burned from somewhere, so he must have all the videos on his computer or somewhere else." She finished her margarita. "It was hard to leave the office without taking at least my discs with me. I didn't want him to have them. But, since the videos were for sure stored elsewhere, that would do little good, and if mine were the only ones missing and he discovered that, he'd know what I had done."

"So you left them?" I asked.

She nodded.

"Another smart move," Nicole said. "It's best if he doesn't know that the three of us know about the videos."

CHAPTER 36

IT WAS NEAR noon before Victor Mendoza finished with April. He was indeed insatiable. She sat on the edge of the bed, too tired and too humiliated to cry. What she felt was anger, and fear, and a sense that she was completely isolated and trapped. She was in the hands of a man who showed no mercy and little feeling except for his own needs. Victor had used her in ways she had never experienced. Nothing was off the table and she had no choice but to comply. She tried to bargain, which got her nowhere, and she tried to resist, to which he slapped her, hard, across the face, saying, "Do what I say, bitch." She did. The worst was that when he left, he stopped at the door and looked at her. "You're special. Great body." He laughed. "You're going to make me a wad of cash."

He left no doubt what was what. She was going to be trafficked. The questions were where, to who, and why. The why was easy, but the where was a question. Victor had mentioned they had to make a stop and then they would head south. Did he mean some Caribbean island, or South America, or someplace she'd never heard of? Did it matter? She was sure none held a pleasant future for her. But it was the who that left her mind racing. Would it be someone who was actually worse than Victor? Was that even possible? Victor was a predator, but something inside her told her she just might be headed toward an apex predator. Someone who could buy women and do with them as he pleased. Maybe in some country that possessed few rules and was controlled by thugs and drug cartels. The scenarios that rumbled through her brain were ugly, and uglier.

She had to do something or she would die. Not here and now, but soon. Once her usefulness or novelty wore off, she would be expendable. She had few doubts about that. If someone buys and uses women, what happens when he grows tired of her and needs a new supply? There were four girls on the yacht now, including her, and each was a consumable item. What was it Andrew had said? That he needed to sell some equipment he no longer needed. No doubt the man buying her would feel the same way. Then what? Would she be killed, placed in some hellhole brothel until she was completely consumed, or both?

First order of business would be to explore the boat. Could she? Was she allowed to leave her cabin? If not, what would happen if she were caught? Could it be worse than the last three hours? Did it matter? The one thing she couldn't do was nothing.

She stepped into the hallway and turned right. She came to a set of stairs and slowly climbed them. Near the top, she saw they led to the bridge. Two men sat in chairs, facing forward, the instrument that steered the vessel before them. They talked with each other in Spanish.

She retreated back down the corridor to another, narrower flight of steps. She quietly ascended them and found that they led to the rear deck. She stepped into the bright sunlight and cool open air. It felt almost cleansing, calming, even as her heart thumped against her chest.

She shaded her eyes with one hand and scanned forward and aft, but saw no one. Then she caught a flash of blonde hair. She stepped farther on to the deck and saw a girl leaning on the aft railing, gazing over the yacht's wake. She wore cutoff jeans and a lime green halter top. She held a cigarette in one hand. April moved toward her.

"Hello," April said.

The girl turned, her startled look quickly evaporating when she saw April. "You must be the new girl," she said.

"I'm April."

She hung the cigarette on her lip. "Chloe."

April walked to where she stood. "Is it okay for us to be out here?"

"Where are we going to go?"

"I just didn't want to make Victor angry."

"Oh, you've met Victor," Chloe said, more a statement than a question.

April nodded.

Chloe took a drag and exhaled the smoke skyward. "I figured that's where he was going when he left my cabin this morning. Pleasant, isn't he?"

"Not the word I'd use."

"Me either." She flicked the cigarette into the churn of the ship's wake.

April examined the girl before her. She had to be five-nine with long, slender legs, a beautiful face with high cheekbones, a pert nose, very pale blonde hair that glistened in the sunlight, and intense blue eyes. She could have been in movies, or a model.

Chloe tugged a pack of Marlboros and a lighter from her hip pocket. She shook one up and offered it to April. April declined, so Chloe lipped it from the pack and lit it. Again, she exhaled the smoke up and away from April where the ocean breeze carried it out over the water. "Roberta said they picked you up down near Tampa?"

"I think so," April said. "At least that's what I was told."

"Where were you?"

April looked back toward the bow of the yacht. It rose and fell over the waves. To think that just yesterday she was onboard *After Hours*, sunning on the deck, enjoying the best life had to offer. It would be lunchtime now. Paulo would have prepared something lavish. Lobster salad, or shrimp scampi, or some other amazing dish that was as good as you could find in the classiest restaurants. She would be at the shaded deck table eating with Andrew. The son of a bitch. How did she miss what he really was? When did he decide to do this? Was this his plan all along? It had to be. This kind of operation didn't simply happen. It had to be orchestrated.

April told Chloe of her time with Andrew and how he had tricked her onto his boat and had sold her to Victor. She asked, "Do you know Andrew Heche?"

"Never heard of him."

"I wish I never had," April said. "What about you? How'd you end up here?"

"Stupidity. They grabbed me in New Orleans." She took another drag from the cigarette, turned, and leaned her forearms on the railing again. "I fell for a line of crap from this insanely good-looking Hispanic guy. He said he was an entrepreneur from Colombia and was in New Orleans on business. He wore a nice suit and had a gold Rolex. He flashed cash. He took me to some club and then down to the Riverwalk. It all seemed so relaxed and actually wonderful. He was charming." Another long drag from the cigarette. "Then he wasn't. We walked back down Magazine Street. A limo pulled up and I was shoved in the back. Bag over my head; wrists and ankles bound." She sighed. "Like a fucking spy movie. So, I ended up here on the trip to hell."

"You seemed resigned to that," April said.

She waved a hand. "Do you see any other options?"

April rested her hands on the railing's cool metal. "What's going to happen to us?"

Chloe glanced at her. "Exactly what you think."

"What are we going to do?"

"If you have any ideas, I'm open. Trust me, I've wracked my brain for something, but I don't see any way out of this."

Chloe's resignation matched what April had felt with Emanuella and Roberta. All three seemed to have surrendered and accepted their fates. Were things really that hopeless? She looked toward the water. "We could jump."

A soft laugh. "Yeah, that'd work. Middle of the Gulf without land or another boat in sight. But maybe you're right. There're worse things than drowning."

Were there? Were they headed toward something worse?

"Any idea where we're going?"

"Venezuela eventually," Chloe said.

"What?"

"That's where we'll meet the guy who's paying for all of this. For us."

"Jesus."

"Jesus jumped ship a long time ago, honey, and he ain't where we're going."

"There has to be a way out," April said.

"Like I said, if you think of one, I'm all over it."

April knew Chloe was right. They were in the Gulf's open water, no safe haven in sight, making taking a plunge and probably drowning the only option. Would it really be that bad?

"Any idea how long it'll be before we get there?" April asked.

"All I know is that we're headed up to Pensacola to pick up another girl and get some supplies. After that, I think we'll head toward Venezuela. I'm not a hundred percent sure though."

"How do you know that?"

"Not for public consumption, okay?"

"I don't see any public around here," April said.

"I speak a little Spanish. I'm nowhere near fluent but I studied it in school, and in New Orleans I worked in a bar with a bunch of folks from Mexico and South America. I picked up quite a bit. At least I understand some of what's said." She glanced at Chloe. "Victor and his guys don't know that, so they speak more freely than they probably should."

"When will we get to Pensacola?"

"The plan is to get everything done tonight. That's why we're hauling ass right now. I heard that if we don't make it, we'll hang out at sea for another day." She shrugged. "These guys do everything in the dark."

CHAPTER 37

IT WAS JUST past noon when Nicole and I walked Lorie out to her car. To say she was on high alert didn't cover it. Her gaze swept the lot, the road, the beach, like a rabbit fearing a lurking pack of coyotes.

"Relax." Nicole hugged her. "Everything's going to work out."

"I hope so, but part of me says I should've stayed low to the ground and kept my mouth shut."

"Would that have made things better?" I asked.

"Probably not."

"You did the right thing," Nicole said. "Everything you told us helps a lot."

Lorie didn't seem convinced. "What happens now?"

"You go about business as usual and let us do what we need to do."

"Which is?"

Nicole gave me a glance. "We'll talk with Ray and Pancake and come up with a plan."

"For sure we'll take a hard look at Andrew Heche," I said. "Knowing Ray, he'll want to see if we can neutralize those videos."

"How? I mean Jonathon has quite a collection."

"Which probably includes us." I nodded to Nicole.

"No. Your room wasn't wired."

"Are you sure?" Nicole asked.

"I am. Only a half a dozen of the suites are, and yours wasn't one of them."

That was good news. If memory serves, Nicole and I hadn't left much to the imagination. Nicole is somewhat of an acrobat. And an exhibitionist. I'd hate to see our naked butts pop up on the internet. With Nicole involved, it'd get millions of hits. Might be good for Paris, and Pam, and the Kardashians, but for Nicole it wouldn't boost her career. Not to mention that her parents would be mortified.

"The DVDs you found," I said. "When was that?"

"A couple of weeks ago."

"Do you think that's all of them?"

"I don't know. But I do know that Jonathon's big on redundancy, so he'll have them on hard drives too. Maybe more than one."

Which would complicate things. "The ones you saw were in a locked filing cabinet in Jonathon's office?"

She nodded. "That's right. He has three four-drawer cabinets in his office, and I found them in the one that's usually locked."

"The others are open?" Nicole asked.

Lorie nodded. "He must keep all the private stuff in the locked one."

"Where is it in the office?" I asked.

"They're lined up along the wall. The black one is the locked one. The others are gray. Why?"

"Just anticipating Pancake's plan."

"Who is this *Pancake*?"

"A longtime friend who works for Ray," I said. "He's a P.I. and knows computers inside and out."

"I don't see how that helps," Lorie said. "Jonathon keeps everything under lock and key."

"You found them," I said. "Pancake has his ways in and out of places most people don't know exist."

"You're sure no one else knows you found the videos?" Nicole asked.

"I'm sure."

"Not even Robin?"

"No one," Lorie said. "It wasn't easy. I was confused and scared. I wasn't sure what it meant." She sighed. "That's not true. I knew. I mean, they were either for his personal kicks, which is creepy, or they were weapons for control and extortion, which is scary. Either way, it was knowledge I almost wished I didn't have."

"But you do," I said. "And you were right to tell us."

"Either way, I sensed it could be dangerous if they knew I had seen them." She looked at me. "I had a bunch of sleepless nights wrestling with what to do. Run away, stay and act as if I knew nothing, go to the police. In the end, I figured any of those would expose me and then who knew what would happen." She kicked a loose pebble. "The hardest part was not telling Robin. She's good people and deserved to know."

"It's good that you didn't tell her," I said.

She gave a weak shrug. "In the end, I felt it would only put her in the same danger I felt. And if she talked to anyone it'd come back on both of us."

"Like I said earlier, a smart move," Nicole said

Lorie looked out toward the beach, a glisten of moisture in her eyes. "This is such a mess."

"Just be cool and don't worry," Nicole said. "Go back to TLM and act as if nothing is different."

"Easy for you to say, you're the actress."

"You'll do fine. I have faith in you."

"I wish I had the same faith," Lorie said.

Nicole smiled. "Consider it your first acting gig."

"It's crazy, I know, but after all Jonathon and Rhea have done for me, why do I feel like I'm betraying them?"

"But not betraying yourself," Nicole said. "Or April."

"Which is the real focus here," I said. "We still need to find her and make sure she's OK."

Now tears appeared in her eyes. "She is. She has to be."

"Let us run with the ball," Nicole said. "I'll call when we know more."

"If you need anything, or feel truly threatened," I said, "get out and call us."

We watched Lorie drive away.

"What do you think?" I asked.

"She'll do fine. She's a smart and tough young lady."

CHAPTER 38

NICOLE CALLED STEPHANIE DeLuca, telling her we had a few more questions for her. When she asked what questions, Nicole deflected her by saying we'd drive over and talk in person. Stephanie wasn't thrilled but agreed.

While Nicole blasted us in the direction of Destin, I called Pancake. He was at Ray's.

"How'd things go with Tony Amato?" I asked.

"He actually turned out to be a reasonable guy."

"Anything there?"

"Nothing that helped us. Yes, he and April had a thing, but he hasn't seen her in months and knows nothing about her disappearance."

I brought him up to date on what we had just learned from Lorie.

"Videos?" Pancake asked,

"Apparently around a hundred of them," I said.

"I got some snooping to do," Pancake said. "You guys headed this way?"

"After we revisit Stephanie DeLuca. She's on the videos, which might make her remember a few things."

"It just might."

"Have you found anything on Andrew Heche?" I asked.

"Just some business stuff with Jonathon and Gordon. A convoluted money trail, but I'm making progress."

"Lorie confirmed what Robin had told us. April was definitely with him at his place when last seen. Plus, check out a girl named Mia Santos. She's another friend of Lorie's and was also last seen at Andrew's. Maybe six months ago."

"That don't sound none too good."

"No, it doesn't. The party line is that she hooked up with some high roller and took off. The same story they're rolling out about April."

"You're getting good at this P.I. stuff," Pancake said. "Or maybe it's Nicole." He laughed and disconnected the call.

Nicole and I decided that the time for a polite conversation with Stephanie DeLuca had passed and a harder, more in-your-face discussion was needed. April's clock was ticking and we needed to gather all the information we could.

"What is this about?" Stephanie asked as we gathered in her living room.

"Your past," Nicole said.

Stephanie recoiled. "What are you talking about?"

"The sugar baby site."

Stephanie's shoulders rose, her spine straightened, and her eyes widened. "I don't understand."

"We know you were on one of those sites, and you had a few clients as it were."

"What is this? What do you want?"

"Relax," I said. "We weren't exactly honest with you before. We're P.I.s and we're looking into the disappearance of April Wilkerson. Her mother hired us."

"I thought she went off with some guy," Stephanie said.

"She did. It's the who and the where we're concerned about," Nicole said.

"I don't see what that has to do with my . . . with me."

"April did the same thing before she joined the TLM staff."

Realization weighed heavy on Stephanie, and her head and shoulders drooped. "Okay. I did do that stuff. Years ago." She looked up at us. "Not my best decision."

"Your secret is safe," Nicole said. "That's not our concern. We're most interested in your time at TLM."

Stephanie looked stricken. No doubt she knew exactly what we were talking about.

"We know what was expected of you while at TLM," I said. "You and many of the other girls. Please understand we aren't judging, we're investigating."

She sighed. "I thought all that was behind me. Dead and buried."

"It's not," Nicole said. "Not yet anyway."

Stephanie swallowed hard. Not easy, as I was sure her throat was dry and tight about now.

"Tell me," she said.

"First a question," I said. "Did Rhea know of your sugar baby involvement when she recruited you?"

Stephanie took an audible breath. "Yes."

"Do you think that's how she found you?" Nicole asked.

Stephanie nodded. "She as much as said so. Said that TLM was a better version of the same thing." She seemed to shrink further into her chair. "I'm so stupid." Her gaze hit the floor and then elevated toward us. "There's more, isn't there?"

"It's not good news," Nicole said. "I won't sugarcoat it. Jonathon had videos."

Now Stephanie's face froze, paled. "Of what?"

"Of private activities that took place out at the farm."

"Meaning?"

No doubt she knew, or feared, exactly what was coming.

"He recorded many of the encounters between members and the staff," I said. "Including you."

"Oh God." She buried her face in her hands. "I can't believe this."

"We're working on retrieving them," I said.

She looked up. "You can do that?"

"Maybe. What we want to know is if you have any more information that might help us find April."

"She really is missing?"

"She is," Nicole said.

Stephanie gave that some thought. "I haven't seen or heard from her in a long time. I have no idea where she might be."

"She was last seen down in St. Pete with a guy named Andrew Heche."

"That creep?"

"I take it you know him?" I asked.

"I do. I've been to his place. I've been to parties there and out on his yacht."

"So was April the last time we have a location for her."

Stephanie looked at me, then Nicole. "Surely, you don't think he did something to her?"

"Do you?" Nicole asked.

"He's a complete asshole. But kidnapping—or—or something worse, I can't even imagine."

"It's the *something worse* we're most worried about," I said. "She's not the first girl to go missing under his watch. Do you know Mia Santos?"

"Not well but I remember her. She came to the farm around the time I left."

"She too was last seen with Heche."

Stephanie now completely deflated. "You're thinking he did something to them, aren't you?"

"We don't know," Nicole said. "It's a consideration. We do feel that whatever happened to her and to April are connected."

Stephanie wound her hands into a knot. "This is a nightmare. I can't believe it." She looked at us through tear-filled eyes. "If Jim learns of any of this, it will crush him. Me, too."

"We'll do everything we can to make sure none of this comes back your way," Nicole said.

"But you aren't sure you can, right?"

"We can't be sure of anything," I said. "But we're going to try to take those videos out of Jonathon Lindemann's hands."

"How?"

I shrugged. "We haven't figured that out yet."

CHAPTER 39

WE LEFT DESTIN, drove straight to Ray's, and joined him and Pancake on the deck, Pancake's nose in his laptop, Ray reading a document that lay on the tabletop before him.

"How'd it go?" Ray asked.

"Stephanie DeLuca has had happier days," Nicole said. "She's shaken and then some."

"She should be," Pancake said.

"I don't like the sound of that," I said.

"It looks worse than it sounds."

"You found the videos?" I asked.

"It wasn't all that hard. I hacked Lindemann's computer and he had them all tucked away in a folder he ingeniously labeled 'Private.' I'm starting to question his brainpower."

"Arrogance," Ray said. "He thinks he's bulletproof."

"Stupid would work too," Pancake added. "But then, aren't most bad guys? They think they have everything all buttoned up and only when it's too late do they realize they forgot to zip their fly."

"Colorful comparison," Nicole said.

"I knew you'd like that." He bounced an eyebrow. "I got a million of them."

"So," I said. "Back to the videos."

"I found around a hundred and fifty of them." Pancake indicated his laptop. "I copied them in case Lindemann tried to dump them."

"Did you find Stephanie on any of them?" Nicole asked.

"I'm only about a third of the way through checking them out, but yeah, she appears in three of them. Two different rooms, three different guys."

"She's recognizable then?" Nicole said.

"Oh, yeah. Everyone is. Each room had three hidden cameras so everything was captured from multiple angles and in high def."

"Who was she with?" I asked.

"Let's see." He tapped the keyboard of his laptop. "Quentin Mason, Gordon Buchanan, and Will Buckley."

"Buchanan is one of Jonathon's closest friends," Nicole said. "They have a lot of business connections."

"That's true," Pancake said. "I've got a bunch of info on that."

"We met him," I said. "We also met Will Buckley. He hit on Nicole."

"He was simply being friendly," Nicole said.

"His eyes peeled your clothes off."

She ruffled my hair. "So do yours."

"And you like it."

"I do."

"Any sign of April Wilkerson?" I asked.

"Two videos of her that I've found so far. Same for the other girls you told me about. Lorie Cooper and Robin Meade. Well, four for Robin."

"When was the most recent one of April?" Ray asked.

Pancake examined the computer screen. "I'm compiling a list of dates, times, and who's involved for each video." He scrolled, his brow furrowed, then he said, "Looks like six weeks ago. With that Andrew Heche dude."

Even I could see the sinister nature of that timing. "That would've been three weeks before she went to his place in St. Pete and disappeared."

"Bingo," Pancake said. "It gets better. So far I've only found one video of that girl you told me about. Lorie's friend Mia Santos. She worked at TLM for over a year and was videoed with Heche about eight months ago. From what you told me, that'd be a couple of months before she dropped off the radar."

"It could be a coincidence," I said, knowing that wasn't likely.

"It's not," Pancake said.

"What do you know about Heche so far?" Nicole said

Pancake nodded to Ray.

"He's been in business with Lindemann and Gordon Buchanan for nearly twenty years," Ray said. "Property construction and management, investments, setting up IPOs, financial counseling, and the like. He has a huge waterfront estate in St. Pete and an eighty-foot yacht he calls *After Hours*. His portfolio puts him north of half a billion."

"Adult money," I said.

"Which is another interesting area," Pancake said. "He, Buchanan, and Lindemann are joined at the hip financially. I mean, each has their own little pot of gold, but they also share a half a dozen accounts all over the world. Spain, Saudi Arabia, Jamaica, Singapore, and a couple of other places that are known for hiding assets and money movement."

"Are you talking about money laundering?" Nicole asked.

"Probably. Let's say they're at least obscuring their assets. If this whole TLM thing is a Ponzi scheme, it's an easy way to rob Peter to pay Paul. The investors would never know that month by month their accounts are actually leaking funds because any paperwork provided by Lindemann would reflect huge gains and the dividend checks would keep coming as more and more people shoved cash into Lindemann's pocket."

"Bernie Madoff," Nicole said.

"Exactly."

"This is amazing," Nicole said. "The nerve it takes to do that."

"Sociopaths don't have nerves," Pancake said.

"Tell them the rest," Ray said.

"There's more?" I asked.

"I've been digging around in Lindemann's finances since we took on this case. He has tons of accounts, not just in the U.S., but as I said earlier, all over the world. The connections between them aren't always apparent but fortunately every time money changes locations it generates a digital footprint. Not always easy to follow, but they're there nonetheless. Bottom line is that most of the threads involve money from Lindemann's businesses and from TLM members who invest with him. But a few were odd."

"In what way?" I asked.

"So far I've found a total of eight deposits for exactly two hundred K each that originated from Venezuela, bounced among several of Lindemann's accounts, and finally made it into one of his private Singapore accounts."

"Drug money?" Nicole asked.

"Could be. They all occurred over the past two years and each came from a bank in Caracas that's known to have ties to the drug trade as well as militia funding and money laundering. But the hooker here is that one was six months ago, another three weeks ago. Which would correlate with the disappearances of Mia Santos and April Wilkerson."

Nicole sat up in her chair. "Are you saying these girls were sold to some guy in Venezuela?"

"It would fit," Pancake said. "To add to the mystery, half of each two-hundred-K deposit was then almost immediately transferred from Lindemann's Singapore account into a Jamaican account that Andrew Heche and Gordon Buchanan own."

"They're all in this together," I said.

"So it would seem," Ray added.

"You're thinking this trio is trafficking girls out of TLM to some dude in South America?" I asked.

Pancake opened his hands. "Don't know, but I'm not finished following the trail."

"Let's say that's true," Ray said. "If so, they've sold eight young ladies over a two-year time frame. Since that farm only opened a year or so ago, it would mean they were doing this beforehand. Maybe snatching young ladies from the Tampa area."

"Which I'm just beginning to get into," Pancake said.

"What are we going to do?" Nicole, asked. "Call the police or the FBI?"

"Not yet," Ray said. "If they know we're on to them, the computer data will be wiped, the DVDs will disappear, and we'll have little proof."

I looked at Pancake. "Can't you simply hack back in and copy his hard drive?"

"I could. It would take hours. It took over an hour to download the videos. Lindemann's Wi-Fi setup ain't the fastest on the planet. What I need is a direct connection."

Nothing about that sounded good. Not to me anyway. Ray and Pancake might think all this clandestine crap is fun and games, but to me it meant danger and anxiety.

"Tonight," Ray said. "We'll go in, and Pancake can do his copying, and we can grab all the DVDs we can find."

"I explored most of the property when we were there," Nicole said. "So I know where the buildings are, where Jonathon's office is, and how to get in and out."

Of course she did.

CHAPTER 40

RAY AND PANCAKE had a plan. Didn't they always? Pancake explained it to Nicole and me and I didn't like it. It involved breaking and entering and theft. More or less like all their schemes. I remembered a few where gunfire broke out. I remembered throwing baseballs at bad guys and firing a snow globe at an armed cop. I remembered Nicole tackling another armed dude.

See why I hate Ray's and Pancake's plans?

The good news was that the plan didn't kick off until midnight so Nicole and I had the remainder of the afternoon and evening to do as we pleased. Which turned out to be a bite at Captain Rocky's followed by a bit of acrobatics in Nicole's bed and then a nap. I fell asleep feeling like a condemned man who had received his final meal and conjugal visit.

When midnight rolled around, we hooked up with Ray and Pancake at Ray's place. Pancake unfolded a map and then placed three black-and-white 12x18 satellite images on the kitchen table. Where he got them, I don't know, but he has his ways. I noticed the time stamp said they were only eighteen hours old. Even more amazing.

"Right here is the farm." Pancake indicated the map where he had used a black marker to outline Lindemann Farms. "It doesn't show on the map, but if you look here at the satellite images, you'll see this dirt road." His finger tapped a spot on the picture. "That's here." Now he fingered a red line he had marked on the map. "It spurs off the paved road just east of the farm and circles toward the back where it apparently ends."

"That's where we'll enter the property," Ray said.

"The downside," Pancake said, "is that it's a one-way in-and-out deal. The good news is it doesn't get much traffic. Maybe none. It seems to simply play out and fade into the trees."

Nicole pointed to a spot on one of the images. "It ends just beyond that pond. Robin and I walked out that way. It's near the back of the property."

"We rode ATVs out there on our first visit," I said. "When Rhea showed us around."

"If you follow this path through the trees, you come out here." Again, she pointed to the map. "This building is where staff stays, and here are the business offices. Next to the lodge."

"Where's the entrance to the building?" Pancake asked.

"There are two," I said. "The front faces the lodge and a small parking area between. The other in the back faces that way." I indicated the northeast wall. "It faces the building where the girls stay."

"There's a thick growth of trees between the two," Nicole said. "It's impossible to see one building from the other."

"Good," Pancake said. "This is looking easier by the minute."

Of course it is.

"Do Jonathon and Rhea stay at the lodge?" Ray asked.

"They do," I said.

"Where?"

I glanced at Nicole and got a half shrug in return. "We don't know."

"Probably near the office," Pancake said.

"No," I said. "We stayed in a corner suite. The front windows overlooked the lodge entry area and the side ones faced the office building."

"That helps," Ray said. "At least they can't peek out the window in the middle of the night and see something out of place."

Like us. Trespassing, burglarizing, and breaking a dozen other laws. I could almost visualize us in Chief Billie Warren's jail trying to explain ourselves while she scowled and flexed her considerable muscles.

At the risk of being redundant, do you see why I hate getting snarled in Ray's world?

Before we left, Ray and Pancake checked their weapons and, satisfied they were loaded and in good order, slid them into shoulder holsters beneath their jackets. They didn't offer one to either Nicole or me.

The trip to Magnolia Springs in Pancake's dually pickup only took thirty minutes. Had Nicole drove it would've taken less time, but Pancake moved along fairly quickly. Lindemann Farms appeared quiet as we rolled past. Of course, we couldn't see the lodge or the office or really anything from the county highway. The dirt road was exactly as advertised and did indeed melt into the trees as if it had run out of energy.

Stealth being a major asset, everyone wore black clothing with black baseball caps, except Nicole who wore a knit one that allowed her to stuff her blonde hair inside. Helping our endeavors, a bank of clouds had rolled in from the Gulf and obscured the moon. It wasn't raining, or even drizzling, but I did feel an occasional random drop of moisture. Probably dripping off the pines we walked beneath.

Winding our way across the property and past the staff lodging, which seemed dark and quiet, we easily reached the office building. Ray worked the rear lock and we were inside in less than a minute.

I positioned myself near the front window, cracking the curtain open just enough to see the lodge. The exterior lights and a few inside lights were on, but nothing looked out of the ordinary, and for sure

I saw no shadows moving around. Now, if everyone would be kind enough to sleep tight until we got out of Dodge, that would be great.

Pancake attacked Jonathon's computer while Ray worked to open the locked black filing cabinet. I heard him rummaging inside.

"Here we go," Ray said.

He lifted the metal box from the bottom drawer and placed it on the coffee table. Nicole sat on the sofa and zipped open the canvas bag Pancake had brought with him. She lifted out several stacks of blank DVDs, while Ray did the same with those in the metal box. The exchange was made and Ray returned the box to the cabinet and relocked it.

Ray had said his thinking was that if Jonathon looked in the drawer and saw his secret little container was there and still filled with his precious DVDs, he'd think everything was kosher. At least with only a casual inspection. If he actually tried to play one of the discs, that'd be a different story.

Pancake sat back in Jonathon's chair, hands clasped over his abdomen, the computer's screen reflecting off his face.

"How's it going?" Ray asked.

"Smooth." He tapped a couple of keys. "Jonathon is good about labeling all his folders in plain, simple language. Already having the videos will make things go faster."

Not fast enough. Time seemed to slow to a crawl. Nicole joined me at the window.

"Everything okay out there?" she asked.

"So far." I glanced at Pancake. "How much longer?"

"Soon. Five minutes tops."

In more like three minutes, Pancake shut down the computer and disconnected the external drive he had brought with him. He placed the drive in the bag with the DVDs while Ray gave the room a final once-over.

Then, we were out the door and into the trees once again. Twenty minutes later we were in Pancake's truck and turning off the dirt road onto the highway.

No doubt the easiest Ray adventure I'd ever been on.

"You get everything?" Nicole asked Pancake.

"Sure did. All his financial and business stuff so I can dig even deeper. He has one of those password apps. The ones that are encrypted. Hopefully, he'll have all his account passwords in there."

I noticed he skipped right over the encrypted part.

"I also installed a bit of special code on his hard drive," Pancake said. "It'll allow easy access to anything he does moving forward. And prevent him from deleting and sharing files."

"You can do that?" I asked.

"Easy peasy. It'll also record any conversations he has in his office."

"Really?" I asked. "How?"

"Simple. It uses the built-in microphone and creates an audio file I can grab at will."

"Doesn't sound simple to me."

Pancake grunted. "It is."

"Don't strain your brain, Jake," Nicole said. "It'll give you a headache."

Pancake laughed. "Maybe he'll use that to pass on sex later."

"It won't work," Nicole said.

CHAPTER 41

FOR OVER AN hour, April's face remained plastered to the porthole, searching the darkness. She had been at it so long that her neck and shoulders stiffened and her eyes burned from probing the nothingness beyond the glass. No stars, no moon, no ships, no city lights. Were they truly headed for Pensacola? Or did Victor lie and they were actually steaming toward Venezuela? Maddening. She wanted to scream, to collapse on her bed and cry.

She swiped the gathering tears from her eyes and continued her vigil. Then a faint glow shimmered on the horizon. Or was it her imagination? At first, she couldn't be sure, but as the lights brightened and expanded, her doubts evaporated. It had to be Pensacola. God, let it be. She continued watching as they drew closer, and indeed the city lights widened and intensified. The engine's rumble softened. The silhouette of the dock, where two smaller boats snugged against one side, materialized.

This would be her last chance to escape. If that was even remotely possible. From what she had been told, Venezuela would be the next stop and then all hope would be lost. The problem with her loose plan was that it would require a jump and a swim. The jump was one thing, the swimming another thing altogether. She had never been strong in the water.

She wore jeans, a tee shirt, and shoes but no socks, thinking the less weight she had the easier it would be to stay afloat. Part of her felt that was silly, even ridiculous. How much did wet socks weigh anyway? Compared to her jeans and shoes they added little. The proverbial spitting in the ocean. Why was she obsessing on things that mattered so little when she had huge obstacles to overcome? She knew the answer. Fear, pure and unadulterated, had literally wound her brain into knots.

Through that chaos, two major problems rattled in her mind. When was the best time to jump? When they neared the dock or when they were leaving? Or maybe while they were tied to it, when the ship would be most stable. Which led to the other problem. The crew. How could she avoid being seen and intercepted before she even got a chance to jump? It seemed to her that during approach and departure would be best, as they would be occupied with the procedures required to dock and undock. She had witnessed this process several times on Andrew's yacht. But, even though they would be focused on their tasks, more crew members would be on deck, increasing the chance her flight would be detected.

Fuck. How did she get here? She knew the answer to that, too. Stupidity and being so naive that she trusted a snake like Andrew. She knew he was a self-absorbed, smarmy ass who only wanted her for the sex she provided, which for her wasn't all that good. Yet she stayed behind for the adventure, for the chance to hang on to a life she had only dreamed about. So freaking stupid. Why hadn't she left with Lorie and Robin? They were back at the farm warm and snug in bed.

Her hate for Andrew Heche and her deep, visceral fear of what was to come drove her toward what she felt was an increasingly foolish plan. Did she have the nerve to jump into the dark water or would she freeze at the railing? If she even got that chance. Did she have the ability to swim to shore? Did she have a choice? Was Venezuela really worse than drowning?

The engine fell silent and she felt the yacht bump the dock. She heard voices and saw that lines were being tossed from the vessel to two guys on the weathered wooden platform. The yacht rocked as the ropes drew it closer.

April decided her best chance of escape would be while the boat was tied to the dock. She moved toward the door. She grasped the handle, took a calming breath, and froze.

Footsteps approached.

She scurried back to her bed, pulled the covers up to her neck, and rolled to one side, feigning sleep. She heard the door creak open. She didn't move.

"Hey." The voice was rough.

She opened her eyes, blinked, looked around as if confused. She carefully rolled over, taking care not to expose her clothing, and focused on the man in the doorway. He was one of the crew. She didn't know his name but had seen him several times. The scariest of a scary group. Dark eyes, a thick mustache, and a permanent scowl that only added to his intimidating nature.

"What's going on?" she asked.

"We've docked. Stay in your room."

She rubbed her eyes. "Where are we?"

"Don't matter. Just stay here. If you leave this room, it will not be good for you."

"What if I need to go to the bathroom?"

"Hold it. Understand?"

She nodded. "How long?"

"Short time. Half an hour." He smirked. "Then we leave and you can visit the head."

"What time is it?"

"Almost *cinco*. Five." He looked her up and down. "Tell me you understand these orders."

"I understand."

"Make sure you do." He left.

She listened to his footfalls recede. She rolled out of bed and parted the curtain just enough to peer through the porthole. The two men she had seen on the dock now stood next to a stack of boxes. They began lifting them and passing them to the crew members on the deck. No doubt fresh supplies for the trip to Venezuela. A third man appeared. Victor. She heard him bark orders but couldn't make out exactly what he was saying.

Okay, she had missed the opportunity to jump on the way in and now there was too much activity for her to make a run for it. She would have to wait for departure.

Doubts crept into her head. Could she do this? Did she have the nerve, or the ability? *Stop it*, she scolded herself. *You have to try.*

A man walked down the dock and into view. He was tall and wore a black windbreaker and a dark cap, which gave him a menacing aura. Worse, he grasped the upper arm of a young woman, who offered some resistance, but not enough. He greeted Victor and then literally lifted the girl and deposited her on deck. Victor looked her over and gave a wave to the man, who turned, headed back up the dock, and disappeared from her view. Victor roughly dragged the girl toward the front of the yacht.

Now there are five of us, April thought.

A pang of guilt rose. If she escaped and left behind Emanuella, Roberta, and Chloe, and this new girl, could she live with that? Did she owe them a chance to go with her? In the end, she saw no reasonable way to bring them into her plan before the yacht would be too far out to sea. Besides, their only hope, her only hope, was that she somehow escaped.

She felt the engines rumble to life. The ropes were tossed from the dock onto the boat, and it began to back slowly toward open water.

It was now or never.

She opened the door to her cabin and looked both ways, seeing no one. She slipped down the hallway to the rear steps and began to creep up them. Halfway to the deck, she heard footsteps above moving toward her. She froze. A man's legs appeared near the top of the stairs. She silently pleaded that he wouldn't descend toward her. He stood motionless for a few seconds before turning and moving out of sight toward the bow.

She eased up to the level of the deck and looked both ways. No one visible. It was still dark, but the predawn was beginning to eat away the darkness. She crawled toward the rear of the vessel. A storage locker sat near the stern railing, and she settled behind it. Her heart beat so hard she was sure it was audible. Her hands shook and she felt panic rising in her chest.

Get a grip.

She rose just enough to see over the locker and scanned the deck. A single crew member stood near the starboard rail, facing forward.

She twisted on her haunches and saw the dock and the town of Pensacola slowly receding. She estimated she was two or three hundred yards from shore, but that distance expanded rapidly.

Now, she thought.

She took a deep breath and hurled herself over the railing and braced for impact. The fall took forever it seemed. She hit the water hard, her breath exploding from her chest, and the wet darkness enveloped her. She bobbed to the surface and gasped a breath. She treaded water and turned toward the yacht. No movement, no one running to the aft rail, no shouting or yelling or anything.

Tears pushed against her eyes. She had done it. She had actually done it.

She turned toward shore and began to dog paddle.

CHAPTER 42

LAST NIGHT, IT was after three a.m. before Nicole and I crawled into bed. We were out within a quick minute of hitting the sheets. I must have descended deeply into the REM world because when my cell phone buzzed, I rose from the depths slowly, my brain foggy. I felt Nicole's hips against my side. Scrunched into a ball, lying on one side, she began to stir.

I managed to unwind the sheet enough to roll toward the nightstand and retrieve my phone. The screen told me two things: it was seven a.m., and the caller was Pancake. I answered, my voice thick with sleep.

"Wake up, sleeping beauty," he said. "You guys hit the streets a running and meet me and Ray at the Pensacola PD."

That made no sense. Less than four hours of sleep and he was up and at it and wanted us to hop over to Pensacola.

"Why?" I asked.

"They found April Wilkerson."

I didn't know whether I liked the sound of that or not. "What do you mean *found*?"

"She's OK. The guy I talked to said she was jabbering about being kidnapped and jumping off a boat and swimming to shore."

I sat up. So did Nicole, a concerned look on her face.

Pancake continued. "She apparently came into the PD with that story. She called her mother and her mother called Ray. Her mother is on the way over from Jupiter. We're headed that way to sort this out."

"So why do you need us there?"

"Not really you. Ray says he wants Nicole to talk with April. Something about a woman's touch."

"Good. I'll send her?"

Now Nicole had a big old question mark behind her eyes.

"Get your ass up, plop in the passenger's seat, and hold on while she rolls that way."

"OK, OK. We're on the way." I disconnected the call.

"What's going on?" Nicole asked.

"That's Pancake. April's at the Pensacola PD with a pretty wild story."

"What happened? Is she OK?"

"I think so. I'll tell you what little I know on the way."

We made it to Pensacola in record time. Nicole passed every car she could but, to her credit, only three times on the right. We raced by two police cars on the way, both headed in the opposite direction, but they seemed to pay no attention to us. I had seen this many times and was beginning to believe she was invisible to law enforcement. Well, except for the few times when she did get pulled over. Then she opened a shirt button or two, flipped her hair into just the right position, and offered up that smile. The one that had the officer apologizing for pulling her over and offering his card, telling her she could call anytime if she had any problems.

We reached the Pensacola Police Department unscathed and once inside were greeted by the desk sergeant who directed us down a short hallway to an interrogation room. Ray and Pancake sat across a table from April Wilkerson, who was wrapped in a blanket and sipping hot chocolate. Ray made the introductions.

Ray stood. "I want you to run through it again for Jake and Nicole. We'll check in with your mother and see what her ETA is and make a couple of other calls."

"To who?" April asked.

"For one, the FBI. If that yacht has other girls on it as you say, they'll have it located and stopped."

"They can do that?"

"They'll have to get the Navy and the Coast Guard involved, but yeah, they can do that," Ray said.

Ray and Pancake left and Nicole and I sat.

"Are you OK?" Nicole asked.

"I am now. But if you'd asked me that a few hours ago I'd have had a different answer."

"Tell us what happened," I said.

"I've already told it twice. To the police and to Ray and Pancake." She gave a headshake. "What kind of name is that?"

I laughed. "He gets that a lot, but it's what I've called him since we were kids."

April sighed, forked her fingers through her hair, and said, "It's truly amazing that I'm here."

"Take your time," Nicole said. "Tell us the whole story."

April did. Her work at TLM, her visit to Gordon Buchanan's estate, the parties there and at Andrew Heche's estate, the party on Andrew's yacht, how Lorie and Robin left but she remained, thinking she and Andrew would cruise the Gulf for a few days and she would follow them. How her phone disappeared so she couldn't call her mother. She said she was sure Andrew had taken and destroyed it. The meeting with the other boat and her transfer in the dark, far from shore. The other girls she met onboard, and the fact that she was sure the vessel was headed to Venezuela at that very moment.

Finally, she sighed. "I still don't know how I did it, but I literally hurled myself off the yacht and somehow made it to shore."

"Jake and I've been there," Nicole said.

Boy, have we.

"Really?"

"Long story."

"I assume Ray told you who we are and what we've been doing," I said.

"He did. Even the part about looking into TLM." She drained her hot chocolate, placing the empty cup on the table before her, staring at it for a beat. She looked up at me. "Do you think Jonathon and Rhea are involved in this?"

"Do you?" I asked.

"They'd have to be, wouldn't they? I don't think Andrew would have done any of this without their consent. Maybe even their help."

"Go with the latter," I said.

She nodded. "Makes sense."

"What I'm going to tell you goes no further," Nicole said. "At least for now."

"You mean there's more?" April asked.

"They took videos." Nicole went on to explain what we had found, and that yes, April was in some of them.

April appeared defeated. A low groan escaped her throat. "This is a total nightmare." Her eyes glistened. "My mom will be devastated."

"Moms are resilient," I said. "And understanding."

"You don't know my mom," April said. "This will humiliate her."

Her? What about April? Was their rift about more than trust fund money? I thought back to our phone conversation with Clarice Wilkerson. Her boy toy, if that's what he was, in his red Speedo hanging with her at the pool. How her hair and makeup had been flawless. How she'd seemed more angry than truly scared.

"We do have some good news," I said. "We grabbed the DVDs Jonathon made, and Pancake set up some kind of thing in Jonathon's computer to block him from sharing them."

"So they won't pop up on the internet?" April asked.

Nicole reached across the table and laid her hand over April's. "We hope not. But you can never be sure."

"Mom would be mortified if they did. So would I."

Interesting that again she focused more on her mother's reaction than her own.

"Hopefully, that will never happen," Nicole said.

"Thanks for telling me," April said. "I hate it, but at least I'm prepared."

"We thought you needed to know."

"How'd you manage to do that?" April asked. "Get the discs and that other stuff?"

"We'd rather not say," I said. "But Pancake's very clever."

"Fuck Jonathon and Rhea," April said. "How could they do this? I was loyal to them. I worked hard. I did crap for them that I'd never do in my former life."

"We know," Nicole said. "Many of you did."

April held back tears. "And now this. They, and that snake Andrew, selling me to that Victor dude. This is freaking evil on steroids."

Was it ever.

Ray came into the room. "An FBI agent is coming over to get the ball rolling on this." He looked at April. "Their office is nearby so it'll only be a few minutes. Unfortunately, you'll have to tell him the story yet again."

"Can he really find that yacht and get to those other girls?"

"He can," Ray said. "I talked to your mother. She's an hour away."

April sighed. "This is going to be fun."

"She seems concerned about you," I said.

"Yeah, she's good at that. Acting concerned. But in the end this will all be my fault and a big inconvenience for her."

I reminded myself not to complain so much about Ray. Probably wouldn't work, but it's the thought that counts, right?

CHAPTER 43

SPECIAL AGENT ROBERT Whiting arrived fifteen minutes later. The local FBI office was that close to the police department. He wore the typical "special agent" suit, this one gray, with a navy-blue tie. His short buzzed dark hair carried a slight silvering at the temples. The haircut plus his erect posture indicated a military background. To me, he looked like a Ray clone. He carried a leather briefcase.

He and Ray shook hands, then Ray introduced Pancake, Nicole, and me to Agent Whiting. I mean, Special Agent Whiting. In my limited experience, FBI agents are prickly about that *special* designation. His square jaw remained fixed, his handshake firm.

Ray brought him up to date on what we knew, and then we walked down to the small conference room where April sat, working on a second cup of hot chocolate.

Whiting introduced himself and sat across from April. He opened his briefcase and removed a writing pad, a ballpoint pen, and a small recorder.

"Ms. Wilkerson," he began.

"Call me April," April said.

"OK." He actually smiled and his face didn't crack. Maybe I had read him wrong. "Time is critical here, so let's get right to it."

April nodded.

Whiting punched on the recorder and went through all the official stuff. The date, time, location, his name, and April's name, as well as those of us in the room.

"Tell me how this started," Whiting said. "How you ended up on that yacht."

April told the story again, though this time an abbreviated version as if she felt like she was on the clock. Which she was.

"So Andrew Heche belongs to TLM, which by the way, I'm aware of. He took you out on a cruise for a couple weeks. Which you willingly did. Is that correct?"

"Yes. But had I known what he had planned, I wouldn't have."

Another smile from Whiting. Either he was actually a nice guy, or he was employing well-trained interview techniques. Trying to relax April and make her think he was her friend.

"I suspect not," Whiting said. "He then met with another yacht out in the Gulf, at night, and you were transported to that yacht. There, you met three other girls, and you believed each of you were captives."

"Which we were. They were taking us to Venezuela to sell us to some guy down there."

"How do you know that?"

"Andrew told me. He said I was *equipment,* that's the word he used, and he was selling some old equipment."

Whiting scribbled some notes on his pad.

"Then Victor, Victor Mendoza, he's the guy that owned the other boat, told me that for the time being I belonged to him." Tears welled in her eyes. "He made me do some awful things."

"Did he tell you he was taking you to Venezuela?"

April considered that. "He never said that to me but Chloe, one of the other girls on the boat, overheard the crew talking about it."

"But you didn't hear that yourself?"

April shook her head. "They all spoke Spanish so I didn't understand anything. Chloe did. They never knew she understood, but she did. She said she learned it in school and in some bar she worked at in New Orleans."

"How did you end up here in Pensacola?"

I knew that Whiting already knew the answer so he must have been testing April to make sure her story remained consistent and to officially document it.

"Chloe had heard we were going to dock here briefly to pick up supplies and another girl." She looked at me and Nicole, then back at Whiting. "I saw them bring her onboard." She looked down at the tabletop. "I was so angry, and so scared. I knew that the opportunity to carry out this wonderful plan I had created in my mind was right there in my face. Some plan. Jump off a boat and swim to shore." She stared at Whiting. "I'm not a good swimmer."

"Good enough it seems," he said.

"Thank God. Anyway, as soon as we pulled away from the dock, I crept out of my room and up to the back deck." She sniffed, swiped a hand across her nose. "Standing at the railing I almost chickened out, but I knew this was it. Now or never. I jumped."

"Did they know you had jumped?"

"I don't know for sure, but I don't think so. At least no alarm was sounded, and the boat kept heading out to sea. But I was busy trying to stay afloat and not drink half the Gulf."

Whiting nodded. "You said the owner, or at least the guy in charge, was Victor Mendoza. Are you sure?"

"Absolutely."

"Do you know him?" I asked.

"We are aware of Mr. Mendoza," Whiting said. "And his activities. We've just never been able to get to him." He looked at April. "But you, young lady, just might have given us that opportunity."

"I hope so. And get to Chloe, Emanuella, Roberta, and whoever the new girl is."

Whiting tapped his pen on the pad. "You're sure the yacht was named *El Jugador*?"

"Yes. It reminded me of 'juggler.'"

"It means *The Player*."

"Oh," April said.

Yeah, oh. The name fit in some perverse way.

Whiting clicked the ballpoint. "And Victor Mendoza plays a very dangerous game."

April screwed down her eyes, face. "What now?"

Whiting closed his notepad. "Track down and detain *El Jugador* and Victor Mendoza. Already have the Navy and the Coast Guard on it. He won't get far. Thanks to you, this time we'll have him red-handed."

"What about Andrew?" April asked.

"He will be dealt with. After we build a case."

"How long does that take?"

"Not long. We'll need to take a formal statement from you, of course. Then, we'll generate the warrants and pay him a visit."

"I'm scared of him," April said. "He's very rich and powerful."

Whiting nodded. "So is the FBI."

"What about Jonathon Lindemann?" I asked.

"Same thing. We'll build a case and see where it goes."

"It's more than trafficking," Ray said.

"We have evidence of money laundering and probably tax evasion," Pancake said.

"You do?"

"I have his entire hard drive downloaded."

"How?"

"It was easy," Pancake said. "He don't know do-wa-diddy about encryption."

Whiting considered that. I could tell he was wondering exactly how Pancake had done that, and more importantly if such evidence would hold up in court.

"I added a little something that'll prevent him from deleting files and, just in case, shoved them into the cloud in a protected file."

"Clever."

Pancake grinned. "That's me."

Wasn't that the truth.

CHAPTER 44

I WATCHED AND listened as Special Agent Whiting, cell phone to one ear, briefed his regional director. His gaze remained on April, who added occasional nods to confirm that what he was saying was true. Whiting relayed that the yacht was indeed *El Jugador* and that it was being captained by Victor Mendoza. He added that there were four captive women onboard. After listening a beat he said, "That will definitely complicate things, but the main thing is to stop the vessel and board it." Another full minute of listening. "I'll text the names and descriptions of the three girls that April Wilkerson knows, but the fourth one came on as she escaped so we have no info on her."

He hung up. April then told him about Chloe, Roberta, and Emanuella, describing each. Whiting thumbed the info into his phone as she spoke.

"Anything else?" he asked.

April shook her head. "Just get them off that ship."

Whiting sent the text, then said, "The plan is to treat this as a routine inspection to avoid any conflict and a potential hostage situation. Hopefully, Mendoza won't panic and do anything stupid."

"It would also not be in our interest if he doesn't communicate with anyone that he's been detained," Ray said. "I'm thinking it's better if

Jonathon Lindemann and Andrew Heche have no idea we're on to them."

"Good thought," Whiting said. "But priority one is to get those girls out safely."

"No doubt," Ray said.

"I'll pass along those concerns. The Navy can monitor his radio traffic, and if need be, jam his communications." He stood. "I've got to make a couple of calls and get the investigation on possible money laundering rolling." He glanced at Pancake, then Ray. "Join me and we can go over the information you've managed to gather so far."

Ray and Pancake followed Whiting from the room, leaving Nicole and me with April.

"Are you feeling any better?" I asked.

"Yeah. I can't believe I jumped off that boat."

"But you did," Nicole said. "A very brave move."

"I was scared shitless."

"I know. I think I mentioned earlier that Jake and I had a similar experience. That was all the scary I ever wanted."

"Do you think they'll really be able to rescue the others?"

"I do," I said. "This guy, this Victor dude, is a smuggler and trafficker. The last thing he'd want would be to get crossways with a Navy cruiser. Once they track him down, and they will definitely do that, I'd bet he'll be very cooperative."

"What about Andrew?" April asked. "Will they arrest him?"

"With your testimony I think that would be a given."

"I don't know." She sighed. "He's rich and powerful and has Jonathon on his side. That's a lot of money and influence. Enough to get the best lawyers on earth. I can see it now. My word against his. He'll definitely have all the cards."

"But you have the truth on your side," Nicole said. "Plus, between the FBI and Pancake, they'll turn up plenty to hang him."

April managed a smile. "Literally, I hope."

"Probably not that," I said. "But he might never see blue sky again."

"Hopefully, Victor follows him."

"He will," Nicole said.

April sighed. "If they believe my story."

"They will," I said. "You're forgetting about the other girls. The ones still on Mendoza's yacht. They have the same story to tell."

"Unless they get killed in the process."

I guess the earlier reassurances, from Whiting, and from Nicole and me, that all would go smoothly on the high seas and the other girls would be safely rescued didn't ease April's concerns. The truth was that I didn't know Victor Mendoza, had never even heard of him, and had no idea how he would react. For sure, if he was in the international sex trafficking business his moral compass was broken. Killing some "equipment," as Andrew Heche had referred to April, wouldn't cause a blip in his sociopathic brain. He just might dump the evidence—the girls—into the Gulf. I hoped that wasn't the case.

"I think the Navy can handle them," I said, trying to convince myself as much as April that this drama would end in a good place.

I could almost feel the fatigue that settled over April. Her body sagged into her chair, her face slackened, her eyes a pool of irritated redness. As if all the energy had been sucked from her. Understandable considering her past twenty-four hours.

I heard the door behind me snap open and turned that way. Clarice Wilkerson exploded into the room, her boy toy in her wake. She wore tight jeans, a bright red silk shirt, her fashionable round sunglasses, and a hat whose brim was nearly shoulder width.

"Oh, darling," Clarice said. She rushed to where April sat, bent over, and hugged her. "Are you all right?"

"I'm fine now."

"I can't believe this." Now she looked at us. "Thank you for finding her."

"We didn't," Nicole said. She glanced at April. "She did it herself." Back to Clarice. "She's the one that jumped into dark water and got away."

"Pretty brave stuff," I added.

"Of course, she shouldn't have been in this predicament in the first place," Clarice said. "I told her to stay away from those people. Those TLM criminals."

"Mother, this is not the time for you to get on your moral high horse." She nodded toward the boy toy. "Particularly since you're still dragging around Sean."

Sean. Of course. The perfect name for a surfer-dude distraction.

Clarice removed her hat, placed it on the table. "I'm sorry, honey. That was insensitive of me."

I was beginning to think Clarice didn't do sensitive.

Clarice looked at me. "Have they found that yacht that took my April?"

Her April? Interesting.

"The FBI, the Navy, and the Coast Guard are on it," I said.

"There are four other girls onboard," April said.

"Oh, their poor mothers."

Not to mention the poor girls themselves.

"Excuse me."

It was Ray. He nudged Sean out of the doorway and he, Pancake, and Whiting walked in. Introductions followed.

"So you're Ray Longly," Clarice said. She shook his hand, lingering a bit too long, her gaze locked on Ray.

Clarice surely knew how to use what she had. How to draw men into her orbit. Or was I once again being too cynical? Of course, she didn't know Ray was immune to that sort of manipulation.

Clarice looked at Whiting. "What's the FBI doing to find these criminals?" She dabbed an eye. "They nearly took my daughter to South America for Christ's sake."

Whiting didn't flinch. "The Navy already has the ship located and are closing in as we speak."

"Good." Now she took off her sunglasses. "I want those animals prosecuted to the full extent of the law."

"They will be," Whiting said.

"They better be," Clarice said. "After what they did to my April."

"Job one right now," Whiting said, "is to safely extract the remaining girls."

"Of course," Clarice said.

Of course.

"When can I take April home?" Clarice asked.

"Soon," Whiting said. "After we go over to my office and she provides her formal statement on Andrew Heche, she's free to go." He turned to April. "Then we'll be in touch if we have more questions. Which I'm sure we will."

April nodded. "And please let me know about the others. I won't be able to relax or sleep or anything until I know."

"Will do." Whiting glanced at his watch. "I need to call the office and get them set up for you." He left the room.

"Are you ready to get home?" Clarice asked April. "We can leave as soon as that FBI guy finishes your interview."

"I'm not going to Jupiter with you."

"Don't be silly. Of course you are. After what you've been through, you need rest and to be with family."

"I'll be with friends. You and Sean can go back to your place."

"My place? It's your home, too."

"Not really."

Clarice recoiled as if slapped. She recovered quickly though. "How ungrateful."

"Ungrateful is stealing an inheritance from your daughter."

"Honey, it's not stolen. It's waiting for you. As soon as you're twenty-five."

"No, it's all about power and control with you. I'm an adult. I can make my own decisions. I don't need you controlling and second-guessing everything I do."

"Apparently, that's not true," Clarice said. "With this mess you've gotten into, I'd say you need some adult supervision."

"Adult as in sleeping with some beach creep half your age? If that's your idea of supervision, I'll pass."

I noticed Sean didn't flinch. He'd probably heard this before. Interestingly, neither did Clarice. She simply let go an exasperated sigh.

"You can be so difficult."

"Well, it's no longer your problem," April said. She glared at her mother. "You better get on the road. It's a long drive to Jupiter."

CHAPTER 45

THE NEXT MORNING, before heading to Ray's for what he called a "debriefing," Nicole and I swung by Captain Rocky's and grabbed a bag of breakfast burritos, and as a special request from Pancake, an order of onion rings. Onion rings for breakfast? The big guy never fails to amaze.

Yesterday, after meeting with Special Agent Whiting and Clarice at the Pensacola Police Department, Ray said that Nicole and I could have the day off—I avoided saying that, one, I didn't work for him, and two, I had every day off. Meanwhile, he and Pancake would continue delving into the world populated by Jonathon Lindemann, Andrew Heche, and Gordon Buchanan, they being the major bad guys in this Greek play. We took advantage of it by hanging out on the beach, and the hot tub, and Nicole's bed. My kind of day.

As soon as we walked onto Ray's deck, Pancake grabbed the bag of onion rings and began marching through them like popcorn.

"Did you bring any ketchup?" Pancake asked.

"There's some in the fridge," Ray said.

"Sit tight," Nicole said. "I'll get it."

She returned and handed the bottle to Pancake.

"Thanks, darling," he said. "I'll leave a tip for you."

"Oh, lucky me."

Pancake squirted some ketchup on a large, unruly ring and popped it in his mouth. "The tip is to dump Jake. You'd be better off."

"Yeah, but he's fun to hang with."

Pancake grunted.

To step out of the crosshairs, I asked Ray, "Anything new?"

"Lots. You know Victor Mendoza's yacht was tracked down and boarded." He had called us yesterday to deliver that bit of news. "The girls were rescued unharmed, and the ship impounded. After chatting with the FBI, Emanuella Carlo and Roberta Winslow will be returned to Houston, and Chloe Murphy to New Orleans. The fourth girl, Tara Lynn Brennan, is safely home in Pensacola. Apparently, her story parallels those told to April by the other girls. Some smooth talker met her in a bar and convinced her to go to a party with him. He took her to Victor Mendoza instead."

"This is a network," Nicole said. "One with procurers everywhere."

"It is," Ray said. "And the deeper we look, the bigger it gets."

"Does Jonathon Lindemann run it?" I asked.

"Nope," Pancake said. "He's actually a small player in the scheme of things."

"But he's involved," Nicole said.

"Up to his ears."

"I bet he's scrambling about now," I said.

"Not yet," Ray said. "At least I don't think so. The Navy did indeed block communication in or out of *El Jugador*, and they don't think anyone was notified of the engagement. Their examination of the onboard communication systems tentatively confirmed that. They'll do a deep dive later."

"So Jonathon and Andrew know nothing about what's gone down?" I asked.

"Looks that way. I'm expecting a call from Whiting any minute now to confirm that." He nodded to Pancake. "Pancake came up with some interesting stuff."

Pancake wiped his mouth with a napkin. "Let's get this out of the way first. I've put together an entire package of Lindemann's financial transactions. They touch places all over the world. I'll be sending it to Whiting later today."

"And?" Nicole asked.

"Sure smells like money laundering to me."

"How can you tell?" I asked.

"It has to do with dates, times, and places of origin and destinations of the monies. Cash goes in one door and in short order out another. Over and over until it's washed." He shrugged. "I've seen tougher trails to follow. The FBI and Treasury will be able to pick up on all that and confirm it. And freeze or seize the accounts."

"When?" Nicole asked.

"That's up to them, but these cases take time to build. Weeks or months."

"Which is good?" Nicole asked. "Right? They won't know this is going on right now?"

"That's correct," Ray said. "Means they're still fat and happy and think everything is copasetic. Gives the FBI time to get everything squared away so the case will stick."

"OK," I said. "What about the trafficking?"

Pancake finished off a burrito, followed it with an onion ring, and spoke around it. "I told you about the eight two-hundred-K deposits from Venezuela."

I nodded.

"The two that corresponded with the disappearance of Mia Santos and then April. That leaves six others. They also followed the same pathway. The same bank, to one of Jonathon's Singapore accounts, and then half on to Heche's and Buchanan's Jamaican account."

"So there are six other girls out there?" Nicole asked.

"Looks that way." He wadded the burrito wrapper and two-pointed it into the trash can behind and to Ray's right. "If not more."

"Who are they?" I asked.

"Don't know," Pancake said. "We'll need to see who went missing from TLM, Tampa, or at least somewhere in Lindemann's world."

"This man is pure evil," Nicole said.

"Worse than that. I found two dozen similar transactions. Over the past four years. All through Lindemann's Singapore account and Heche's and Buchanan's Jamaican account. These payments originated in Saudi Arabia, Thailand, Ghana, and Paraguay."

"You're kidding," Nicole said.

"Wish I was."

"Did those girls work at TLM?" I asked.

Pancake shrugged. "Don't know yet. I would suspect not. That would be too many folks disappearing from one place. I'd suspect they have another source."

"Like the guys that grabbed those girls onboard *El Jugador* with April," Nicole said.

"That'd be my guess," Ray said. "Young ladies disappear every day."

"We'll put that on the list of things we'll have to squeeze out of Lindemann," Pancake said.

Pancake could squeeze. No doubt about that.

Ray's cell buzzed. He answered and listened for a full two minutes, a couple of nods, a furrowed brow, then he thanked the person and hung up. "That was Whiting. They drilled down on the communication equipment aboard *El Jugador*. No outgoing messages. Also, they forced Mendoza to contact his guy in Venezuela and tell him that they had some engine trouble but were getting it taken care of and would be a couple of days late getting into port."

"Buys us some time," Pancake said.

"I have a question," I said. Ray, Pancake, and Nicole looked my way. "Why would Jonathon, Gordon, and Andrew do this? I mean, two hundred K is small potatoes to these guys."

"Kicks," Pancake said. "Grins. Fun and games. All that crap that insanely rich dudes do for entertainment. Sociopaths don't need a reason to do crazy shit."

Still didn't make sense to me, but maybe that's all it was to them. A sick game.

"I'm worried about Lorie," Nicole said. "I feel like I should call her and make sure she's OK."

"Me and Pancake have been kicking around a plan," Ray said. "Along with Whiting. Contacting Lorie fits into that."

"Oh?" I asked.

"Pancake sent everything he had to Whiting, and they're planning to take down Buchanan and Heche on the money laundering and Ponzi scheme scams. That's an easy one. But the sex trafficking charges are stickier. At least as far as snaring Jonathon and Rhea in it."

"Don't they have enough with what the girls are saying?" I asked.

"Yes, and no," Pancake said. "Jonathon's still insulated to some extent. At least on selling these girls for trafficking. A smart attorney could argue he knew nothing about it and Buchanan and Heche simply went rogue."

"It seems clear to me."

"But maybe not to a judge and jury," Ray said. "Jonathon has videos of Buchanan and Heche with multiple girls, but none of him doing the same. He can deny, but they can't."

"I guess," I said. "So, what do we do?"

"Turn Rhea," Pancake said. "Then it's a different story."

"How do we do that?" Nicole asked.

"Call Lorie," Ray said. "Make sure all is still quiet on that front. Then have her set up a meeting with Rhea away from the farm. Tell her you two have some questions about TLM but are interested in joining."

"Ray and I will crash the meeting so to speak," Pancake said. "And make her an offer. One that shortens her time in prison garb if she'll roll over on Lindemann."

"I'm not sure she will," I said. "She seems very loyal to Jonathon."

Pancake grunted. "Funny thing about prison time. It breaks a lot of conspiratorial bonds."

Nicole lifted her cell phone from the tabletop. "I've got this."

Of course she did.

CHAPTER 46

IT TURNS OUT Nicole did have it. She called Lorie, placing her phone on speaker. Lorie answered after a single ring.

"Can you talk?"

"Oh, hey," Lorie said. "I'm in the middle of something. Can I call you back in five minutes?"

"Sure."

Lorie disconnected the call.

"She must be with Rhea," Nicole said.

We waited. Five minutes became ten. Then fifteen.

"Do you think she's balking?" Ray asked.

"She's in a difficult situation," Nicole said. "Knowing what she knows and having to act clueless. Not an easy task. But I feel she'll come through."

Lorie did indeed call back. When Nicole answered she said she was on speaker and that I was there along with Ray and Pancake.

"Sorry it took so long," Lorie said. "Rhea is planning some big event down in Tampa at Andrew's place in a couple of weeks and it's been a bit crazy. I'm outside right now so I can talk. What's up?"

"Is everything cool?" Nicole asked.

"Seems to be."

"Nothing out of sorts?"

"If you mean do they suspect I know about the videos, the answer is no. Both Jonathon and Rhea seem perfectly normal."

That's good news. It means they didn't know Victor Mendoza was captured and that April and the other girls had been rescued. Of course, Lorie knew nothing about the trafficking. Not yet anyway. Probably for the best right now. She has enough secrets to keep under control. Knowing that girls are being sold might be too much for her to handle right now.

"Good," Nicole said. "I knew you could do it."

Lorie laughed. "I'm glad someone did. I surely didn't. But it actually feels kind of cool that I know something that they don't. Sort of like being a spy or something."

"Keep it that way," I said.

"That's the plan. So what's up?"

"Can you set up a meeting with Rhea and us?" Nicole asked. "Jake and I?"

"Sure. When?"

"Lunch today?"

"That's short notice. Let me check. One of my duties here is to handle their calendars. I keep Rhea's and Jonathon's schedule on my phone. Let's see . . . she's open until a three o'clock meeting she and Jonathon have."

One neither of them will make, I thought. Handcuffs tend to put a chill in the air and make business meetings uncomfortable.

"Their meeting's at the farm?" I asked.

"Yeah. Some new member coming in from Dallas."

"Tell her Jake and I will be in Fairhope today and would like to buy her lunch and talk about TLM," Nicole said. "Tell her you think we're ready to join. Do you think that'll get her there?"

"Sure, but what's this about?"

Nicole hesitated, glanced at Ray.

"This is Ray Longly. It's best that you don't know. One less secret to keep. Let's just say that we might have a way to bring all this to an end, safely and quickly. We simply need to sit down for a private chat with Rhea."

"That sounds very spy-like."

"It is," Nicole said. "We don't want Jonathon around when we talk, so lunch away from the farm seems like the best solution."

"Okay. I'll ask her and get right back to you."

"One more thing," Ray said. "Is Jonathon at the farm now?"

"Yeah. He's in his office. I know he has a bunch of calls, and then that three o'clock meeting."

"So he should be at the farm all day?"

"I think so. He for sure doesn't have anything on his schedule."

CHAPTER 47

THE LUNCH MEETING would take place at Stella's Bistro, one of the most upscale places in Fairhope, the kind of place where high rollers like Nicole and me would dine. That's me, Jake Longly, high roller and mover and shaker. Maybe not, but it was the role Nicole and I were playing.

We had eaten at Stella's a couple of times before, back when we were investigating the murder of Emily Patterson. Quaint, quiet, very European, and we thought the kind of place that would make Rhea comfortable.

Lorie and Rhea were seated at a table near the back when we arrived. Nicole had grabbed a table for six since Ray and Pancake were with us. I also saw Special Agent Whiting and two other suited-up guys two tables away. Also part of the plan.

At first, Rhea had been surprised when Ray and Pancake walked in with us but relaxed after the introductions and after Pancake explained that he and Ray were also interested in TLM. Ray sat across from her, Pancake at her left side.

"Jake and Nicole have told us about TLM and it seems like a solid organization," Pancake said. "We thought we'd get the details from the boss."

Rhea's face lit up, obviously flattered. "That would be Jonathon, but I am his right hand."

"And you're a lovely right hand," Pancake said,

Always the charmer.

"Aren't you the charmer?" Rhea said.

See, told you.

"I take it you know everything about TLM then," Ray said.

"I do. I helped Jonathon create it, and now I run all the day-to-day operations."

Our waitress appeared but Ray said, "Give us a minute, please." After she walked away, Ray leaned back in his chair. "So nothing goes on at TLM that you don't know about?"

Suspicion rose in Rhea's eyes. She looked at Ray, Pancake, back to Ray. "You're a P.I."

"I am. Glad you did your research."

"What's going on here?" Rhea asked. She fidgeted in her seat.

"We're here to make you an offer," Pancake said.

Now Rhea looked at Lorie. "What is this?"

Lorie shrugged. "I don't know."

"Look at me," Pancake said. "Tell us about April Wilkerson."

Rhea paled, took in a breath.

"Or maybe Mia Santos?" Ray added.

She wadded her napkin, tossed it on the table, and started to rise. Pancake grabbed her arm.

"Sit," he said. "We're here to help you."

Rhea settled back in her chair, jerking her arm from Pancake's grasp. "Help me with what?"

"With shortening the time you spend behind bars," Ray said.

This time Rhea made it to her feet. "I'm not going to listen to this."

"Sit down," Nicole said. "You need to hear this."

Rhea hesitated, then dropped back in her chair. She crossed her arms over her chest. "OK, I'm listening."

"I'm going to be honest with you," Ray said. "You aren't leaving this restaurant without handcuffs, but how tight those cuffs are depends on the decisions you make right here, right now."

"You can't arrest me."

"No, I can't. But they can." Ray nodded toward the three agents.

Whiting gave a small wave.

"FBI," Ray said. "We're going to take Jonathon down at the farm when we leave here. But you need to decide which side of this you're on."

If you looked up "defeated" in the dictionary you would find a picture of Rhea Wilson staring back. You might also find her image under "confused" and "terrified."

"We know about the money laundering and the Ponzi scheme you and Jonathon have been running. We, and the FBI, have the entire money trail. From Zurich to Singapore and everywhere in between. But that's not why we're here."

Rhea dropped her head and shoulders a couple of inches as if trying to avoid the next shoe to drop. No doubt she knew what was coming. A truth she never thought she'd have to face. I almost felt sorry for her, but not really. She sold young women to miscreants all over the world, which made her more or less unredeemable.

"We were hired by Clarice Wilkerson, April's mother," Pancake said. "When April dropped off the radar, she became concerned and reached out to us." Pancake opened his hands. "So here we are."

"She ran off with some guy," Rhea said.

"You take that attitude and it'll add a couple of decades to your time in lockup," Ray said.

"Rhea," I said. "April was found and rescued."

An audible intake of breath by Rhea.

"Yeah," Nicole said. "Along with four other girls."

"April was sold by your buddy Andrew Heche to a guy named Victor Mendoza, and they were on the way to Venezuela when the U.S. Navy stepped in," I said.

"We know that many other girls have been involved," Nicole said. "Not just girls from you and Jonathon and TLM, but from all over. We know it's all part of a worldwide sex trafficking ring."

"It's been going on for years," I added.

"The FBI is doing its due diligence on all that right now," Ray said. "Jonathon and his buddies Andrew Heche and Gordon Buchanan are going down today."

"What we're offering," I said, "is a way to soften your fall."

"It's entirely up to you," Ray said. "But you have to decide right now."

Rhea considered that. "What are you offering?"

Bingo.

"The FBI and a Federal Court will ultimately decide that, but it depends on exactly what you can offer us," Ray said.

"You have inside information," Pancake said. "You know where the bodies are buried, so to speak. You know how the money train works. You know how to locate the girls who have gone missing from TLM over the past few years. All that might become clear once we finish with Jonathon's computer, but right now that information is your bargaining chip." He leaned down and looked her in the eye. "If you're smart enough to use it."

"So I'd have to give up Jonathon?"

"He's done anyway," Ray said. "We're talking decades whether you help or not. It's all the others involved where you might be able to help." He shrugged. "So consider it giving up them, not Jonathon."

"Do I really have a choice?" Rhea asked.

"Not if you want to see blue sky again before you're too old to enjoy it," I said.

She bowed her head and remained perfectly still for over a minute. She looked up. "OK."

"One last question," Pancake said. "Does Jonathon have any guns?"

"One. It's a Glock he keeps in his desk drawer."

While Whiting's colleagues walked Rhea down the street toward their car, we gathered with him outside Stella's. We stood in the shade of a tree and waited as he completed a call to his office.

"The judge is reviewing our arrest warrants right now," Whiting said. "We should have his blessing shortly. An hour, max. Then we can move on Lindemann." He glanced up the street to where Rhea Wilson slid into the back seat of the nondescript FBI car. "Getting her to flip is major and having her in custody means she can't warn Lindemann that we're coming his way."

"Unless someone else has already clued him in," Pancake said.

"Part of the conversation I just had was about our guys down in the Tampa area. They're squatting on Heche and Buchanan, and so far, neither has shown any sign that they know. At least there's been no change in their routines." He shrugged. "So as soon as the judge signs off on everything, we'll take all three in custody at the same time."

I could see the tension in Pancake's shoulders and jaw. He was in action mode, his face adopting that let's-go-kick-some-doors-down look. Waiting never meshed well with that.

"We'll head on over to the farm and put eyes on Jonathon," Pancake said. "Make sure he doesn't smell that something's off and fly away."

"I think it'd be better to wait for the warrant," Whiting said. "Keep this all kosher."

"He'll never know we're there," Ray said.

CHAPTER 48

JONATHON LINDEMANN HAD a lot of balls in the air, which was not unusual. The truth was that he loved it. Sitting around and wasting time was never part of his makeup. He finished his preparation for the three o'clock meeting Rhea had arranged. Some monied cattleman from the Dallas area. Could this guy be an entryway into more Texas money? Rhea thought so. Most of Jonathon's clients resided in Florida or at least the southeast corner of the country. Maybe this guy would get him a foothold in the Lone Star State. That would be nice, and profitable. Texas has money, lots of money.

Jonathon would take his own read during the meeting. On paper the guy looked solid, but Jonathon trusted his own face-to-face assessment over anything on a computer screen.

He began looking into his travel schedule. Hectic would be the proper word. He had a couple days here at the farm before departing for Charlotte, and then on to Atlanta, Jacksonville, and Miami, and ultimately to St. Pete for Andrew's next party. He didn't make it to all of Andrew's bacchanalias, but Andrew had said this one would be epic. His word. Over a hundred people, with many holding an interest in TLM and Jonathon's investment prowess. But the cherry on top was that Andrew said he had a new girl coming. One that was insanely hot and would make a good addition to the TLM staff.

Andrew ended it with, "She's absolutely giddy about meeting the great Jonathon Lindemann."

How could he not attend?

He tapped the keyboard and opened the photo of the girl that Andrew had sent. Hot wasn't nearly strong enough. Blonde hair, blue eyes, and a micro bikini that hid none of her incredible body. A welcome slice of R and R at the end of a series of mostly boring business meetings.

His cell rang and he answered.

"What the hell is going on?"

It was Hector Alvarez.

"Hector," Jonathon said. "How's the weather down in Venezuela?"

"I'm more concerned about the weather in Pensacola."

"What are you talking about?"

"Victor Mendoza and *El Jugador*," Hector said.

"He's headed your way with the merchandise."

"That's why I'm calling. We might have a problem."

A chill crept up Jonathon's spine and his scalp tingled. Not only from what Hector said but from the way he said it. A layer of menace lay over his words. He had only met Hector once, and that was enough. He didn't like him—and to be honest—Hector scared the hell out of him. He could visualize his scrubby beard and dark eyes and the single gold tooth that flashed when he smiled. More a sneer than a smile. One that said, fuck with me and you'll die. He knew for a fact that Hector had killed many men. Either by his own hand or by one of his trained cartel killers. He had never been comfortable working with Hector, but the money was good and easy, so he rationalized that Hector was far away, so any problems with him seemed remote. But now he felt as if Hector were standing right in front of him with a gun in his hand. Or was he over-reading this? Maybe the problem wasn't really a problem.

"What is it?"

"Victor was supposed to be here today, but he called and said they had some engine trouble and would be delayed."

"Those things happen," Jonathon said.

"Do they? I've known Victor a long time. I know *El Jugador*. I sold the yacht to him. It's a very reliable vessel, and Victor maintains it with a certain meticulousness."

"Still, things can go wrong."

"Of course, but I'm curious by nature. I reached out to some contacts. The news I received wasn't to my liking."

The chill along Jonathon's spine intensified. "What news?"

"*El Jugador* might have been impounded by the U.S. Navy and the FBI."

Now Jonathon felt dizzy, and a cold sweat lacquered his face. "No way. I would have heard."

"Would you?"

"Of course." That was a lie. "Sit tight. Let me look into it."

"You do that. And bring me some good news." Hector ended the call.

What the fuck? Did the FBI really have Victor Mendoza in custody? If so, had April talked? The two were joined at the hip. If one, then the other. Which meant this whole sordid business would come right to his door. Unless Victor had killed her and dumped her before he was captured. Victor was one mean son of a bitch, so he just might have. But could he hang his future, his freedom, on that? He almost laughed. Here he sat hoping that some degenerate had killed a young woman. What did that make him?

He knew this entire enterprise was a bad idea. Knew it was risky and the profit peanuts. But Andrew and Gordon felt otherwise. Not for the money—neither of them needed that—but for the game as Andrew put it. Some fucking game.

He should have ended this a year ago when he considered it. Too late now.

He dialed Andrew Heche's number. It rang once and went to voice-mail. He hung up and dialed Gordon Buchanan. Same thing.

He stood and paced the room. What the hell was going on? What should he do? How could he extricate himself from what might be coming his way? He turned toward his desk.

Time to dump some files and secure others in a computer far away and out of the reach of the FBI. He sat, faced his computer, and quickly navigated to the file where he kept the info on the transactions he and Andrew and Gordon had made with Hector. He hit DELETE.

ACTION NOT ALLOWED

What?

He tapped DELETE again.

ACTION NOT ALLOWED

He hammered a finger on the delete button again and again with the same response.

He'd have to erase and reformat the entire drive. He went through the steps to accomplish that.

ACTION NOT ALLOWED

What the hell was going on?

He had to reach Andrew. He'd know what to do. He dialed the number once again and like before it immediately jumped to voicemail.

"Andrew? Call me right now. We have a problem."

CHAPTER 49

"ANDREW? CALL ME right now. We have a problem."

That's what I heard through the door to Jonathon's office.

How did we get here? Lurking just outside Jonathon's inner sanctum? Only a wooden door separating us from a possibly desperate dude with a Glock in his desk drawer?

This was so Pancake, so Ray, and so not where I wanted to be.

During the drive from Fairhope to Lindemann Farms, Pancake had unfolded his plan, which was basically to take Jonathon down and hand him to the FBI all wrapped with a bow. He didn't elaborate on the details, but I pictured Jonathon bouncing off a wall or two and Pancake laughing. I'd seen that movie before.

We had again parked along the rear of the property, and as I climbed out, I asked, "Shouldn't we wait for Whiting?"

"Nope."

"Why not?"

"Because Jonathon's probably destroying evidence or something like that," Pancake said.

"He doesn't know what's happening," I countered.

"He could. He's mega rich and probably has connections within connections. Maybe a bunch we don't know about. If he even gets a hint of what's coming his way, he won't sit idly by and do nothing.

He'll go into self-preservation mode and destroy everything within his reach."

"I thought you did something to his computer that blocked him from deleting files," Nicole said.

"Just the stuff I found. There might be more here and there that could be important to the case against him. Besides, grabbing his computer while it's intact and not having to rely on the copies of his hard drive I made will sit better in court. Less for his defense to work with. You know, claim tampering with the evidence and all that crap."

"Still, shouldn't we let the FBI handle that?" Nicole said.

Pancake grunted. "While they push paper around, crucial materials could go up in smoke."

That made sense and I told him so.

His response: "Of course it makes sense. I always make sense." He smiled at me. "Plus, I ain't big on waiting."

So, off we went through the trees, giving the employees' building a wide berth and luckily not running into anyone, until we reached the TLM administration building.

That's how I found myself standing next to Nicole and behind Ray and Pancake. Ray had a gun, Pancake had a gun, Nicole had a year of Krav Maga training. I had a baseball. Okay, not a great weapon, but it had worked in the past and it's all I had. Which is why I stood behind Pancake.

Ray twisted the knob and shoved the door open, hard enough that it slammed against the adjacent wall.

Jonathon looked up and recoiled. His eyes focused on Ray and Pancake who came through the door with long strides. Then he noticed Nicole and me.

"What is this?" Jonathon asked.

"Put the phone down," Pancake said. "Step away from the desk."

"Who the hell are you?"

I had to hand it to Jonathon. Given the circumstances, I mean, staring into the face of an angry Pancake, he didn't wilt. He stood erect, shoulders squared, eyes narrowed.

"I'm the angel of fuck you up," Pancake said. "Now do as I say."

By now we had all moved into the office.

Jonathon stiffened. "Get the hell out of my office or I'll call the police."

"Go ahead," I said.

Jonathon stared at me. "Then tell me what you want."

"You," Pancake said.

"You can't break into someone's private domain and threaten them."

Pancake smiled. "Yet here we are."

I could feel Jonathon's bluster wane. Pancake had that effect.

"What's this about?"

"April Wilkerson," Nicole said.

"What about her?"

"A little late for that," I said. "The FBI has her. And the other girls Victor Mendoza had onboard."

Pancake nodded toward the computer before Jonathon. "Bet you tried to clear the evidence, didn't you?"

Jonathon stared at him but said nothing.

"I figured that, so I fixed it so you can't."

"Give it up," Ray said. "The FBI has Andrew Heche, Gordon Buchanan, and Rhea in custody. There are three agents coming for you. It's over."

The motion was quick. Jonathon ripped open the drawer and his Glock appeared. He pointed it toward us. Ray and Pancake removed their weapons.

A standoff.

Just great. Another day with Ray.

Nicole took a step to her left, out of the line of fire, and then two more toward Jonathon. "You don't want to do that. They will kill you."

Jonathon angled his weapon toward her. "Not before I kill you."

I gripped the baseball. Could I take him out with a fastball? Not likely.

Ray leveled his weapon at Jonathon. "Put the fucking gun down."

"And if I don't?"

"You have until I count to three."

"If I so much as flinch, she's done."

"One," Ray said.

The explosion concussed my ears. Nicole staggered backward a couple of steps but remained upright. My heart jumped into my throat. Nicole's head turned slightly and I saw her eyes were wide open, but she otherwise looked fine. I looked at Jonathon. A dark hole now decorated the middle of his forehead, he wavered, seemed to hang in suspended animation for a second, then collapsed.

Pancake lowered his weapon. "I ain't big on counting either."

CHAPTER 50

THREE WEEKS LATER, Nicole, Pancake, Ray, and I sat at my table on the deck at Captain Rocky's, knocking back margaritas. Sunset approached, and the low sun painted the sand orange and twinkled off the ripples in the calm water. Pancake motored through half a dozen fish tacos, a mound of fried calamari, and a family-sized order of pulled pork nachos.

Once again, my life was good, even great, and all had returned to normal. Lazy and comfortable. The way I liked it.

Between mouthfuls, Pancake and Ray brought us up to date on each of the players in the TLM drama. Most importantly, Special Agent Whiting and his superiors, though not happy with how things went down, had ultimately decided that Pancake's shooting of Jonathon Lindemann was justified and no charges would be coming his way. It took a few trips to Pensacola for interviews by each of us to accomplish that. It helped that we all told the same story—the true one—and that Jonathon had no story to tell.

Gordon Buchanan and Andrew Heche were tightly locked away with no bail, since their numerous offshore accounts made them flight risks. Despite the fact that most of those accounts had been frozen and the others would be soon, the judge felt the duo just might have hidden money that wasn't on the radar. Even their $600-an-hour attorneys couldn't alter the judge's decision and apparently the fact that further motions on the issue would be a waste of time.

The sex trafficking network that Hector Alvarez ran was slick and well-oiled with many tentacles. The hub was his palatial compound near Caracas, Venezuela. Beachfront and buffered from scrutiny by thick jungle growth. It served as his drug distribution center and a playground for his wealthy clients and friends, complete with young women to entertain his visitors. Thus the need for a steady stream of new flesh. What happened to the girls after their usefulness waned? According to Pancake, Alvarez handed them off to lower-level dealers in smaller villages for their own prostitution operations where most were sold on the streets for a few pesos. It didn't take much of an imagination to know where that would end.

Eleven girls, including Mia Santos, had been rescued from Hector Alvarez's grasp by a group of folks Pancake said were friends of Ray's. According to Ray, the U.S. government had no solid jurisdiction in Venezuela, even though an American citizen, maybe several, were involved, so any use of U.S. special forces would have spun up an international incident. Ray felt handling it privately would be best. Privately being a group of ex-Navy SEALs and Delta Force guys out of Birmingham. A flight to Aruba, an assault on Alvarez's beachfront compound, and a major firefight. All the girls and the special ops guys had escaped unscathed while Hector and fourteen of his thugs didn't see dawn. No great loss.

TLM had been shut down, a given with Jonathon Lindemann dead, and the money laundering and Ponzi scheme charges would now fall on Buchanan and Heche and three lawyers involved in the scam. Pancake opined that those filings coupled with the sex trafficking charges would likely lead to a hundred or more years for each of them. Again, no great loss.

Rhea Wilson turned on all of them and for her cooperation her plea deal would confine her in a cushy federal lockup for only five years. To me, that seemed light, but her testimony did leave the others involved with no wiggle room.

I thought about TLM and what it could have been. Self-improvement and financial security are worthy goals, and on paper that's what TLM was all about. But greed and corruption can erode even the most noble enterprises. That surely fit Jonathon Lindemann. No doubt he was a charismatic speaker and could influence others to better themselves, and no doubt he understood the markets and made money. Just not fast enough or large enough for his needs, or his ego. So he ripped a bunch of pages from the Madoff playbook and ran with it. I guessed like every other crook who has tried to run the same game, he didn't grasp the concept of chickens coming home to roost.

But the worst part was the trafficking of young women. Again, bringing them into TLM and helping them become the best version of themselves and showing them the path to financial success were lofty goals worthy of applause. Selling them to some drug smuggler in South America was so far over the line that the line evaporated. I still didn't get it. The couple of hundred thousand he made off each girl was a drop in the bucket when compared to the other monies his schemes generated. Why would he do that? Was it just for kicks as Pancake had said? It made no sense. With Jonathon dead, we'd never know what motivated him.

Nicole's cell buzzed. She answered. "Hey." She put it on speaker, saying it was April. "I'm here with Jake and Pancake and Ray."

"Good," April said. "I wanted to thank all of you."

"You did the hard part," I said. "Jumping off Victor Mendoza's yacht was no small feat."

"Yeah, but you guys brought the whole thing down," April said. "I heard the FBI found Mia in Venezuela and brought her home."

Well, not exactly the FBI, but let's go with that.

"That's a fact," Pancake said. "Along with ten other girls. The icing on the cake is that Hector Alvarez didn't survive the raid."

"I'm glad I never met him," April said.

"Are you OK?" Nicole asked.

"I am. I'm in Jupiter with my mom."

Not what I expected.

"All good?" I asked.

"I wouldn't go that far, but definitely better. Mom and I've done some talking. A burying of the hatchet, so to speak."

"That's great," Nicole said.

"Mom dumped Sean—the creep—and I've moved back in. For now, anyway."

"That sounds like a good first step," I said.

"Best of all, she decided that after all that went down, I was adult enough to handle my own money."

"So you're a rich lady," Pancake said.

April laughed. "You might say. I'm going back to school for some post-graduate studies and then I'll be ready to enter the world of adulthood."

"Welcome to the club," I said.

Pancake and Nicole gave me a look. I guess I wasn't the one to welcome anyone to adulthood.

PUBLISHER'S NOTE

We trust that you enjoyed *Cultured*, the sixth novel in the Jake Longly Thriller Series. While the other five novels stand on their own and can be read in any order, the publication sequence is as follows:

Deep Six

Jake Longly and Nicole Jamison explode onto the thriller scene in *Deep Six* when their quiet Alabama shore town takes on corruption, vendettas, and cartels—complete with murders and lavish yachts.

"Corruption, vendettas, cartel killers, oh my! *Deep Six* puts the fun back into late-night reading with this fast-paced romp through murder and mayhem. Prepare to flip the pages."

—Lisa Gardner, *New York Times* best-selling author

A-List

Reluctant P.I. Jake Longly and his girlfriend, Nicole Jamison, head to New Orleans and an A-list actor who woke up on location with a dead girl in his bed.

"D. P. Lyle hits it over the fence with *A-List*. This mystery, featuring former Major League pitcher and reluctant P.I. Jake Longly, is fast-paced, slick, and funny. Bad times in the Big Easy mean a great time for readers. Head to New Orleans with Jake, and enjoy the trip."
—Meg Gardiner, best-selling author

Sunshine State

Sunshine State throws Jake and Nicole into the bizarre case of a convicted serial killer who now claims: *Two of those seven murders I confessed to are not mine—but I won't tell you which two.*

"*Sunshine State* sizzles with just the right mix of action and mystery, a rollicking roller-coaster ride on a track lined with thrills and spills."
—Jon Land, *USA Today* best-selling author

Rigged

Rigged finds Jake and Nicole trying to sort out the murder of Jake's best friend Tommy "Pancake" Jeffers's first love from back in the sixth grade.

"Snappy dialogue, fun characters, smart writing, a juicy mystery—all had me flipping pages until I reached The End. Jake and Nicole remind me of my favorite mystery duo, Nick and Nora Charles, with a modern twist. The Jake Longly series never fails to entertain."
—Allison Brennan, *New York Times* best-selling author

The OC

Jake's and Nicole's fun in *The OC* is rudely interrupted when Nicole's girlfriend triggers a desperate search for a deadly stalker.

"*The OC* is a poignant and wickedly funny tale. Lyle's prose is stylish, smart, and compelling. Another grand slam in an immensely entertaining series."
—Sheldon Siegel, *New York Times* best-selling author

We hope that you will read the entire Jake Longly Thriller Series and will look forward to more to come.

If you liked *Cultured*, we would be very appreciative if you would consider leaving a review. As you probably already know, book reviews are important to authors and they are very grateful when a reader makes the special effort to write a review, however brief.

For more information, please visit the author's website.
www.dplylemd.com

Happy Reading,
Oceanview Publishing
Your Home for Mystery, Thriller, and Suspense